Jacquie D'Alessandro

Kiss The Cook

ZEBRA BOOKS
Kensington Publishing Corp.
www.kensingtonbooks.com

Lois O. Erickson

**Outstanding praise for the novels of
Jacquie D'Alessandro!**

Kiss The Cook

"This story works on so many levels. Melanie and Chris are believable, multidimensional characters. Melanie's spry, wisecracking Nana and Chris's matchmaking mama add humorous color to the tale, which snaps along at breakneck pace. And humorous and dramatic moments are handled equally well. Bon Appetit!"—*Affaire de Coeur*

"Pulsating with sexual tension and a cast of marvelous characters whose dialogue is fresh and filled with passion, this delicious tale is a definite keeper."—*Rendevous*

Love and the Single Heiress

"Stuffed to the brim with D'Alessandro's trademark laugh-out-loud humor, this crowd-pleasing Regency-era romance gallops along in winning style, keeping readers in suspense until the exhilarating finish."—*Publishers Weekly*

"Engrossing romance with an undercurrent of danger . . . keeps readers glued from the very first page. Catherine and Andrew's chemistry gives added joy, as do the chapter excerpts from the sinful advice book. *Love and the Single Heiress* belongs on the keeper shelf!"—*The Best Reviews*

"Highly recommended . . . I was delightfully amused by the premise right from the opening pages . . . completely heartwarming. The things Andrew does to woo Catherine melted my heart. His ultra romantic gestures and considerate nature, coupled with his strong, masculine allure, make him quite the irresistible hero. A well-written tale, delivering humor, emotion, and ample romance. Don't let it go by!"—*Romance Reviews Today*

The Bride Thief

"This charming, funny romp is destined to delight readers with its fast pace, snappy dialogue, winsome characters and the sweet yet sexy love story. This "feel good" read brings smiles galore while tempting readers to keep turning pages."—*Romantic Times*

Books by Jacquie D'Alessandro

KISS THE COOK*

NOT QUITE A GENTLEMEN

LOVE AND THE SINGLE HEIRESS

WHO WILL TAKE THIS MAN?

WHIRLWIND AFFAIR

THE BRIDE THIEF

WHIRLWIND WEDDING

RED ROSES MEAN LOVE

*Published by Kensington Publishing Corporation

ACKNOWLEDGMENTS

I would like to thank the following people for their help and support on this project:

My editor, Ann LaFarge; my agent, Damaris Rowland; and my critique partners, Rachelle Wadsworth and Karen Hawkins.

Thanks also to Stephanie Bond Hauck, Martha Kirkland, Pat Van Wie, Wendy Etherington, Donna Fejes, Jenni Grizzle, Carina Rock, Susan Goggins, and the members of Georgia Romance Writers.

And thanks to my mom and dad, Kay and Jim Johnson, for all they do.

ONE

Melanie Gibson eased her beat-up, rusted-out lime-green Dodge into the circular drive of the soaring office building at One Atlanta Plaza. This was her last delivery for the night and she prayed she'd find an open parking space. She craned her neck, peered around, and sighed. Not a parking spot in sight. A solid row of cars lined both sides of the wide driveway.

She looked at her watch. Ten past seven. If she didn't deliver the order of food in the next five minutes, the customer wouldn't have to pay for it. That was the guarantee of the Pampered Palate—Gourmet Food To Go.

"If we don't deliver on time, it's on us," Melanie muttered under her breath. "Since I was clearly insane when I came up with that slogan, I'm making an executive decision to change it tomorrow to, 'You'll get your food when you get it, and be damn glad about it.' "

She glanced at the large warming container of food in the backseat and made another executive decision: If she pulled around to the back of the building and parked in the lot, she'd never make it in time. Almost two hundred dollars' worth of food. She could not afford to be late. She pulled up alongside a dark blue Mercedes and double-parked.

I'll only be upstairs for a few minutes, she rationalized, hauling the heavy red-and-white-striped warmer into her arms. *Besides, whoever owns the Benz will be here 'til midnight, working overtime to afford it.*

She slammed the car door with a thrust of her hip and awkwardly maneuvered herself and her ungainly package through the revolving door. She'd certainly be glad when she got her bank loan and could buy her catering truck. Then she could use the special delivery entrances and forgo this double-parking/revolving door ordeal.

When she entered the lobby, a blast of air-conditioning greeted her and she almost groaned with pleasure. Atlanta was into the second week of a record-breaking July heat wave and the Dodge's air-conditioning consisted of rolled-down windows.

After scribbling her name on the security roster, she rushed into an open elevator car and pushed the button for the thirtieth floor. No way was she going to be late. No way. The elevator zoomed upward, then opened with a quiet ping. Melanie stepped out with a sigh of relief.

Whew! Made it! She placed the box on the carpet outside the outer glass doors leading to Slickert, Cashman, and Rich, Attorneys at Law. Great name for a bunch of lawyers. Kinda like the way her gynecologist's name was Dr. Seamen. She raised her hand to ring the bell and froze. Leaning forward, she stared through the glass with disbelief. Her stomach fell to her toes.

The digital clock on the reception desk glowed in the deserted waiting area. It read 7:40.

She looked at her watch. It still read 7:10.

"Damn, damn, *damn!*" She shook her wrist and held the timepiece up to her ear. Nothing. Zip. *Nada.* She slapped the watch's face. No signs of life. Like the Wicked Witch of the East, her watch was not merely dead, it was really most sincerely dead.

But how could that be? She'd just bought the blasted thing last month—a twenty-eighth birthday present to herself. The Kmart special had just cost her two hundred dollars in food. Two hundred dollars she couldn't afford to lose.

She glanced down at the box at her feet and suppressed an urge to kick it. Fifteen gourmet dinners, all the condiments, plates, cutlery—everything for a Pampered Palate meal. And if she announced herself to Slickert, Cashman, and Rich, Attorneys at Law, the meal would be on her.

She eyed the food, tempted beyond all endurance to gather up the heavy box and slink away, but she knew she couldn't. If she didn't live up to her promises, her fledgling business would suffer. She'd worked too hard and too long to risk her reputation with one of her best customers. Besides, a ravenous Cashman or a starving Slickert might slap her with a lawsuit.

Nana always said the only way to swallow a bitter pill was to do it quickly and get it over with, so Melanie took a deep breath and rang the bell. She tapped her foot, waiting, mentally cursing Mike, her delivery man. Of course it wasn't Mike's fault he was sick, but having to make this batch of deliveries herself had turned a bad day into the day from hell.

The day had started when her alarm didn't go off and she woke up forty-five minutes late. Then there was no hot water for her shower. In her haste, she got shampoo in her eye, burned her fingers ironing her shirt, and got a run in her stockings. All before she arrived at work—an hour late.

Speaking of late, where are these people? She rang the bell again and knocked on the glass door for good measure. Another minute went by with no response.

Great. They'd probably given up on her and gone home. A weary sigh escaped her. Now what? She wasn't about to leave the food here in the hall. What if they'd all left? If they weren't there to get their food, she was going to bring it home. Why leave it for the mice?

Hefting the heavy warmer into her arms, she struggled back to the bank of elevators. *I'll go down to the lobby and call the lawyers. If they don't answer, I'm outta here.* The elevator door *shushed* open and she shoved in the box with her foot. When she stepped in after it, her heel got caught in the narrow space between the doors. She gave her stuck foot a heave and the heel snapped off cleanly.

Jeez. Calgon, take me away. Far away. Yanking the broken heel from the crack, she limped onto the elevator and jabbed the L button with her broken shoe. She sagged against the wall, closed her eyes, and wondered what she'd done to bring the wrath of God down on her head. Must be her tendency to speed in the Dodge, she decided. Or maybe the fact that she'd kicked Tony Pasqualio's shin in the third grade had finally come back to haunt her.

But couldn't those evils be canceled out by some good stuff? She loved animals and kids, and she was kind to senior citizens. *I always hold the door open for strangers, I feed stray cats, and I don't cheat on my taxes.* She looked down, groaned, and squeezed her eyes back shut. Her toes were sticking out of a gaping hole in her hose. Apparently third-grade shin-kicking carried more weight with higher beings than holding doors open.

The elevator stopped on the twenty-fifth floor. Melanie peeked her weary eyes open a crack and caught a glimpse of masculine tassel loafers stepping into the elevator. By the time she opened her eyes all the way, the man had turned his back to her and repushed the L button.

Just as well. She was too exhausted to make conversation. Her eyes drifted shut, traveling down the man's back as they did so. Tall. Suit jacket flung over one arm, burgundy leather briefcase. His white dress shirt fitted across broad shoulders. Her gaze dipped lower. Charcoal gray suit pants to match the jacket. Nice butt. She inhaled deeply and caught a whiff of spicy-clean cologne. Whoever he was, he smelled great. A lot better than she did. She smelled like fried chicken and Caesar salad. Her eyes settled again on his backside. Yes, indeed, he had a *really* great butt.

Christopher Bishop stepped into the elevator, barely noting the fact that another person was in the car, and pushed L with a sigh of relief. He was tired. Bone weary. He glanced at his watch. Seven forty-five. Another fourteen-hour workday. He rolled his aching shoulders and sighed. Since he'd made partner at his accounting firm, his workload had become murderous. He couldn't wait to get home, ditch the suit and tie, get into his sweats, grab a beer, and relax. And food. Something to eat would be real nice.

While he watched the lit numbers drop, he became aware of an aroma . . . a mouthwatering, drool-inducing aroma in the elevator. Fried chicken.

His nostrils twitched and his stomach let loose a ferocious growl.

He turned his head and noted the woman leaning against the back wall. Her eyes were closed and she looked about ready to drop. His gaze traveled over her, noting her disheveled reddish-brown hair, wrinkled white man-tailored blouse, short black skirt, and . . . one shoe? She stood lopsided, but she had great legs. *Really* great legs, even though her bare toes stuck out of a hole in her hose. The words PAMPERED PALATE were embroidered on the pocket of her shirt and printed in red block letters on the sides of the large box that sat at her feet. He'd obviously found the source of the tantalizing aroma.

Pampered Palate. Now why did that sound so familiar? He'd probably ordered an eat-it-at-your-desk lunch from them. A frown scrunched his brow. No, it was something else. He searched his mind, but his exhausted brain cells refused to function. It would come to him—eventually.

The elevator *pinged* and the door slid open. Almost groaning with relief, Chris hastily crossed the marble-tiled lobby.

"Thank God it's Friday," he muttered with a weary nod to the security guard. A whole weekend to rest. Sleep late. Read the paper. Do the crossword puzzle. Fifteen minutes. He'd be home in fifteen minutes. His car was right out in front—he'd left it there when he ran back up to his office to pick up some forgotten papers. He pushed his way through the revolving doors, debating whether he wanted to watch the Braves game or a *Titanic* documentary. The thought had no more than entered his head when he stopped dead.

Someone—some idiot—had double-parked and

blocked him in. He strode over to the offending ve-
hicle and peered in the window of the dilapidated
Dodge.

The car was empty.

"Terrific. The owner probably abandoned this
junk heap." He straightened and blew out a long
breath. "What else can go wrong today?" No sooner
had the words passed his lips than a huge raindrop
landed smack on his nose.

Chris closed his eyes and shook his head. "I had
to ask."

Lugging the heavy warmer, Melanie limped in one
shoe across the lobby to the security desk. The guard
dialed Slickert, Cashman, and Rich and handed her
the phone. She let it ring twenty times. No answer.
She hung up and called the Pampered Palate.

"Pampered Palate," a gravelly voice said at the
other end. "Gourmet To Go. It's on time or it's on
us. May I help you?"

"Nana, it's Melanie. I'm—"

"Melanie! Thank goodness you called," Sylvia Gibson said. "The lawyers canceled their order not five
minutes after you left."

Melanie huffed out a breath. "Great. I'm here now.
What happened?"

"I don't know. Some emergency. They all had to
leave. Looks like we'll be eating chicken for a while."

"I guess so." Melanie blew her hair out of her eyes.
"How are things going there, Nana? Is everything all
right?" Melanie worried that her seventy-five-year-old
grandmother would overwork herself.

"Everything's great. Mike's brother came in to

help out with the deliveries, and Wendy's manning the front register."

"Good." She glanced at her watch, forgetting it was broken until she saw it still read 7:10. "I'm leaving now. I'll see you within half an hour."

"Take your time, dear. All's well here. The evening rush is over."

Melanie hung up, thanked the guard, and hefted the heavy box into her arms. She limped across the lobby, then struggled with the revolving door, maneuvered herself around, and stepped outside.

That's when she discovered it was raining.

Actually, rain could not describe what was coming down. It was pouring. Pouring as if to make amends for a century-long drought. Torrents of water rushed from the canopy protecting the doorway. The rain fell in a veritable sheet, large drops that splashed up a good six inches once they hit the sidewalk.

"It figures." Of course her umbrella was in the car. Even though the Dodge was close by, Melanie knew she'd be drenched by the time she reached it. *Looks like I'll be getting my bath sooner than I wanted.*

She kicked off her one unbroken shoe, tossing it and its heel-less mate into a trash can. Drawing a deep breath, she made a run for it.

A deluge of stinging rain pelted her, soaking her before she'd taken a dozen steps. She scurried across the cement, intent on reaching the sanctuary of the Dodge. While struggling to balance the box and unlock her door, she heard a car door slam.

"It's about time you got here," a deep voice said.

Melanie paused and looked up. A tall man stood under a big black umbrella. He'd obviously come from the Mercedes she'd blocked in. He frowned at her over the roof of the Dodge.

Uh-oh. Mr. Mercedes looked pretty pissed. She squinted through the wet darkness and shook her streaming hair from her eyes. No smile, bunched-up eyebrows, set jaw, possible teeth grinding. He sounded pissed, too. Hopefully he didn't harbor latent homicidal tendencies. She wished she hadn't abandoned her shoes. The only weapon she had was a fried chicken leg. Well, she'd beat him to death with it if she had to.

She lifted her chin. "I beg your pardon? Are you speaking to me?"

"You should beg my pardon. I've been waiting out here for almost fifteen minutes." He peered at her through the rain. "Where I come from, people who double-park run the risk of getting their tires slashed."

"Must be a lovely neighborhood," she muttered under her breath. Realizing he had a legitimate complaint, she said, "Look, I'm really sorry. I only needed to run upstairs for a minute—"

"Since I've been waiting for fifteen minutes, that's not really true, is it?"

Melanie's anger flared to the surface. *Well, excuuuuuse me, Mr. Mercedes.* She had already apologized. Did this bozo want a blood oath?

"Like I said, I'm sorry. I'll just get in my car and toddle on home." Suddenly wondering if Mr. Mercedes was angry enough to turn violent, she opened the car door, shoved the box of food across the seat, and slid in, quickly slamming and locking the door. She looked over and was relieved to see him get back into his car.

Melanie stuck the key in the ignition and turned it. A weak *grrrrrr* sounded and nothing else. She tried it again. An even weaker *grrrrr* came out. On the third try, nothing. She thunked her forehead on the steering wheel.

"This day has to end . . . this day has to end . . . this day has to end!" She turned the key again, but only silence met her ears.

A tap sounded on the driver's window and Melanie yelped in fright. She looked up and saw a face peering at her from beneath a black umbrella. Touching her palm to her beating heart, she took a deep breath. Mr. Mercedes. She rolled down the window an inch.

"I don't mean to harp on this," he said in a distinctly sarcastic tone through the crack, "but when you said you were leaving, I sort of assumed you meant sometime tonight."

Ha, ha, ha. Very funny. Mr. Mercedes was a veritable Jerry Seinfeld. Smothering a groan of annoyance, Melanie turned the knob to lower the window farther.

The knob came off in her palm.

She squeezed her eyes shut and mentally cursed the Dodge in six languages. Pulling herself together, she looked up at Mr. Mercedes. She couldn't see much through the crack in the window, but what she *could* see didn't scream *serial killer.* At least he didn't have CRAZED MURDERER tattooed on his forehead.

He was just a tired businessman trying to get home from work. Of course, he seemed a tad irritated, but who could blame him? She was a bit out-of-sorts herself. Deciding her choices were to face Mr. Mercedes or rot in the Dodge, she opened the door. He backed up to give her room to get out.

"Look," Melanie said, standing under his umbrella, trying to keep her impatience under control,

"I'm really sorry about this, but now it seems that my car won't . . ."

Her voice trailed off as she got her first look at Mr. Mercedes. Good grief. Melanie stared at him and her breath deserted her body in a *whoosh*. Must be a trick of the light, and the sheen of the rain. No man could be that gorgeous.

He stood at least six two, and his face looked like something out of a Ralph Lauren ad. All sculpted planes, bedroomy blue eyes, and a firm, square jaw complete with sexy five o'clock shadow.

A stark white dress shirt contrasted with his ebony hair and accentuated his broad shoulders. He'd loosened his conservative paisley tie, and his shirtsleeves were rolled back, exposing tanned, muscular forearms. Dark gray dress pants hugged his lean hips. Her eyes traveled back up his long length. No doubt about it: The good-looks god had clearly favored this guy. He had to be married. She looked at his left hand. No ring. Probably gay.

"Your car won't what?" he asked, bringing her thoughts back to her present problem.

Melanie snapped her gaze back up to his face. He was staring at her, frowning, his annoyance evident. "Start," she replied. "My car won't start."

"Are you sure?"

"Positive. I don't know much about cars, but I know when one won't start. It growled at me twice, then died."

His gaze shifted over her shoulder to look at the Dodge. "No offense, but it looks like it was time for it to go."

Melanie took immediate umbrage. Nobody insulted her car. She drew herself up to her full five feet eight inches. "Hey, this car is a classic. It's in perfect condition. Almost. It might not be as fancy as your wheels, but it gets me where I've got to go . . . or at least it did until a few minutes ago."

"Mind if I give it a try?" he asked. When she hesitated, he looked skyward. "Listen, lady, I'm not about to steal your car, okay? I'm tired, I'm hungry, I'm soaked from the knees down, and I'd like to get out of here sometime before midnight. Until that piece of . . . er . . . your car gets moved, I'm stuck."

Sheesh. What a grouch. And at least he was only wet from the knees down. She was soaked through to her skin. "Be my guest," Melanie said, sweeping her hand in a grand gesture toward the driver's seat.

"Thanks. Here," he said, passing her the umbrella. "Hold this."

He slid into the driver's seat and yelped in pain, pushing up his hips as high as the steering wheel would allow.

"Watch out," Melanie warned. "There're a couple of broken springs in the seat."

He sent her a withering look. "Thanks."

"No problem."

He turned the key in the ignition. Nothing. "You said it growled at you?" he asked, looking up at her.

"Twice. Then it died."

"Well, I'd guess that your battery is dead. Do you have jumper cables?"

Melanie shook her head. " 'Fraid not."

He muttered something under his breath that Melanie didn't catch, but based on the look on his face, she decided that was probably for the best.

"Maybe the person who's parked in front of you or behind you will show up," she suggested, hoping it was true.

"Based on the day I've had, they've probably gone

on vacation and won't be back 'til Christmas." He took a deep breath. "I might as well jump you—"

"Whoa, buddy. Hold it right there." Melanie backed up several steps. "If you touch me, I'll scream. I've got chicken legs and I'm not afraid to use them."

He stared at her as though she was an escapee from the home for the criminally insane. "What the hell are you talking about?"

"If you think I'll stand here and let you jump me—"

"Your *car*. I'll use my jumper cables to jump-start your car."

Melanie felt her face flush with embarrassment. "Oh. Right. I knew that."

He muttered again and shook his head. "I'll just pop the hood." He slid across the seat, got one leg out of the car and stopped. Melanie stared down at him and waited. He jerked forward a few times but didn't move.

"What's wrong?" she asked.

He looked up at her with an unreadable expression. "You said something about broken springs in the seat?"

Melanie nodded. "Yeah. Why?"

"It seems my pants are . . . snagged."

"Snagged?"

"I'm stuck."

"What do you mean?"

He sent her a potent glare. "Which word are you having trouble with—*I'm* or *stuck*?"

"Sheesh. There's no need to be sarcastic."

He wiggled his butt a bit. Melanie could almost hear his teeth grinding together. "Stuck. Caught. Trapped. I can't move."

Melanie shook her head in sympathy. "Bummer.

But I know just how you feel. I've ruined a dozen pair of hose on those darn springs."

He stuck his hand under himself and yelped. "Jesus! Look at this! I'm bleeding!" He withdrew his hand and held up fingers smeared dark red. "I'll probably get tetanus from this rattletrap."

Melanie bent over, grabbed his hand, and peered at it in the dim interior light. Then she sniffed. "Barbecue sauce."

"Excuse me?"

"That isn't blood. It's barbecue sauce. A stray packet from a previous delivery order, no doubt. Here." She reached under the seat and handed him a wad of paper napkins.

He wiped his fingers and scowled at her. "So, my pants are ripped *and* stained."

"Seems so. Hope you know a good dry cleaner."

"Great. That's just great."

Melanie considered pointing out to him that the barbecue sauce wasn't doing her upholstery any good, but it didn't seem like something he would appreciate hearing.

"I think I could use a little help here," he said testily.

"Oh. Sure." Melanie rested the umbrella between the open door and the car roof and leaned in across him, trying to see where his pants were caught. "Sorry," she mumbled, pushing her way in. "Gotta crawl over you. Passenger door doesn't open."

Chris stared down with disbelief at the woman sprawled across his lap. Her short skirt was hiked up and barely covered the essentials. Since her backside was practically in his face, he couldn't help but notice the curve of her hips. She had a great butt. At the moment, however, her long, lean legs, encased in ripped hose, stuck out the open door, dangling in the rain. He prayed none of his coworkers happened by. This definitely did not look good.

Something pinched his rear and he sucked in a breath. What the hell was she doing to his ass?

"Hey, lady," he said, annoyed to be placed in this awkward spot, "if you're so anxious to cop a feel, I'd rather find a more private place."

She pushed herself up and glared at him. Her head was only inches from his and with the aid of the interior light, Chris got his first good look at her face. Her hair was half plastered to her head, half sticking up at crazy angles. She looked like she'd stuck her finger in an electric socket.

Her mascara had run, forming black moons under her eyes. They were big, limpid, chocolatey-brown eyes and they studied him with clear exasperation. She had creamy skin, and a battalion of pale freckles marched across her straight nose. Two deep dimples winked at him from the sides of her mouth. Despite his annoyance, his eyes lingered there for several heartbeats. She had the most incredible, lush mouth he'd ever seen.

His gaze dropped. Her shirt was soaking wet and clung to her like a second skin, clearly outlining soft curves encased in a lacy bra. The words PAMPERED PAL-ATE were embroidered on the pocket. She was the woman from the elevator. He breathed in. She smelled like fried chicken.

"Listen, you pervert," she said, her eyes flashing, "I was *not* copping a feel. I was trying to save your pants."

She was breathing hard, and every time she inhaled Chris felt her breasts pressing against him. Soft, full breasts that made his groin tingle and his heart speed up. *Jeez, I must be losing my mind.* She looked like a drowned rat. This woman was nothing but a pain in the ass—literally. He was simply suffering from malnutrition-induced dementia. Of course he would be affected by a woman who smelled like chicken. It had nothing to do with the sexy curves plastered against him.

Wanting her away from him as soon as possible, he said, "If you'll just move, I'll save my own pants."

She scooted off him, stood and grabbed the umbrella. "Fine. But don't blame me if—"

The sound of material ripping was unmistakable.

"Uh-oh," she said.

Gritting his teeth, Chris got out of the car. He peered inside and saw a good-sized piece of dark material on the seat. Hoping it wasn't what he suspected, he picked it up, dangling it between his fingers.

Dark wool.

Like from a man's suit. *His* suit. His *brand-new* suit.

"Oh, boy. That doesn't look good," she said. "Looks just like my panty hose did." She peered around at his backside, then straightened. Her amusement was clear. "Hmmm. I see you're a boxer man."

Chris mentally counted to ten. The sooner he jumped her car, the sooner she'd be on her way, and the sooner he could get home. Without a word, he popped her hood, then walked to his car to get the jumper cables. He left the umbrella with her. There wasn't any point in bothering with it—his suit was already ruined, and the rain was tapering off a bit.

She stood under the umbrella and waited while he attached the cables.

"Okay," he said, several minutes later. "Turn the key."

She slid into the car and turned the ignition, and the engine coughed to life. Chris almost jumped for joy. He quickly disconnected the wires from both cars and replaced the cables in his trunk.

"I think that should do it," he said, slamming the Dodge's hood.

"Yes. Thank you very much." She smiled, and two deep dimples winked at him. "My name's Melanie Gibson. But everyone calls me Mel."

He stared at her. "Your name's Mel Gibson?"

"Yup. What's yours?"

He couldn't believe he was standing in the rain talking to a lunatic woman who thought she was Mel Gibson. "I'm Peter Pan."

She looked him up and down, then shook her head. "I don't think so. Peter Pan wore green tights." She waggled her eyebrows at him, Groucho style. "I already know you're wearing white boxers."

In spite of himself, Chris felt a chuckle rumble in his chest. He quickly smothered it. Why the hell did he feel like laughing? He was angry. Inconvenienced. Wet. Hungry. His suit was ruined; probably his shoes, too. *I'm deranged from lack of food.*

"So, are you going to tell me your name?" she asked. "Don't be shy. Believe me, it can't be worse than mine. No matter how hard I try, no one will call me Melanie."

He held out his hand. "Christopher Bishop. Call me Chris."

She shook his hand, and Chris immediately noticed how soft her skin was. And how cute her dimples were. A warm tingle zoomed right through him. *Jeez, I'm really losing it.* This woman was so completely not his type, it was laughable. He preferred small, curvy, blue-eyed blondes. *She* was tall, lanky, and dark-eyed. Not to mention a mess.

But there was something about her—he had no idea what—that had all his senses standing at attention. He shook his head. Obviously the final stages of malnutrition were setting in.

Her look turned serious. "I'm really sorry I blocked you in. And about your pants." She reached into her shirt pocket and withdrew a card. "If you send the repair bill to me, I'll be happy to pay it."

He took the wet card and studied her closely. Now that home was again fifteen minutes away, his annoyance ebbed somewhat. The rain had dwindled down to a mere drizzle. "I doubt they can be repaired, but thanks anyway." He leaned closer and sniffed. "I saw you on the elevator. You smell like fried chicken."

She cocked an eyebrow at him. "Wow. Words I've always longed to hear."

He laughed. "I meant, I smelled you in the elevator and . . ." His voice trailed off and he shook his head. "Somehow that doesn't sound right, either."

"That's okay. I smelled you in the elevator, too. You're wearing my favorite men's cologne. It smells much better than chicken."

"Not if you're starving, it doesn't," he said. Almost as if he'd planned it, his stomach let out a loud growl.

"Well, Christopher-call-me-Chris Bishop, you sound hungry, and I happen to have two hundred bucks' worth of Pampered Palate food in my car. Could I interest you in a meal? As a way of saying thanks?" She smiled at him. "We make the best fried chicken in Atlanta."

Since he was ready to eat the windshield wipers off

the Mercedes, he didn't even consider refusing her offer. "Sounds good."

She handed him the umbrella and leaned into the car, once again affording him a heart-stopping view of her long legs. She straightened and handed him two boxed dinners. "Here you go. Enjoy."

"Thanks."

"Least I can do. Well, I'd better let you get home to your dinner." She slid into the Dodge and waved to him. He nodded in return and walked to his car.

Melanie clicked her seat belt into place and pushed her wet hair behind her ears, trying not to watch him as he climbed into the Mercedes. Whooooeee. Christopher Bishop was, for lack of a better word, a complete hunk.

He was gorgeous when he frowned, but when he'd smiled at her, he was downright devastating. Dry, he was beautiful. But wet he was stupendous. Looking at him, with his dress shirt molded to his muscular arms and chest and his hair combed back by his hands, she got a clear image of what he must look like coming out of the shower. She thanked God she wasn't a cartoon character—her eyes would have bugged out two feet and her tongue would have rolled out onto the ground.

Well, she'd never see him again. Good thing, too. Any guy who looked that good and smelled that good was a hazard to her mental health. She knew first-hand that men who looked like Christopher Bishop couldn't be trusted. Brokenhearted women probably littered the sidewalks around his house. Yup, he had *girl in every port* written all over him. She exhaled loudly. *Been there. Done that. Never again.*

She put the Dodge in gear and pulled forward,

driving to the end of the curved driveway. The moment her foot touched the brake, the car stalled.

"Oh, no. Not again."

Melanie turned the key. Growl, growl, silence. She turned it again. Growl, silence. One more turn. Silence. She looked around her. At least she wasn't completely blocking the driveway. Cars could get around her. She was just contemplating the wisdom of screaming and pulling out her hair when a horn tooted. She looked out her window and saw the Mercedes pull up next to her.

She felt around on the seat for the knob to open the window. Finding it, she jammed it back on and rolled down the window. Christopher Bishop looked at her from the driver's seat of his car.

"What's wrong?" he called.

"I stalled out."

"There must be something more wrong than the battery," he said, frowning. "Probably faulty spark plugs, or a wet distributor cap."

"Oh." Faulty spark plugs. And her thingamabob was wet. Swell.

"I'd try drying it off for you, but there's not much point as long as it's still drizzling."

Melanie muttered a mild oath. Now what? It would seem a call to Nana was in order. She rolled up the window, opened the door, and slid out. No point bothering with the umbrella. The rain was now nothing more than an annoying drip-drip, and she was soaked anyway. And barefoot. It seemed this day was just getting worse by the minute.

She'd only taken two steps when she heard Chris yell, "Where are you going?"

She turned. He stood next to his car, munching

on a chicken leg. "I'm going to call someone to pick me up."

He hesitated a second, then said, "I could drop you off . . . but I warn you, it's gonna cost you some more food." He took another bite and grinned. "It's great chicken, by the way."

Melanie considered his offer. Nana would have to close up shop to rescue her. Besides, her grandmother shouldn't drive—she was a hazard on the road. That was why Melanie had made the deliveries tonight—she'd been elected by default.

Christopher Bishop seemed like a decent guy. He certainly wasn't hard to look at, he smelled great, and he hadn't made any untoward gestures when she'd been sprawled across his lap. Besides, she had pepper spray in her glove compartment. She'd bring it with her. One false move and the guy would be toast. Pepper toast.

"How much more food?" she asked, walking back toward the Dodge.

"How much ya got?"

She laughed. "Okay, Christopher. I'll trade you a ride to the Pampered Palate for two more chicken dinners. It's just a few miles down the road. On Peachtree."

"Deal. Let's go."

While he transferred the heavy box from the Dodge to the Mercedes, Melanie grabbed her purse and stuck the pepper spray inside. Hey, a girl could never be too careful.

She slid into the soft leather passenger seat of the luxurious Mercedes and sighed. A Billy Joel tune flowed from the CD player. "Nice car. It still smells new."

"I only bought it two months ago," he said, easing

his way into the Friday-night traffic. "A present to myself for making partner."

"You're a lawyer?" she asked, praying he wasn't from Slickert, Cashman, and Rich.

"No. Accountant."

"Ah. And you work in that office building?"

"Yup. Twenty-fifth floor."

She cocked her head toward the CD player. "You a Billy Joel fan?"

"Everybody from New York is a Billy Joel fan."

She stared at his profile. "You're from New York?"

"That's not a crime, you know."

"Of course it isn't. I'm originally from the Big Apple myself."

"I thought I detected a bit of an accent. What part of New York?"

"Long Island. You?"

"Westchester." He looked over and smiled at her. "Seems like everybody in Atlanta is from somewhere else. What brought you down south?"

"I couldn't afford New York. Atlanta's a happenin' place, the weather's great, and it's affordable. So here I am." She tapped her bare foot to the music. "Have you lived here long?"

"Since high school. My dad was transferred during my sophomore year."

She winced in sympathy. "That must have been tough."

"At the time, I thought it was the end of the world." He shot her a sheepish grin. "I think I set a world record for complaining."

"Considering the way you carried on about being blocked in, I'm not surprised to hear it," Melanie teased.

"Very funny. So, how long have you worked for the Pampered Palate?"

"Ever since it opened six months ago." She hummed along to "Uptown Girl" for several seconds, then added, "Actually, I own it."

His brows shot up. "You own the Pampered Palate?"

"Yes. Well, me and the bank. That fried chicken is our best-selling item. It's Nana's secret recipe and she guards it with her life."

"Nana?"

"My Grandma Sylvia. I've always called her Nana. We live together and she helps out in the kitchen."

"Do you usually make your own deliveries?"

Melanie shook her head. "My delivery man called in sick at the last minute. Nana offered to step in, but as much as I love her, she's a menace on the road. Sort of a cross between Mario Andretti and Mr. Magoo. Anyway, we offer free delivery on orders over a hundred dollars. That's mostly corporate accounts."

She slanted him a sidelong look. "Our motto is, 'If it's not delivered on time, it's on us.' That's why I double-parked." She jerked her head toward the backseat. "I had five minutes to get that box of food upstairs or I was out two hundred bucks."

"Why do you still have it?"

"The customers had some sort of emergency. They called and canceled the order, but I'd already left."

"Who was it for?"

"Slickert, Cashman, and Rich, Attorneys at Law. Thirtieth floor. I wonder what happened."

"Walter Rich was rushed to the hospital," Chris said.

"Oh, no! Is he okay?"

"I think so. He slipped and fell. His leg is broken and he might have cracked a few ribs. The ambulance came around seven."

"How awful. Which hospital was he taken to?"

"Piedmont, I think."

"I'll have to call and find out how he is," Melanie said. "He's such a nice man, and one of my best customers. He looks just like—"

"Santa Claus without the beard," Chris finished for her. "My firm audits them. Walter's a great guy."

Chris maneuvered the Mercedes into the small parking lot adjacent to the Pampered Palate. "Here we are. I'll help you with the box."

Melanie held the door for him and they walked into the small front room of the brightly lit store. No one was there behind the glossy dark green granite counter, decorated with a vase of cheerful flowers and a stack of takeout menus. The gleaming parquet floor lent the small space a cozy feel, while the cream-colored walls gave it a dignified air. No tables. The Pampered Palate was strictly takeout.

When she saw him looking around, Melanie said, "I know it's small, but I'm hoping to expand. I want to buy a delivery truck and do private catering on the weekends, then eventually expand into a full restaurant."

"Ambitious goals," he said, nodding, "but if your food is any indication of your talents, I'm sure you'll succeed."

"Thanks." She set her purse on the counter. "I really appreciate the ride. It was very nice of you, especially considering the inconvenience I caused you."

"What are you going to do about your car?"

Melanie shrugged. "I'm not sure. The only person

I know who knows anything about cars is my delivery man, and he's sick."

"You can't leave it parked in that driveway the whole weekend. It'll get towed."

Towed. She hadn't thought of that. Just what she needed—another expense. "I'll think of something," she said.

He set the box down on the counter, and Melanie smothered a laugh. The rip in his pants was a good six inches across. A patch of white boxers stuck out, complete with a smear of barbecue sauce. She smiled and pulled out two dinners.

"Hey, Melanie!" Nana's scratchy voice reached them. The energetic woman who walked in from the kitchen was a cross between Julia Child and Richard Simmons. She stared at Chris. "Jiminy Cricket. Who's the babe magnet?"

Melanie coughed to cover up a laugh. "Nana, this is Christopher Bishop. I had some car trouble and he gave me a ride."

"Sylvia Gibson," Nana said, sticking out a flour-encrusted hand.

Chris shook her hand and said, "You make the best fried chicken in Atlanta, ma'am."

Nana blushed and patted her short, frizzy, bright red hair. "Call me Nana. So, you after my grand-daughter or what?"

"Nana!"

"She's a great cook and she's single," her grand-mother continued, unrepentant. "Drives a piece of crap for a car, but she won't give it up. She's stubborn but good-hearted, and loves kids and pets." She peered at him over her bifocals. "What do you think?"

Melanie groaned and covered her eyes with her

hands, but Chris just smiled. He leaned close to Nana's fire-engine red hair and said, "I think I'm going to charm her out of some more chicken, then see if I can talk her into parting with some cheesecake."

Nana laughed and slapped her knee, sending her knee-high stocking down to her ankle. "Well, good luck, son. Mel hasn't parted with any cheesecake in quite a while. I keep telling her to loosen up a little, but does she listen to me? No. All she does is work, work, work."

She turned to Melanie, who felt as if the fires of hell were burning in her cheeks. "I'd hold onto this one if I were you. He's cute, smart, and he's got a great butt. Needs some new pants, though. I don't care for this fashion of lettin' your drawers hang out of holes in your pants. At least the hole's in the back, otherwise his—"

"Thank you, Nana," Melanie broke in hastily. "Why don't you head back to the kitchen? I'll be right there."

Nana fixed Chris with a stern glare. "You fix up those britches, young man, before you call on my granddaughter."

Chris gave a smart salute. "Yes, ma'am."

"And clean that barbecue sauce off your ass," Nana said over her shoulder.

Melanie smothered a chuckle, not sure what amused her more—Nana's remark or the look on Christopher Bishop's face.

He cleared his throat. "Your nana is . . ."

"Outspoken? Irrepressible?" Melanie supplied.

"Actually, I was thinking she was pretty great." He smiled, and it did odd things to Melanie's knees.

"She reminds me of my mom. Keeps forgetting I'm not six years old."

Melanie laughed, but her laughter slowly faded as she looked at him, really looked at him for the first time in the bright light. His good looks were no illusion caused by darkness or rain. He was a veritable DNA masterpiece.

Whatever gene pool he swam out of deserved its own display at the Smithsonian. Thick, wavy mahogany brown hair beckoned her fingers to ruffle through it. His dark blue eyes reminded Melanie of her favorite color from her childhood Crayola crayons, midnight blue. His mouth was sensuous, his lips full and firm. An unbidden image of him kissing her flashed through her mind. Full-blown lust slammed into her so hard she gasped.

"What's wrong?" he asked. "Do I have chicken stuck between my teeth?"

An embarrassed laugh escaped her. "No. I was, er, just . . ."

"Staring." He took a step closer to her, and Melanie's heart shifted into overdrive. "You were staring at me."

Melanie averted her eyes, ready to deny his words when she caught a glimpse of her reflection in the glass door. Her short, curly hair stuck up from her head at all angles—like hundreds of tiny vacuum cleaner hoses had sucked it up. No shoes, torn stockings, wrinkled shirt. And her face. Good grief, her face.

Just her luck. Here she stood, looking like the creature from the black lagoon, with the winner of the *GQ* "Man of the Year" contest. *Story of my life. I've got permanent when-my-ship-comes-in-I'll-be-at-the-airport syndrome, while* he *looks like he'd never miss the boat.*

"Are you okay?" he asked.

Melanie shook her head. "I just caught a glimpse of myself. Yikes. I'm surprised you didn't run screaming from the store the moment we arrived."

He stepped closer and tilted his head, studying her like an art patron assessing a Picasso. "You look like a raccoon," he pronounced.

She pasted a sticky-sweet smile on her face. "Thanks. I guess I won't take offense, since the source of that opinion is a guy whose ass is hanging out of his pants."

"Touché." Laughing, he touched a finger to the black smudge under her right eye. "I have three sisters. I'm used to this look." He smiled at her. "Besides, I bet you clean up pretty good."

Melanie tried to swallow and couldn't. The moment he touched her with that single gentle finger, all the spit in her mouth dried up and left her tongue feeling like dust.

He glanced at his watch and frowned. "Listen, it's late and I need to go before I fall asleep on my feet." He picked up the two boxed dinners she'd set aside. "Thanks for the chicken."

Melanie cleared her throat. He was the most gorgeous man she'd ever met, and he was leaving. She'd never see him again. Good. Fine. She didn't have time for men anyway. Men were nothing but pains in the tush. She knew that all too well. Yes, indeed. She could thank her ex-fiancé for that lesson. Todd Jenkins had taught her all she needed to know about men. And the better-looking they were, the worse they were. This guy probably had more notches on his bedpost than Mick Jagger. Yup, it was a good thing he was leaving. She wanted nothing to do with—

He touched her arm. "Okay?"

She stared at him. Clearly he'd been talking to her while her thoughts ran away. "Huh? Okay what?"

"You must be more tired than I am. I said I have to go." He held out his hand. "It was, er, *interesting* meeting you. Thanks again for the dinner."

"Thanks for the ride."

Melanie thought she sensed a momentary hesitation in him, almost as if he was reluctant to leave. She discovered she was holding her breath. Was he going to ask her out? *Oh, sure. I look like something the cats dragged in that the kittens wouldn't eat.* Not that it mattered. She didn't want a guy cluttering up her life.

"Good luck with your car." He flashed her a smile. "Brush your hair, okay?"

Smart aleck. "Change your pants, okay?"

He laughed. "Deal." Balancing the boxes in one hand like a professional waiter, he walked out the door. Melanie stood rooted to the spot for a good two minutes.

"Jiminy Cricket," said Nana from behind her. "He's a real hunk."

Turning around to face her grandmother's knowing eyes, Melanie adopted what she hoped was a casual air. "I suppose a certain type would find him attractive."

"What type is that?"

Melanie sighed. "The female type."

"So why'd you let him get away?" Nana smacked her lips. "I woulda hog-tied that sucker and made him my love slave."

Melanie couldn't help but smile. "I'm not looking for a love slave. I'm not looking, period. A man is the last thing I need."

"Phooey. A man is *exactly* what you need. A little passion, a little lust, they're great for the soul."

Maybe. But Melanie had a sinking feeling that a *little* passion and a *little* lust would not be the problem where Christopher Bishop was concerned.

Thank goodness she would never see him again.

TWO

Chris entered his sparsely decorated Buckhead condo and breathed a sigh of relief. He plopped his briefcase in the ceramic-tiled foyer and was half undressed by the time he reached his bedroom. Leaving his ruined clothes in a heap on the bathroom floor, he stepped into the shower and allowed the stinging spray to massage away his stress-induced aches.

It didn't take long for his neck and shoulders to feel better, but there was one ache that he couldn't seem to wash away—the ache brought on by Mel Gibson's lush body pressed up against him. He shook his head. He was definitely going to have to call her Melanie. If anyone got wind of the fact that he was having erotic thoughts about Mel Gibson, he'd have some explaining to do.

He turned off the shower and grabbed a towel. Rubbing his hair dry, he tried to recall the last time a woman had turned him on so much so fast, and couldn't think of one. Not one of the women he'd dated in the last several years had ignited more than a fleeting spark.

And neither had any of the women his determined-to-see-her-single-son-married mother constantly threw in his path. He shuddered, recalling the last "perfect girl" Mom had introduced him to. Turned out Miss Perfect was looking for a candidate to father her child. She had a thing for accountants and was anxious to discuss "loopholes." He'd barely made it away from her alive.

He pushed away the unpleasant memory and pulled on a clean pair of sweats, then headed toward the kitchen. Popping the top on a beer, he settled in at the built-in snack bar with his Pampered Palate dinner.

Pampered Palate. He stared at the blue and red logo on the container and frowned. That name set off a chorus of bells in his mind, but he still couldn't pin down the source.

His gut told him it was work-related, but his memory refused to cooperate and tell him why the Pampered Palate and the name Melanie Gibson struck a familiar chord in him.

Melanie Gibson. Hmmm. Chris washed down a bite of cole slaw with a swig of beer and shook his head. By all accounts he should be furious with her. The woman and her dilapidated car had *headache* written all over them. The next stop for his new suit was the dumpster, and his shoes would probably suffer the same fate.

But something about her had prompted him to offer her a ride. Maybe it was her forlorn expression when her car died the second time. Or maybe it was because if one of his sisters had been in a similar fix, he'd want someone to give them a hand. Maybe it was simply her fabulous fried chicken.

He thought of her, in those wet, clinging clothes, sprawled across his lap, trying to unsnag his pants, and he blew out a breath.

Fried chicken. Yeah. Right.

He'd taken one look at her delectable curves, those big mascara-smudged eyes, and those moist, full lips and lost his mind. Lust had smacked him with the force of a two-by-four to the face. She was cute, funny, and unassuming—definitely very attractive in spite of her disheveled appearance. And he really liked the way she'd laughed off her raccoon eyes and Bride of Frankenstein hair. Something about her strummed a chord in him—a note no one had plucked in a long, long time.

But the timing stank.

His life was just beginning to be uncomplicated. He reflected on the difficulties he'd faced since becoming "man of the house" after his father's sudden death twelve years ago. He'd struggled to put himself through school, then spent the last eight years helping his mother put his sisters and brother through college. The youngest, his brother Mark, had finally graduated two months ago. Chris made partner soon after that, and now his life, and his finances, were finally unencumbered.

And for the first time in two years he didn't have his brother for a roommate. Mark had moved out right after graduation. No more worrying about walking in on each other while a date was there. No fighting over the bathroom or the remote. And Mark was a neat freak. They got along fine, but Chris was secretly relieved that he could finally leave a dirty dish in the sink without receiving a lecture.

He loved his family, but he was thirty years old and he wanted to play. He wanted to leave his socks on the floor, let dust bunnies grow under the sofa, blast his stereo. He imagined popping off to the Caymans for a weekend, having a beach fling, hanging out with his buddies.

But it seemed that being partner at Waxman, Barnes, Wiffle, and Hodge left little time for jaunts to the Caribbean. Worse, the women interested in beach flings bored him, and his buddies were either married or shortly due to wander down the aisle. Still, he'd waited a long time to live the footloose, fancy-free bachelor life, and by damn he was going to!

Unfortunately Melanie Gibson didn't strike him as a one-night stand sort of girl. No, she was not at all the type of woman he wanted to meet *now*. Maybe in five years. She had *long-term* written all over her, and for now he wanted his long-term to be no more than two hours. Three hours tops.

Still, it hadn't been easy to walk away from her. He swallowed a mouthful of baked beans and found himself wondering what she was going to do about her car.

Shaking his head, he forced his thoughts into another direction. He wanted to date sleek, blond, model types. Why would he want a lunatic brunette who drove a rusted-out '77 Dodge?

An image of Melanie sprawled across his lap flashed in his mind and he groaned. Okay, he knew why he would want her, but he had to forget her. He'd never see her or her dilapidated car again. That was good. Definitely very good.

The phone interrupted his thoughts, and he snatched up the receiver. " 'Lo."

"Christopher, how are you, dear?"

"Hi, Mom." He bit into a chicken thigh and prayed Lorna Bishop wasn't going to announce that she'd fixed him up with another of her friends' daughters.

He should have known better.

"Guess what?" she asked.

Chris's warning antennae immediately rose. He knew that innocent voice, that innocuous question all too well. He stifled a groan.

"Can't imagine, Mom."

"Well, you know the family cookout we're having on Sunday to celebrate Mark's new job?"

He'd completely forgotten, but he knew better than to say so. "Yes. The cookout Sunday. What about it?"

"Well, Cousin Ralph called. He and Margie are bringing along Margie's second cousin's neighbor's sister for you to meet. Her name is Zoë Kozlowski. Ralph says she has a *great* personality. She's twenty-nine, looking to settle down, and—are you ready?—she's a *florist*. Isn't that exciting? I just love flowers. I'm sure you two will have *so* much to talk about."

Uh-oh. The warning bells in Chris's head reached alarming proportions. He had to do something and quick, or Mom would be picking out china patterns with Zoë Kozlowski the florist within the week.

"Mom, I appreciate this, but I can get my own dates."

"Of course you can," Mom said, her voice cheery but determined, "but you don't get them. All you do is work, work, work. If you got your own dates, I wouldn't try to fix you up."

Promises, promises. "Mom, I date. I've just been really busy at work."

"Humph. When's the last time you met a nice girl?"

Chris closed his eyes and prayed for patience. An image of Melanie Gibson flashed in his mind, and his eyes popped open.

"Tonight," he improvised in a jiffy. "In fact, I had a date tonight." Sort of. Kinda. *Okay, I'm a big fat liar, but these are desperate circumstances.* He imagined Zoë I'm-looking-to-settle-down Kozlowski, and the picture wasn't good. God help him. Besides, the story wasn't a total lie. The part about meeting a nice girl tonight was true enough.

"How wonderful! What's her name?"

Chris pinched the bridge of his nose. *Me and my big mouth.* "Her name is Melanie."

Lorna chirped out a barrage of questions. "Have you known her long? What's she like? What does she do? Where does she live?"

"I haven't known her long. She lives with her grandmother, and she owns the Pampered Palate."

"Pampered Palate? What's that?"

"A gourmet food takeout place."

Chris could almost hear the wheels turning in his mother's pretty, matchmaking head. "So she cooks."

"Uh, yeah."

"Wonderful! Tell her to bring a dessert to the cookout. I can't wait to meet her. Your sisters will be so excited you've met someone. We'll see you both on Sunday! Oh, and tell Melanie to bring her grandmother if she wants. Two o'clock. Oops! There's the doorbell. Gotta go!, Bye."

The dial tone sounded in Chris's ear. He placed the receiver back on the cradle and thumped himself on the forehead. His mother had missed her calling. She should have enlisted in the military—she could outmaneuver General Colin Powell. Now she expected him to bring his "date" on Sunday, not to mention dessert.

He finished his beer in a single gulp, reviewing his choices. There was Zoë Kozlowski, the florist with the "great personality," or Melanie Gibson, the gourmet cook with the killer bod who had his libido dancing the Lambada.

Neither one, he suspected, would do his mental health any good.

Well, tomorrow night he had a *real* date with Claire Morrison, a marketing executive he'd met several weeks earlier. She was blond, beautiful, and smart, and she'd sent out very definite signals that she had no qualms about kissing—or "whatever"—on the first date.

He wondered how she felt about cookouts.

Late the next afternoon, Chris parked his Mercedes in the Piedmont Hospital lot. Glancing at his watch, he estimated he could spend about thirty minutes visiting Walter Rich and still have plenty of time to pick up his date.

Carrying a cheerfully wrapped copy of John Grisham's latest legal thriller, he strode into the brightly lit hospital, checked in at the information desk, and made his way to Walter's room. When he walked in, he saw his friend sitting up in bed, smiling at a dark-haired woman who had her back turned to Chris.

"Christopher Bishop!" Walter exclaimed when he saw his new visitor. "What a nice surprise."

Chris opened his mouth to say hello, but the words died in his throat as the woman turned around to face him. Big chocolate-brown eyes stared at him with a clearly surprised expression.

"Don't just stand there in the doorway," Walter said. "Come on in and join the party." He indicated the woman with a wave of his hand. "This is Melanie Gibson, a dear friend who took pity on a starving old man and brought me the most scrumptious feast. Melanie, this is Christopher Bishop, an accountant at—"

"One Atlanta Plaza, twenty-fifth floor," Melanie finished for him with a smile. "Chris and I have already met." She stood and held out her hand. "Nice to see you again."

Chris stepped into the room and shook her hand. Same soft skin, same lush lips, same deep dimples. And boy, did she clean up nice. A riotous mop of chin-length reddish-brown curls framed an uncommonly attractive face. His gaze traveled downward. She wore a neon-green T-shirt that read KISS THE COOK, faded Levis, and Nikes that had seen better days. Not exactly come-hither clothes. So why did his heart rate suddenly accelerate? And why did the slogan on her T-shirt seem like the best idea since the invention of the telephone?

"I see you took my advice," she said.

He brought his wandering gaze back to her face. "What advice is that?"

"You changed your pants."

He reached out and gently tugged one of her shiny curls. "You combed your hair."

She laughed. "I didn't have much choice. Every dog on the block would have tried to bury me in the backyard if I hadn't."

"*Ahem!* Remember me?" asked Walter in an amused tone from the bed. "The guy with the broken leg, cracked ribs, and other assorted aches and pains."

Chris leaned around Melanie and smiled at the lawyer. "So sue me. She's prettier than you are." After setting the gift-wrapped book on the nightstand,

Chris pulled over a chair. He sniffed the air. "Do I smell cookies?"

Walter nodded. "Homemade double chocolate chunk cookies." He passed a round tin to Chris. "Melanie baked them for me, and they're *mine*. Since you were kind enough to visit me, you may have *one*."

"What happens if I take two?" Chris asked, reaching into the tin.

"Lawsuit," Walter said without hesitation.

Chris made a horrified face. "Okay! Only one cookie." He took a bite and groaned. "Wow. I think I might have to risk the lawsuit."

Despite Walter's threats, the cookie tin was soon empty. Chris discovered that Melanie not only made the best cookies on earth, she also had the sexiest laugh he'd ever heard—a low, throaty rumble that reminded him of fine brandy. Warm, smooth, and delicious. He was enjoying himself so much, he forgot the time. When he glanced at his watch, he realized that if he didn't leave immediately, he'd be late picking up his date.

He stood. "I'm afraid I have to get going," he said, surprised at his reluctance to depart.

Melanie leaned over and sneaked a peek at his watch. "Good grief. I need to leave also."

"Thank you both for coming," Walter said, giving Chris's hand a hearty shake and accepting a kiss from Melanie. "And thank you for the dinner, my dear. Best veal piccata I've ever eaten."

"My pleasure, Mr. Rich. When you're feeling better, I'll bake you some more cookies."

"In that case, I see a miraculous recovery right around the corner," he replied, his eyes twinkling.

After a final wave from the doorway, Chris and Melanie headed down the hall together. "He's such a nice man," Melanie remarked once they were in the elevator.

"Very nice," Chris agreed. His gaze wandered over her, studying her profile. He wasn't aware he was staring until she turned toward him.

"Something wrong?" she asked, cocking a single brow.

Chris shook his head. "No. I was just realizing I was right."

She gave an unladylike snort. "Oh, brother. A man realizing he's right. Now *there's* a shocker. Good thing I'm not in my heart attack years. I might just keel over." She slanted him a pursed-lips look. "What were you right about?"

"You *do* clean up pretty good."

Chris watched, amused, as a bright pink blush stained her cheeks.

"Oh," she said. "Ah, thanks. You, too."

The elevator door opened and they stepped out. "Where's your car?" Chris asked.

"Parked in my driveway." A sheepish half-smile touched her lips. "I practically dragged my sick delivery man out of bed this morning to help me. He tinkered with the engine a bit and got it started, but I'd no sooner arrived home than the ole Dodge coughed, burped, and spit for several agonizing minutes, then died." She shook her head sadly. "It was painful to watch."

"How did you get here?"

"By cab."

"How are you getting home?"

"By cab. In fact, I'd better call one." She smiled and held out her hand. "It was nice seeing you again."

Chris absently shook her hand. "Yeah. Nice."

She turned and walked away, heading toward the bank of pay phones in the lobby. Chris watched her, his eyes glued to her curvy derrière. He looked at his watch. Even if he set a new land speed record, he would still be late picking up his date.

For reasons he could not logically explain, he found himself jogging across the ceramic tile floor to catch up with her. His mind was saying "I'm outta here," but his feet were not cooperating at all.

"Where do you live?"

She turned, clearly surprised. "Why?"

"I'll give you a ride home."

She eyeballed him. "You look like you're ready for a date. I wouldn't want to make you late."

"I have time," he heard himself say, "provided you don't live in Oklahoma."

She laughed. "Actually, I'm pretty close by. Only about ten minutes from here."

"Great. Let's go."

Chris followed her through the revolving door. The instant they stepped outside, a blast of hot, humid air hit them. He led her to the Mercedes, opened the door for her, then settled himself behind the wheel.

"Where to, lady?" he asked in his best New York cabbie voice.

Smiling, she gave him directions. Except for "Turn left here" and "Make a right at the stop sign," the drive was made in relative silence. Chris spent the ride convincing himself that he'd only offered to drive her home because it was the chivalrous thing to do. It had nothing to do with *her.* Not a thing.

True to her word, ten minutes later he pulled up in front of a small, neat brick ranch. A profusion of pink and white flowers filled the carefully tended

beds, and the postage-stamp–sized lawn was lush and
green. The only thing that looked out of place was
the lime-green, rusted-out eyesore sitting in the driveway.

A young girl, maybe twelve years old, sitting on the
front steps waved. Melanie waved back and said,
"That's my neighbor's daughter. I promised to help
her bake her mom a birthday cake." She unhooked
her seat belt and opened the car door. "Thanks. I
really appreciate the ride. Cab fare kinda strains the
budget."

"My pleasure."

"Enjoy your date."

Date? He stared into her big brown eyes and lost
his ability to think straight. Just looking at her made
him swell against his trousers. With an effort he
snapped out of it. Date. Right.

She slammed the car door, shot him a dimpled
smile, and ran across the lawn to the porch. She ruf-
fled the girl's hair then turned and waved at him
before following the child into the house.

Chris stared at the cozy house. His plans for the
evening somehow had lost their appeal, and he
found himself wishing he could stay and watch her
bake that birthday cake. Her kitchen was undoubtedly welcoming and homey, and he bet it smelled
great.

He puffed out a breath and shook his head. What
the hell was he thinking? He had a date with a real
babe, and here he sat, mooning over a woman who
was clearly not his type.

Good thing she was gone. Her and her big brown
eyes and soft, luscious mouth. He shifted in his seat.
His pants felt uncomfortably snug.

Must have been all those darn cookies he ate.

THREE

Ten minutes into his date with Claire Morrison the marketing executive, Chris realized she was not cook-out material. By the time their dinner was served, he'd summed Claire Morrison up as a self-centered bore, and by the time dessert rolled around, he was ready to stuff his napkin in her mouth just to shut her up.

Tuning out her plaintive complaints about her last boyfriend, Chris studied her from across the table with an objective eye. The woman was undeniably gorgeous. Her tall, slim physique, combined with her shoulder-length blond hair and startling aqua eyes guaranteed she'd attract male attention wherever she went. She was savvy, successful, and had made it plain that sex was in his immediate future—just the sort of woman with whom he envisioned whiling away his bachelor hours.

He couldn't wait to get rid of her.

The woman *hated* everything—her mother, her sister, her job, her apartment, her six ex-boyfriends, and the key lime pie she'd ordered for dessert. Unable to stand much more of her, he quickly paid the check and drove her home. The instant he shifted the Mercedes into park, she slid across the seat. Wrapping her arms around his neck, she kissed him, thrusting her tongue into his mouth.

Chris knew he should be thinking *yippee*.

Instead he was thinking *yuck*.

He let the kiss go on for nearly a minute, hoping she'd ignite some sort of response in him, but she left him totally cold. It was as if his hormones had suddenly packed themselves up in little suitcases and left the country.

She lifted her head and stared at him briefly before scooting back to her seat. After checking her makeup in the mirror, she turned to him. "Dinner was nice, but I don't think we should see each other again."

Thank you, God. "All right." He suspected his male ego should feel deflated, but all he felt was relief. Profound relief.

"You're a nice guy," she added, apparently thinking he needed an explanation, "but there's really no spark here, you know?"

Chris just nodded, happy that she'd said it first.

She exited the car and he drove away, inhaling his first easy breath in hours.

When Chris arrived home twenty minutes later, he had two messages on his machine. Snagging a beer from the fridge, he slipped off his shoes, plopped on the sofa, and pushed the playback button.

The first message was from his mother. "Hi! It's Mom. Just calling to tell you to bring your bathing suit tomorrow. We're all looking forward to meeting your *friend* Melanie. And don't forget, Zoë the florist will be there, too. Looks like you'll be busy!, Bye!"

The second message kicked in. "It's Mom again. Don't forget to bring dessert!, Bye!"

Groaning, Chris stretched out his legs, laid back his head, and closed his eyes. For reasons he didn't understand, he felt irritable and out of sorts. Of course, spending the last two hours listening to Claire Morrison piss and moan about everything under the sun didn't help, but it was more than that.

It was *her.*

Her and her darn cookies. And those big, brown, puppy-dog eyes.

Melanie Gibson.

He couldn't seem to get the damn woman off his mind. Her, and the fact that the name *Pampered Palate* was so familiar. While Claire had incessantly blathered on, his thoughts had wandered to Melanie dozens of times. But what good did that do him? What was the point of thinking about a woman who was all wrong for him, and whom he'd probably never see again?

He recalled his mother's messages and puffed out a breath. Mom expected him to bring a date to the cookout tomorrow. Claire was out of the question, and being fixed up with Zoë the florist held no appeal.

Chris suddenly sat up straight. Actually, his mother didn't expect him to bring a *date*—she expected him to bring *Melanie*. If he could convince Melanie to go, he'd be saved from Zoë *and* satisfy his mother's matchmaking tendencies in one fell swoop. He looked at his watch. It was past eleven—too late to call Melanie. He'd have to phone her in the morning. Or even better, maybe he'd stop by her house. Offer to take a look at her car.

Yeah, that's the ticket. Fix her car, and she'll come to the cookout. Bishop, you're a genius. Everybody wins. Melanie gets her car repaired, I'm saved from the horrors of a fix-up, and Mom will get off my back about not dating.

Of course, his plan meant having to spend the day with Melanie. A slow smile spread across his face.

Oh, well. He'd suffer through it. Somehow.

At 7:45 the next morning, Melanie looked at the thermometer just outside her bedroom window and groaned. It was already eighty-six degrees. Another pizza-oven day.

She dressed in a bright lime-colored sleeveless shirt and neon tangerine shorts. She checked herself in the mirror and gave her mop of curls one last swipe with the comb. A slash of peach lipstick, scrunchy lime socks, and her beat-up Nikes, and she was ready to face the day.

Since she had an appointment with the bank tomorrow, she planned to spend this morning making sure all her business documents were in order. If all went well with the loan officer, she'd soon be buying her new catering truck. Expanding the *Pampered Palate* into private catering was something she desperately wanted and needed for the future of her business. In order to succeed, she had to grow.

But first, she needed caffeine. She brewed herself a cup of tea in the bright, sunny kitchen and spread the newspaper on the large, round oak table. She'd barely tasted her chamomile when the doorbell rang.

Mug in hand, she walked to the door, fully expecting to see one of her neighbors. All the neighbors knew Melanie kept a well-stocked kitchen, and someone was always stopping by to borrow a cup of this or a pinch of that. Melanie didn't mind—in fact, she enjoyed the easy camaraderie she shared with the people who lived nearby.

When she opened the door, however, it wasn't a neighbor but Christopher Bishop, a.k.a. the most beautiful man on earth, who stood on her porch.

His hair was just-out-of-the-shower damp. He wore a pale yellow Polo shirt, Docker shorts, bright white socks, and Reebok tennis shoes. A dusting of dark hair was sprinkled on the most gorgeous legs she'd ever seen on any man. And he smelled good enough to eat.

"Good morning," he said with a lopsided grin.

Melanie knew he was talking to her because she saw his lips moving, but she had no idea what he was saying. Her hormones, however, were apparently very aware that Christopher Bishop was in the area. After hibernating for more than a year, those little suckers were suddenly wide awake and anxious to be entertained.

Yesterday, the sight of Christopher Bishop had jump-started them like they'd been shot in the ass. They had started a veritable hormone-cheerleader kickline. Rah rah rah, sis-boom-bah, they yelled at the top of their tiny hormone lungs. Some action. At last.

Melanie rolled her eyes at her own thoughts. So he was gorgeous. So he smelled great. So he was nice. So what? He was a man, and therefore not to be trusted. A man who'd had a date last night, probably with some woman who'd jetted into town between modeling assignments.

She had no time, no space, and no inclination to start something with anyone. Besides, he was holding a bakery bag. Wasn't there some dire warning about men bearing gifts?

He waved his hand in front of her face. "Hello? You okay?"

Melanie mentally shook herself. "I'm fine. Just surprised to see you. Here. So early."

"I figured you were up because there was no newspaper out front." He peered around her. "Is this a bad time?"

"A bad time for what?"

He held up the bakery bag. "Breakfast."

"Breakfast?"

"Yeah. You know, that meal in the morning that starts off your day." He paused. "Can I come in?"

She opened her mouth to speak, but nothing came out. *Oh boy. I'm in trouble. Big, gigantic, whopper-sized trouble.* Six feet, two inches of the most delectable-looking male she'd ever clapped eyes on stood on her porch, wanting to come in. Her hormones let out a cheer and did the wave.

"Who's at the door?" came Nana's gravelly voice. She peered around Melanie. "Why, if it isn't the hunk!" Nana conducted a thorough inspection of their guest. "Wow, Mel, he's got great legs." She sniffed the air. "Do I smell doughnuts?"

Chris nodded. "Boston creme. Fresh from the oven."

Nana elbowed Melanie out of the way. "Well, come on in, honey, and bring your doughnuts. I'll put on some coffee."

He walked into the pale green tiled foyer. "I hope you don't mind me dropping by like this, but I thought you might need some help with your car."

Melanie's common sense suddenly kicked in. He'd brought breakfast *and* he wanted to fix her car? She narrowed her eyes and told her hormones to pipe down. Something was definitely fishy here. "Why would you want to fix my car?"

A slow, devastating smile touched his lips. "I admit I have an ulterior motive."

"Don't all men?"

He laughed. "More like a proposition."

Uh-oh. This guy probably dated supermodels—hell, he probably *broke up* with supermodels—and he had a proposition for her? Holy smokes. What if it was one of those propositions like Robert Redford made in *Indecent Proposal*—a million dollars for one night of naked splendor and unbridled lust?

Near panic set in. A million dollars? She'd never raise that kind of cash. But wait—no, *she'd* get the money. *And* get to sleep with him, too. Sweat broke out on her forehead. Her hormones switched to the Macarena.

"So what do you think?"

I think I've lost my marbles. You showed up and all my brain cells morphed into liquid and drained out of my body. She licked her dust-dry lips. "What do I think about what?"

His dark blue gaze skimmed over her, lingering on her mouth. "My proposition," he said in a deep, velvety voice that reminded Melanie of candlelight, champagne, and bubble baths. "I think it would work out well for both of us."

Her hormones abandoned the Macarena and started dancing the Peppermint Twist.

He stepped closer to her, until only a few inches separated them, his gaze fixed on her mouth. Heat radiated from his muscled body, warming her skin, and she squelched the urge to fan herself with her hand. *Jeez, it's hot in here.* His woodsy scent wrapped around her like a velvet cloak and it suddenly felt like all the oxygen had been sucked from the room.

"You're staring at me," he murmured, "in a very distracting way."

Ohmigod. He was going to kiss her. Right here in the foyer. He lowered his head. She was going to run. She was going to faint. She was going to—

"Coffee's ready!" Nana yelled.

Melanie jumped back with a gasp. Her hormones groaned in protest.

"Coffee's ready," she repeated in a shaky voice.

"Coffee. Right. That's exactly what I wanted. Coffee."

Melanie led him into the kitchen, mentally berating herself the whole way. This guy was dan-ger-ous. Yipes. Another second and he would have *kissed* her. If not for Nana's announcement, Melanie knew she would, at this very moment, be on the receiving end of what she had no doubt would have been a mind-blowing kiss. She could almost feel the warm caress of his sensuous mouth. Drat! *I mean, good thing Nana spoke when she did.* Her lips still tingled at the thought.

"Nice place," he said, settling his tall frame into one of the chintz-patterned chairs. "Very homey and cozy."

Melanie arranged the doughnuts on a serving plate while Nana poured the coffee into thick blue and yellow mugs.

"Mel was kind enough to let me move in with her a couple years back," Nana said. "I used to live in one of those retirement places in Florida, but I hated it. Nothin' but a bunch of hypochondriac old fogeys down there." She bit into a chocolate-iced doughnut and hummed her appreciation.

Sipping her coffee, Melanie stole glimpses of Chris

over the edge of her mug. He carried on an easy banter with Nana, telling her about his three married sisters and his younger brother. He genuinely seemed to enjoy her company.

Melanie hadn't dated much since breaking off her engagement to her philandering ex-fiancé over a year ago. In fact she'd gone on exactly three dates, all of them disasters, all forced on her by well-meaning friends. Aside from the fact that she hadn't wanted to date those men in the first place, her biggest problem with them was that they all objected to Nana.

None of them, including Todd, her ex-fiancé, would spare Nana more than a quick hello. Todd considered her a troublesome old lady, and the three dates had grumbled that Nana cramped their style. Well, Nana was not only Melanie's roommate, she was Melanie's best friend. And if you didn't like Nana, then the heck with ya.

But that didn't seem to be the case with Chris. He and Nana were yakking like they'd known each other for years. His warm, easygoing manner and teasing smile were a true surprise to Melanie. He couldn't really be a nice guy, could he? All that male pulchritude *and* nice? Nah. Impossible.

He threw back his head and laughed at something Nana said, and Melanie shook her head in wonder. If he wasn't nice, he was doing a damn good imitation of it. Darn it! He *had* to be a creep. She *wanted* him to be a creep. She needed a reason to tell him to get lost so her hormones would sit down and shut up.

He and Nana burst out laughing again, and Melanie's heart squeezed. Her common sense told her this was bad. Exceedingly bad. Her hormones broke out into a rousing chorus of "Our Day Will Come."

"Did you say something, dear?" Nana asked.

Melanie started out of her reverie. "Huh?"

"You were mumbling. Something about hormones." Nana peered at her over her bifocals. "Are you okay? You look flushed."

Melanie grabbed a doughnut. "I'm fine. The coffee's making me hot." *Yup. The coffee's making me hot. That's my story and I'm stickin' to it.*

They polished off the doughnuts in record time. Chris helped load the dishwasher, a gesture that sent Nana into a near swoon. When they finished cleaning up, Nana enfolded Chris in one of her famous bone-crushing hugs. "Any man who brings doughnuts *and* loads the dishwasher is okay in my book." She clapped him on the back with such enthusiasm that he almost fell down. "You're welcome at Casa Gibson anytime, young man." In a loud aside to Melanie, she added, "Don't let this one get away. He's a real honey. Great legs, too." She patted her frizzy hair. "Well, I'd better go fix myself up and set my hair. See you young folks later."

Melanie breathed a sigh of relief. Ten more minutes and Nana would be hinting about something old, something new, something borrowed, something blue.

Chris leaned his hips against the gleaming white countertop and smiled. "Your nana is quite a character."

Melanie's hackles rose. No one insulted Nana and got away with it. "Character? What's that supposed to mean?"

"Hey! Relax. I meant she's great. Very funny. I like her a lot."

Drat. He liked Nana. Didn't think she was a pest. And Nana obviously liked him. Why couldn't he have said what her last date said? Something to the effect that Nana was a crazy old bag. Then she could have sizzled him with a withering glance and told her hormones to take a hike. She glanced over at him. His profile was awesome. She needed a cold shower.

"So, do you want to observe while I look at your car," Chris asked, "or are you going to whip up some dessert?"

"Dessert? We just ate breakfast!"

"I meant for the cookout."

She stared at him. "What cookout?"

He stared back at her. "The cookout at my mother's house. Today. At two o'clock."

She shook her head. "I'm drawing a blank. Am I supposed to know about this?"

He laid his hand on her forehead. "Hmmm. No fever, but your short-term memory is shot."

Melanie stepped back from his disturbing touch. No fever? Coulda fooled her. She felt like she was melting from the inside out. "Refresh my memory."

"My proposition. I fix your car, and you come with me to the family cookout. I need a date so my mother doesn't try to fix me up with every single woman within a fifty-mile radius." He paused. "And we need to bring dessert."

Melanie cocked a brow at him. "Wow. What a romantic invitation. Be still my heart."

A devilish gleam sparkled in his eyes. He took her hand, entwined their fingers, and placed a warm kiss on the palm of her hand. "You want romance?"

"Yes. I mean *No!* I mean stop kissing my hand." She tried to snatch her hand away, but he held on tight, his eyes glittering with unmistakable mischief.

"Nana seemed to like the idea," he said. "She can't wait to go."

"*Nana?*" Melanie croaked. "*My* Nana? When did she agree to this?"

Chris shook his head. "It's terrible how the heat affects some people," he said, his expression filled with pity. "I told you in the foyer. Before breakfast. Nana and I discussed the plans while we were eating. Where were you?"

"I was, er, preoccupied, I guess."

"Well, you seem lucid now. So what do you say?" He dipped his head and looked up at her, a look no breathing woman could possibly be immune to. "C'mon. Nana already said yes. And you'd really be doing me a favor."

"Favor? Well, I guess so. I'd say I owe you one. Probably two, if you're the scorekeeping sort."

He ran his index finger down the bridge of her nose, causing a legion of chills to skitter down her spine. "I'm the scorekeeping sort, and you owe me three," he said softly.

"Three! How do you figure that?"

"One for blocking in my car, one for my ruined suit, and one for jump-starting your car. That's three."

"I gave you chicken, so you're down to two."

"I gave you a ride home. Three."

"I invited you in for breakfast. Two."

"I brought Boston creme doughnuts. Three."

Melanie shook her head. "Oh, all right. Three. Sheesh. You sound more like a lawyer than an accountant."

He shot her a woebegone look that reminded Melanie of a sad puppy.

"Hey!" she protested, suppressing a grin. "Quit

looking at me like that. I bet you practice that look in front of the mirror. No fair."

"I'm desperate. My mother wants to fix me up with some woman who has got two heads, breathes fire, and could eat me in one gulp." He chucked her under her chin. "Come on," he coaxed. "It'll be fun. And you'll get your car fixed for your trouble."

Melanie narrowed her eyes. "If, and I do mean *if* I save your sorry butt from the 'dragon lady,' then you have to call us even on the favor thing."

"You drive a hard bargain, Mel Gibson."

"Damn straight. And I have to be home early. I need to gather some papers for an appointment tomorrow morning."

He held out his hand. "Deal."

Melanie shook his hand, trying to ignore the zing of pleasure that zoomed up her arm at his touch. "Deal. Now haul it outside and fix my car."

He clicked his heels together and saluted her. "Aye, aye, Captain." He brushed past her, then paused in the doorway. "About dessert—Nana said *she'd* bake a cheesecake, so anything chocolate would be great." Flashing her a deadly grin and a big wink, he left. The front door closed several seconds later.

Melanie collapsed in a chair and waved her hand in front of her face in a hopeless effort to cool off.

Yup. She was in trouble for sure.

An hour later, Melanie stepped outside into the oppressive heat carrying a frosted mug of lemonade. Laughter bubbled up in her throat at the sight that greeted her eyes. The only part of Chris that was visible were his legs. The rest of him was under her car.

As much as she didn't want to, Melanie couldn't help but admire those muscular, tanned male legs.

Walking up to him, she tapped his Reebok with her Nike. "I brought you something to drink."

She watched him scoot out, moving sideways like a sand crab. When his head was clear, he stood up and wiped his dirty hands with an equally dirty rag. He was sweaty, rumpled, and sported a smudge of something black on his jaw. How could he possibly look so incredibly sexy?

He took the proffered lemonade and drained it in a series of nonstop gulps that drew Melanie's attention to the strong column of his tanned throat. When he finished, he touched the cold mug to his forehead. "Thanks. I needed that."

"Want some more?"

He shook his head. "Not now, thanks."

The proximity of his glistening skin was having a strange effect on her stomach. Stepping away from him, she asked, "How's it going?"

"Good. I just finished changing the oil. I gave you a complete tune-up and your battery is hooked up to my recharger. All that's left is changing the spark plugs." He indicated the opened hood with a jerk of his head. "Wanna watch?"

"Sure, but I have to warn you: I know diddly squat about cars."

"That's okay. I know diddly squat about making dessert."

Melanie followed him to the front of the car, watching him open a package of what she assumed were spark plugs. She wasn't sure what fascinated her more—the ease with which he selected foreign-looking items from his toolbox, or the way his muscles bunched and flexed while he worked. Whatever it was, she was soon thoroughly engrossed, and surprisingly curious.

She leaned over the engine with him, watching his every move, and asked a hundred questions.

"What's that little do-flickit?"

"That's the air filter," he said, screwing a spark plug into place.

"How about that thingamabob there?"

"The carburetor."

"I've heard of that. What's it do?"

"It vaporizes liquid fuel and controls its mixing with air for combustion in the engine."

"Uh-huh. And the English translation of that is . . . ?"

"It makes the car go *vroooomm.*"

"Ah."

She wiped a bead of sweat from her forehead with the back of her hand. "Whew. It sure is hot out here."

Chris snuck a glance at her and nodded in mental agreement. Hot as hell. And every time he looked at her, in her neon shorts and bright green top, it got a little hotter.

Her skin was the color of warm honey, and his fingers itched to sample its soft smoothness. Her reddish-brown hair was a riotous cap of untamed curls that begged to be touched. Her eyes reminded him of sweet, gooey, yummy chocolate, and her mouth . . . whoa! Her mouth made him think of carnal things that made sweat pool in his socks.

Her finger bounced back and forth and he answered all her questions, falling more and more in lust with each passing minute. His mind tried to convince his hormones that this was not the woman they were looking for—this woman was more than a one-nighter and represented a serious threat to his bachelor freedom—but his hormones were having none of it.

This is the one we want, his hormones said. *This one right here, who doesn't know an oil filter from a brake pad. The one who smells like fresh-baked brownies and stares at you with those big chocolatey-brown eyes. Now do something about it before we get nasty.*

She pointed to something else, asking what it was. When he turned his head to explain the intricacies of the wiper-fluid dispenser, they bumped noses. Chris froze and stared into her startled eyes.

She was so close—so heart-stoppingly close.

Before she could back away, and before he could change his mind, he did what he'd wanted to do since almost the first moment he saw her. He angled his head and brushed his mouth lightly over hers.

He should have expected the electric sizzle that crackled through him, but it was so strong, he nearly groaned. All thoughts of spark plugs, do-flickits, and thingamabobs drained from his head. He reached for her, pulling them both to their feet. Their heads smacked into the raised hood at the same time.

"Ouch!" Melanie yelped, rubbing the top of her head. "Wow. I feel dizzy. I bet I have a concussion."

Chris wrapped one arm around her waist, pulling her close, and ran gentle fingers over the small lump forming on her head. "Me, too."

She gazed up at him. "You think you have a concussion?"

"No. I feel dizzy. And it has nothing to do with hitting my head."

"The heat getting to you?"

His gaze settled on her mouth. "You could say that."

Her eyes widened. "Oh, my. You're going to kiss me again."

"That okay?"

"I'm not sure. The first one almost knocked me unconscious."

He took her face between his hands and lowered his head. "Yeah," he breathed against her mouth. "I know exactly what you mean."

Melanie decided that if their first kiss almost knocked her unconscious, their second kiss—which just sort of melted into their third, fourth, and fifth kisses—blew her socks right off the soles of her steaming feet.

He kissed her gently at first, almost an experimental tasting of lips. When he glided his mouth over hers more insistently, she wrapped her arms around his waist and held on tight. Good thing, too, because a few seconds later he slid his tongue into her mouth and her knees fell off.

She groaned and leaned into him, opening her mouth, eager for the warm invasion of his silky tongue brushing against hers. She hadn't been kissed in so long. And never this well. Never by someone who made her want to crawl into the same clothes with him and never come out. His bare legs brushed against hers and all the blood drained from her head and settled in a hot, bubbling pool in her belly.

His lips trailed a path of heat down the side of her neck while his hands slid down to her butt and hauled her up tight against him. She plunged her fingers into his thick hair and pressed herself closer. Either he was in the habit of carrying a cucumber around in his pocket, or he was as shaken by their kiss as she was.

When they finally came up for air, they stared at each other. "Holy smokes," she said when she could find her voice. "What was that?"

He looked as dazed as she felt. "I think," he said in a velvety rasp that brought to mind satin sheets and hot sex, "that was spontaneous combustion." He buried his face in her neck and breathed in. "You smell incredible. Like fresh-baked brownies and Ivory soap."

"Yup. That's one of my specialties. Ivory brownies. You eat and wash up at the same time. It's a real time-saver."

He touched his tongue to the side of her neck. "Sounds great."

"Glad you think so," she said, her voice a mere whisper. "I baked them just for you."

He lifted his head. "Brownies? For me?"

"Well, for the cookout. You said chocolate, and you look like the brownie type."

"What's the brownie type?"

The yummy, delicious, drool-inspiring, want-to-scarf-you-down in two bites and then go back for seconds type. "You're a male. That makes you the brownie type."

He leaned forward and gently bit the sensitive skin behind her ear. "If they taste half as good as you do, I'll be in heaven."

Melanie inhaled a deep breath and tried to calm her frazzled nerves, but it was hard to do with her hormones jumping up and down, giving each other high fives. "My toes feel like they're being barbecued over a slow flame."

He straightened, a sheepish, lopsided grin touching his lips. "I don't even want to mention what part of *my* anatomy feels like it's roasting over a flame," he said in that same velvety, goose-bump-inducing voice.

Melanie clearly read the desire and passion in his darkened eyes. "I think I have a pretty good idea. It's kinda hard to miss, seeing how it's poking me in the belly and all." She knew she should step back, away from him, away from his obvious arousal, but her feet refused to cooperate. Her feet were very happy right where they were. In fact, her whole body was perfectly content plastered smack up against his.

He cleared his throat and stepped back. "I, ah, think I'm done with the car."

"Oh?" What car? She managed to drag her gaze from his face and saw her Dodge. Memory returned. Ah. *That* car.

"Give me your keys and I'll try it out."

Melanie handed him the keys. "Watch the broken springs. I wouldn't want you to open an artery."

"Thanks," he said, his tone unmistakably dry.

Gingerly sitting on the seat, he slid the key in the ignition. The engine turned over on the third try.

He disconnected the battery recharger and slammed the hood of her car. "That should hold you for a while, but you need to have a mechanic look it over." He glanced at the crack in the windshield and the missing radio antenna. "Actually, what you need is a new car."

"Sorry, but a new car isn't in the budget. I'll just feed this baby a couple quarts of motor oil and she'll be fine." A hot wave of embarrassment washed over her, and Melanie looked down at her Nikes. Two minutes ago they were kissing like they couldn't get enough of each other, and now she didn't know what to say. She was scared to death that he was going to kiss her again.

She was scared to death that he wasn't.

He reached out and entwined their fingers. Lifting her hand to his mouth, he asked, "What's the matter, Mel Gibson? You look nervous." He took a step closer to her, until their bare legs brushed. "Am I making you nervous?"

"Certainly not," she lied in her haughtiest tone. Nervous? He made her more nervous than a dog on its way to the vet. And if he brushed the palm of her hand with his tongue once more, she was going to break out in hives. And probably rip off his clothes.

"You make me nervous," he said against her palm, his breath beating warmly on her skin.

"I do?"

"Big time. Every time I look at you my stomach feels weird."

"Probably ate some bad Boston creme," she suggested with a shaky laugh.

"I don't think so. But we can argue about it later."

"Later?"

"Yeah. I'll pick you and Nana up around one-thirty."

He neatly replaced his tools. Melanie tried not to notice how tanned and strong his arms looked, or how incredible they'd felt wrapped around her. She failed completely. She noticed and she remembered.

"There's a pool at my mom's subdivision," he said when he finished, "so bring your bathing suit. And don't forget dessert."

"Umm . . . dessert, Nana, bathing suit. Got it. Anything else?"

He brushed his mouth over hers in a quick kiss, then tousled her hair. "Nope. See ya, Mel." He ambled off to his car, whistling, like he hadn't a care in the world. Infuriating man. First he kissed her into oblivion, then he rumpled her hair like she was a dog.

After watching him drive away, Melanie walked into the house in a daze. She should have told him that she didn't want to see him again. When he'd offered his proposition, she should have said, "Sorry Chris, but I have no time for you and I don't want a relationship." Somehow that had turned into "Sure, I'll go to the cookout and bring dessert."

And now he'd kissed her. Kissed her until she'd all but melted into a steaming puddle on the driveway. She should have given him and his doughnuts a cheery *adios* and wished him a nice life. She should have slammed the door on his beautiful face. She should have—

Nana tapped her on the shoulder. "You've been standing here in the foyer for a good five minutes, staring off into space. You okay?"

Melanie snapped out of her fog. Okay? Not exactly. She felt like she'd been sucker punched in the heart. "I'm fine."

A sly grin eased over Nana's wrinkled face and she nudged Melanie in the ribs. "Great kisser, huh?"

Fire burned in Melanie's cheeks, but there was no point in denying it. Nana could read her like a book. "Actually, *great* is an understatement."

Nana slapped her knee and let out a whoop of laughter. "Well, it's about time! But I do have one piece of advice."

Good. Advice is what she needed. Levelheaded adult advice from her wise grandma. "I'm listening."

"Better change your shorts before you meet his mama." Nana cast a pointed glance at Melanie's rear.

"Mr. Great Kisser left a motor oil handprint on your butt." With that, Nana walked into the kitchen, chuckling.

Melanie twisted around and groaned. The seat of her shorts bore the black imprint of Chris's large hand. She didn't know much about motor oil, but she suspected it would be nearly impossible to wash it out of cloth. Now they were even on the ruined clothes thing, although she was only out a pair of shorts. He'd lost a suit.

She glanced again at the handprint and heat shimmered through her at the memory of him pulling her close, letting her feel his desire.

She needed to stay away from him.

In fact, she never wanted to see him again.

Damn it, she couldn't wait until 1:30.

FOUR

Chris lounged in a plastic chaise by the pool and struggled to keep his eyes off Melanie.

Talk about mission impossible.

From the moment he'd seen her in her bathing suit, all the blood had drained from his head and settled in his groin, a fact that made standing up without holding a towel or a newspaper in front of him a bit of a problem. For now he lounged, knees strategically bent, cradling an ice-cold can of Coke between his hands, and tried to carry on a conversation with his brother.

Mark was talking a mile a minute, but Chris had no idea about what. "Blah, blah, blah," Mark said. Chris nodded absently and made a few noncommittal noises in response, but he was too busy feasting his eyes on Melanie to follow Mark's story.

She was in the pool, playing in the shallow end with his five-year-old niece, Amanda. Water glistened on Melanie's honey-gold skin, her mop of curls sleeked back to seal-like slickness from the water. Amanda squealed with delight as Melanie tossed her a colorful beach ball.

Chris couldn't understand why Melanie's simple, black one-piece suit had sent his libido into such a frenzy, but it had. Probably because it showcased her long, lean legs, accentuated her slim waist, and hinted at cleavage, leaving him all but panting to see more.

He raked his hands through his hair and sighed. Good grief, the woman had him behaving like a testosterone-inflated fourteen-year-old. He hadn't suffered such a bad case of tongue-tying, palm-sweating, boner-inducing lust since the seventh grade, when Marisa Guacamora had let him feel her Kleenex-enhanced breasts through her cheerleading sweater. If Melanie had worn a bikini, he'd probably have suffered an aneurism.

But worse, and much more frightening than the lust, he genuinely *liked* her. Hell, he liked her a lot. She was warm, intelligent, funny, a great cook, and if his laughing niece was any indication, she was also great with kids. Not to mention a fabulous kisser.

The woman had *threat to bachelorhood* written all over her. He knew he should run—not walk—away from her and her big brown eyes to protect his long-anticipated freedom, but he felt disinclined to move so much as an inch. In fact, it suddenly occurred to him that being a "swinging bachelor" was not all it was cracked up to be. His date last night with Claire was proof of the pitfalls of singledom.

Was it possible that after spending only two months as a carefree man-about-town he was ready to call it quits? Give up the ship, throw in the towel, and involve himself in a meaningful relationship?

No! He wanted to live it up—have all kinds of guy fun. Sow some oats. Date a hundred women. Yeah. That's what he wanted.

Wasn't it?

He'd certainly thought so.

Until two days ago.

He sneaked a peek at Melanie and stifled a groan at the arousing sight of her, wet and sun-kissed, her swimsuit molded to her like a second skin.

All right, so maybe he only wanted one woman. The sexy brunette in the pool. Wanted her so much he thought he was going to explode.

He blew out a breath. This did not bode well for his bachelor lifestyle, but somehow the realization didn't panic him. If anything, it filled him with a sense of relief. No more empty, awkward dates. He could spend all his time and energy pursuing one woman . . . one *particular* woman.

One particular woman? Whoa! The enormity of that slapped him with the force of a brick to the head. He could practically feel his long-awaited freedom evaporating like smoke in a windstorm. No way was he giving up the ship. Damn it, he was going to be a bachelor if it killed him!

Clearly he was suffering from a case of too-much-work, not-enough-play syndrome. And if Melanie was the one his annoyingly particular libido wanted, so be it. Surely if they slept together, she'd be purged from his system along with everything about her that threatened his lifestyle.

As long as he was up-front that he wasn't looking for a long-term relationship, he wouldn't feel guilty when they parted ways. He had nothing to lose and everything to gain by pursuing her. What was the worst that could happen?

She could say no.

His heart thunked in protest. *No* was not an option he cared to contemplate, especially when *yes* was *so* much better.

Hmmm. Sleeping with Melanie. Melanie in his

bed, tousled from a bout of hot sex. That was definitely something to consider.

And where better to consider it than in the pool?

Glugging down the rest of his Coke, he debated how best to slip into the water without anyone noticing his condition. He'd just decided to make a run for it when Mark jabbed him in the ribs.

"She's really something, Chris," Mark said in an undertone. "Every time I look at her, my bathing suit gets tight. I'm so horny I can barely think straight."

Chris slowly lowered the Coke can from his lips. "What?" He must have heard Mark wrong. He didn't just say *horny*. His brother couldn't be lusting after Melanie.

"I said she's something. A totally bitchin' babe. Cripes, what a bod." A wolfish grin lit Mark's handsome face. "I'm not sure what office she's running for, but she definitely has my vote."

Great. His twenty-one-year-old brother had the hots for Melanie. This had to be nipped right in the bud. Melanie was *his*. Well, she wasn't *his*. Yet. But he meant to change that. ASAP.

God, what am I thinking? He raked his fingers through his hair again in frustration. She wasn't his. He didn't want her. Mark was welcome to her.

Okay, he wanted her. But he didn't *want* to want her. And he definitely did not want Mark to want her. If Mark so much as touched her, Chris would have to hurt him.

"Back off, bro," he drawled in as casual a tone as he could manage. "Melanie's mine."

Mark lowered his sunglasses and peered at him over the rim. "Huh?"

Chris lowered his sunglasses and stared right back. "Mine," he repeated. "Hands off."

A crooked smile slashed across Mark's face. "Whoa, big brother. Not that Melanie's not terrific, but I was talking about Zoë." He practically smacked his lips. "She's the one who has my trunks in an uproar."

Chris gave him a blank stare. "Zoë? The florist with the unpronounceable last name?" Chris's mom had introduced them at the house. They'd exchanged pleasantries for a few minutes, then Chris had promptly forgotten her.

"Hell, Chris, are you freakin' blind? Look at her." Mark jerked his head toward the other end of the pool. Zoë lounged on a chaise, her curvy body on display in a hot-pink bikini that barely covered the essentials. Her long, curly blond hair was piled on top of her head, and she was flipping through the pages of a magazine.

"*That's* the florist?" Chris couldn't help but stare for several seconds. The woman was *this close* to getting arrested for indecent exposure.

"That's the florist," Mark confirmed. "I talked to her for a while back at the house. She only works at the flower shop one day a week." He leaned closer. "She's a model for Stacy's Armoire."

"The lingerie company?"

"Can you believe it? Who would have thought that Cousin Margie's second cousin's neighbor's sister would turn out to be a lingerie model. I can just picture her in a satin teddy. Holy hell. Somebody throw cold water on me." Mark sat up and faced Chris. "Look, I know Mom invited her for you, and I know how you're into the bachelor thing, but . . . ah . . . is there any chance you'd consider . . ." His voice trailed off.

Chris smiled and gave Mark a playful punch on the arm. "Knock yourself out."

"You sure? I wouldn't want to step on your toes."

Chris looked over at Zoë. Her hot-pink bikini top resembled two postage stamps connected by a wisp of dental floss. His gaze shifted to Melanie. For some inexplicable reason, her modest black one-piece sent a shivering tingle through him that Zoë's blatantly sexy attire did not. *Damn. I've got it bad.*

"No toes stepped on," Chris assured his brother. "Why don't you mosey on over there? Zoë probably needs someone to rub oil on her back."

Mark clutched his heart. "A dreary job, deserving combat pay, but someone's gotta do it. Can't have all that luscious female flesh getting sunburned." He saluted Chris and made his way over to Zoë. Within twenty seconds he was smoothing oil on her back with one hand and giving Chris a thumbs-up with the other.

Good. Now at least Chris didn't have to worry about his mother shoving Zoë at him the rest of the night.

Of course Mom had changed her tune when he'd arrived with Melanie and Nana. He suspected that his mother hadn't really believed he would show up with a date. She'd taken charge, eagerly greeting and introducing Mel and Nana to the other guests, then settling them in lawn chairs with cold drinks.

Melanie had immediately hit it off with his three sisters, and while his mom and Nana yakked like they'd known each other for years, Chris, Mark, and the brothers-in-law sat at the picnic table, talking sports, cars, and power tools, and drinking beer. Real macho, he-man stuff.

After an hour of chit-chat, everyone except his mother and Nana had wandered down to the pool.

They'd settled their belongings on lounge chairs, and Chris had opened his mouth to ask Melanie if she needed sunscreen, but the words froze on his lips.

She was shimmying herself out of her denim shorts. He'd stood, transfixed, watching her pull her T-shirt over her head. He realized she wasn't trying to be provocative or sexy, and that just made her all the more so.

He'd felt himself stirring against his trunks and quickly sat down. That was forty minutes ago. He was still throbbing, but it was time to get up and jump into the pool. He wanted to be next to her, feel her wet skin sliding against his. Touch her slicked-back hair. Kiss her luscious lips.

He hoped the pool water was chilly because he definitely needed some cooling off. Walking to the edge as quickly as he could, he made a shallow dive.

He surfaced several yards from Melanie and his niece and swam over to them. He stood and was relieved that the water reached his waist. Whew. At least he didn't have to kneel. "Uncle Chris!" five-year-old Amanda squealed. "Toss me high like you did last time!" She turned to her new best friend. "Watch this, Mel. It's *way* cool!"

Chris obligingly tossed Amanda up, catching her before she went under the water. After the fifteenth toss, he pleaded exhaustion.

"Gotta rest," he said, huffing and puffing in an exaggerated way. "I'm an old man." He tousled her hair. "Tell you what. I have a present for my favorite girl in my bag." He pointed to the gym bag under his lounge chair. "Why don't you go check it out?"

Amanda needed no second urging. She hopped out of the pool, ran across the cement, and pounced on the gym bag like a starving dog on a bone. "A new Barbie! And it's the one I wanted! Thanks, Uncle Chris!" Returning to the side of the pool, she planted a wet kiss on Chris's upturned cheek, then scampered over to her mother. "Mom, look!"

Chris walked over to Melanie. "Alone at last."

"Did you actually buy that Barbie doll yourself?" she asked.

Chris ran his gaze over her. He wanted to touch her. Had to touch her. He slid a single fingertip down her wet arm, encouraged by the shiver he felt run through her. "I not only picked out Barbie all by myself, I bought her a teeny-weeny party dress."

"I'm impressed. I would have thought most guys would be too intimidated to buy doll stuff."

"Not me. I love toy stores."

She stood next to him at the side of the pool and stared down at the water. She seemed as tongue-tied as he was. Chris reached over and took her hand, entwining their fingers. He wondered how she would react if he kissed her, if she would mind, with his family all around. He was just about to find out when she spoke.

"Listen, Chris," she said, her words coming out in a rush, "this is kind of embarrassing for me, and I'm sure it is for you, too. I mean, obviously you didn't know she was going to be the way she is, so it's probably best if you just take me home as soon as we get back to the house."

He stared at her, unkissed and clueless. "What?"

She lifted her chin and looked him straight in the eye. "I understand. Really. No hard feelings."

"Okay. No hard feelings. What the hell are you talking about?"

She rolled her eyes and shot him a look that clearly

indicated that men were nothing but dunderheads. "Zoë. I'm talking about Zoë."

"Zoë? What about her?"

She made a fist and gently knocked on his forehead with her knuckles. "Hello? Are you home? I know you invited me today to save you from her, but she's obviously not the blind date from hell. In fact, she looks like she just wandered over from the Playboy Mansion." She pushed her hair back. "I don't want you to feel obligated to be with me. Really. Hey, if I was a guy, I know who *I'd* rather be with."

"Are you finished?"

She nodded. "Uh, yeah. I guess so."

"Good." He imprisoned her with his arms, pushing her back until she was trapped against the side of the pool. He pressed his body into hers, leaving no doubt as to his aroused state. Her eyes widened to saucers. "Since you're not a guy, thank God, I'm going to have to set you straight here." He rubbed himself against her, very slowly and very deliberately. "That's for you. Because of *you,*" he murmured, staring into her brown depths, not even attempting to hide the desire he knew she'd read in his expression. "Just you. I've been hard and aching for you since the moment we got here. Jesus, it's embarrassing." He lowered his head and brushed his mouth over hers. "No matter how hard I try, I can't make it go away. You're driving me crazy."

"But what about Zoë?" she asked, slowly sliding her arms around his waist.

"Not my type," he murmured against her lips. "I talked to her for about five minutes and we ran out of things to say. To be blunt, she's dumber than dirt."

Melanie smiled against his lips. "I'm surprised you

noticed. I talked to her also. She didn't strike me as the brightest bulb on the marquee."

He nipped at her dimples. "Yeah. Not the sharpest knife in the drawer."

"Couple of sandwiches short of a picnic."

Chris laughed. "I think we've made our point."

"Well, I wasn't thinking you'd necessarily want to spend your time *talking* to her."

Chris raised his head. He could see some emotion in her eyes, but he wasn't sure what it was. Jealousy? He hoped so. Hurt? He hoped not. He framed her face in his hands.

"Listen: Big-breasted lingerie models are not my type." He made a gagging sound. "Really. I feel breakfast coming up."

She shot him a clearly skeptical look. "Oh, sure."

Drawing a cross on his chest, he said, "Cross my heart. I prefer brunettes with short curly hair and big brown eyes." He paused for a moment, realizing that that sentence would not have passed his lips even three days ago. What the hell was happening to him? Since the moment he'd met Melanie, it was as if aliens had abducted his bachelor self.

He cleared his throat. "Now Mark, on the other hand, is as happy as a pig in mud talking to Zoë."

"Hmmm. I hope he isn't using any big words."

A grin spread over Chris's face. "You're jealous."

"Damn right. What woman wouldn't want a body like that? I've always dreamed of buying a thirty-eight triple D. And if I looked like that in a bikini, I'd wear one everywhere. Even to the supermarket. I'm pea green with envy."

His grin faded. "That's not what I meant."

She looked away and bit her lip. "I know. I'm sorry. But she's the kind of woman who makes every other woman feel frumpy, lumpy, flat-chested, and suicidal." She shrugged. "It's a girl thing."

"Ah. I see a bit of reassurance is in order." Wrapping his arms around her, he walked backward toward the deep end, pulling her along. His family, he noted, was busy gathering up their wet towels, preparing to leave.

When the water reached his neck he leaned back against the side of the pool and dragged Melanie toward him like he was reeling in a fish. When she was flush against him, he covered her mouth with his.

She hesitated for a second, then wrapped her arms around his neck and whispered his name in a breathy sigh that undid him. He hauled her up tighter against him with one hand while his other hand fisted in her short curls. He slipped his tongue past her lips and groaned when she opened her mouth wide to give him access. His senses reeled and he completely forgot where he was. He felt like a starving man who'd been given a feast; a man dying of thirst who'd been presented with a cool drink.

He slanted his mouth over hers again and again, his hand slipping down to stroke the curve of her buttocks. God only knew where his hand might have wandered next if a loud *ahem* hadn't sounded next to his ear. His brother's amused voice penetrated his passionate haze.

"Sorry to interrupt," Mark said, "but it's time to head back to the house."

Chris lifted his head and glared up at his brother. Zoë stood beside him.

Mark backed up a step and held out his hands, palms up. "Hey! Don't blast me with that look. I'm just saving you the embarrassment of Mom coming down here to get you. The sisters left a few minutes

ago." A wide grin split his face. "They were all a-twit-
ter over the goings-on down here in the deep end. I
told them you were just doing your bachelor
thing . . ." His gaze shifted to Melanie and he shot
her a sheepish grin. "Oops. Sorry, Mel. Just kidding.
Anyway, expect the third degree sometime tonight.
See you back at the house." He wrapped an arm
around Zoë's waist and they sauntered off.

"Jeez," Melanie moaned. "How embarrassing was
that?" She pressed her hands to her flaming cheeks.
"I know I'm blushing. How can I face them? What
will they think of me? I was ready to strip you bare
right here in the pool. What on earth is wrong with
me? I never behave like this!"

A slow grin curved his lips. "You were ready to strip
me bare?"

She sent him a sizzling scowl. "That is *not* a good
thing."

It was as far as *he* was concerned. On his list of
things he wanted most, having Melanie strip him bare
was firmly set in the number-one position. He looked
at the hectic color blooming on her face and was
completely charmed. He didn't know women still
blushed.

Something inside him squeezed tight and he knew
he was in big trouble. Actually, he'd known he was
in deep doo-doo the minute he met her. No woman
had ever affected him this way before. She appealed
to him on every level—mental and physical. It was as
if she'd reached inside his chest and grabbed his
heart and soul with her fist.

And the fact that he preferred the woman in his
arms to the genetically perfect and bodacious Zoë
was just further proof of his problem.

He had a strong suspicion that an emotional minefield hovered just around the corner. He should run, not walk, in the opposite direction to avoid being blown to bits, but he couldn't seem to help himself.

Damn. This woman was putting a real crick in his swinging bachelor plans.

In fact, his swinging bachelor plans were looking more and more unappealing with each passing minute.

Damn, damn, double damn.

FIVE

Back at the Bishop house, Melanie used Chris's old room to change into her clothes. Once she was dressed, she spent a few minutes looking around.

Framed certificates and sports posters hung on the walls. Basketball and baseball trophies stood proudly on the bookshelf alongside pictures. One photo showed Chris in a basketball uniform, posing with his high school team. Melanie picked it up and studied it.

Yikes. He was handsome even in high school. A devilish smile lit his teenage face, and Melanie imagined a corp of cheerleaders fighting over him.

Another picture showed him in a black tux, his arm around a pretty girl in a pink formal. Obviously a prom. Again he looked incredible. Lucky girl. Melanie recalled her senior prom date and grimaced. She'd gone with John Klingerhammer, a boy she'd known since fourth grade who went by the unfortunate nickname of Itchy. He'd panted and pawed her all night until she'd finally jabbed him in the eye with her corsage. She hadn't spoken to Itchy since. He was probably doing time for assault.

She picked up another framed picture and smiled. It showed a teenage Chris and an adolescent Mark in their swim trunks, suntanned, soaking wet, and laughing. Mark's fingers made devil horns behind Chris's back, and Chris was giving Mark a head noogie.

Melanie replaced the photo, trying to banish the vivid image of Chris in his bathing trunks at the pool this afternoon, but it was impossible. The moment she'd laid eyes on him, she'd had to jump in the water to cool off.

His shoulders were strong and lightly tanned, and his chest was sprinkled with an intriguing patch of dark hair that arrowed down and disappeared into his trunks. She'd had an incredible urge to pull the waistband of his trunks out a few inches and see where that enticing line led. He was lean, muscular, and sent everything that was female in her into an immediate frenzied rampage.

And then there was that kiss. *Whooooeee.* She waved her hand in front of her face in an effort to cool the blush heating her cheeks. Being kissed by Christopher Bishop when he was fully clothed had left her breathless. Being kissed by him in the pool, his skin warm and wet, with nothing between them but their swimsuits, had practically killed her. God help her if she ever saw him naked. She'd have a stroke for sure.

Not that she was thinking along *those* lines. Oh, no. The thought of seeing Chris naked was the absolute *farthest* thing from her mind. Anyway, she knew what a naked man looked like. Seen one, you've seen 'em all. Nope. The words *naked* and *Chris* would never be in a sentence that passed her lips. Starting right now.

Besides, after tonight she had no intention of seeing him again. What would be the point? They'd be even on their favors, and although she found him attractive—okay, *desperately* attractive—she wasn't about to get involved. She'd have to make that plain when he drove her home tonight.

And she had no doubt Chris would resume his— what had his brother called it? His *bachelor thing*—as soon as he dropped her off. Clearly, getting rid of him would be easy. And that was good. Yup. Very good.

That resolved, she wandered toward the kitchen, admiring the Bishop home, a cozy brick colonial on a shady, tree-lined street. Children's bikes littered carefully tended lawns, and mothers pushed baby carriages down the sidewalks. Very much like the middle-class neighborhood where she'd grown up.

"There you are," came Chris's deep voice behind her. Before she could turn around, his fingers brushed the nape of her neck. "Hmmmm," he murmured against her ear, "you always smell so good. What is that?"

A shiver twittered down her spine. "Chlorine, I would imagine."

He laughed softly, and his warm breath tickled her ear, pulsing her nerve endings into red alert. She closed her eyes and prayed for strength. The man was going to make her lose her mind. This called for drastic action. Immediate retreat. She drew a deep breath and pulled away from him.

"I think I'll see if your mother needs any help with the food," she said, proud that her voice sounded so steady.

"Good idea. I'm starved." He took her hand and led her to the kitchen. She spent the next twenty minutes helping Chris's mom, who insisted on being called Lorna, with the final dinner preparations. Lorna was very impressed with Melanie's culinary expertise, and before long they were exchanging cooking tips. The kitchen was lively and fun, with Chris's sisters joining in and teasing her about her name.

"We almost fainted when Chris said Mel Gibson was coming over," they reported with a laugh.

Their banter carried on all through dinner. After consuming a veritable wagonload of hamburgers, hot dogs, and salads, everyone sat in lawn chairs under the shade of a huge weeping willow. They were just finishing dessert when Nana leaned over and poked Melanie in the ribs.

"Who's the hunk?" she whispered out of the side of her mouth, jerking her head in the direction of a distinguished gentleman walking toward them.

Melanie shook her head. "Don't know."

The "hunk" turned out to be Bernie Sinclair, the Bishops' next-door neighbor. He pulled up a chair, and Melanie was amused to notice how adroitly Nana maneuvered her chair around until she and Bernie sat next to each other. Within ten minutes they were chatting like old buddies. Within an hour, Nana and Bernie rose, announcing that they were leaving.

"Bernie knows a great little place that plays forties tunes and serves two-for-one margaritas," Nana declared. She thanked Chris and his family for their hospitality and said her good-byes. When she hugged Melanie, she whispered, "Don't wait up!"

"Actually, I should be going, too," Melanie said to Chris after Nana left.

She thought she detected disappointment in his eyes, but he said, "Okay."

After gathering her things, Melanie said good-bye to Chris's family. His sisters hugged her, and little Amanda attached herself to Melanie's leg like a burr. Lorna kissed both her cheeks and enveloped her in a Chanel-scented bear hug. When Lorna invited her to come back anytime, Melanie blinked back the tears pricking her eyes. They were all so nice and had made her feel so welcome.

But her one date with Christopher Bishop was over. And she knew she'd never see any of them again.

Twenty minutes later, after a car ride filled with awkward silences, Melanie breathed a sigh of relief when Chris parked the Mercedes in front of her house. Now all she had to do was say good-bye to him. That was the plan. No problem. Piece of cake. She turned to bid him a fond *adieu,* but before she could open her mouth he said, "Looks like Nana's found herself a boyfriend."

Diverted from her plan, Melanie asked, "Bernie isn't married, is he?"

Chris shook his head. "Widower. His wife passed away three years ago after a long illness. He's a great guy. He's lived next door for as long as I can remember. Since his wife's death, he's been very lonely."

"My Grandpa Will, Nana's husband, died eight years ago. Nana's so lively and vibrant. And alone. It would be great if she could find a nice man to spend some time with."

"And what about her granddaughter?" Chris asked, his eyes dark and probing. "Is she looking for a nice man to spend some time with?"

Melanie looked at her lap. This was her opportunity to tell him. Tell him that she had no room in her life for him. She raised her gaze and forced herself to say the words.

"Look, Chris—"

"Uh-oh. That doesn't sound good."

"You're a great guy, and I had a lot of fun today, but—"

"I don't think I'm gonna like what comes next. Stuff that comes after 'but' is generally not good."

She raked her hands through her hair. "I just don't have time for this. For you. For anyone. The Pampered Palate already takes all my time and energy, and I'm planning to expand. I'm determined to see my business succeed. All my money, all Nana's money is tied up in it. I can't afford to fail.

"To be perfectly blunt," she continued in a rush, "I don't want my attention diverted by a relationship that will eventually die from lack of attention. Then I'll not only have a failed business, but a broken heart on my hands. I've already had my heart broken once. Believe me, once is enough."

"I can understand that," he said in a quiet voice. "My schedule is bad, too. I have to travel a lot, and I've been putting in twelve-, fourteen-hour days for so long, it seems normal. And since I made partner, it's even worse." He reached across the seat and squeezed her hand. "But I'm willing to make time for something important." His eyes probed hers in a way that sent her pulse skittering. "I'm willing to make time for you."

Her heart flipped over in her chest. He wasn't supposed to say these things. He was supposed to say fine, great, gotta do my bachelor thing, see ya, have a nice life.

"There are only so many hours in a day, Chris."

"I know. And since I met you, you've been on my mind every single one of them. I didn't want it, I can't explain it, but there it is." He squeezed her hand and smiled at her. "Hey, relax. All I'm suggest-

ing is that we get to know each other better. Go out.
Have some laughs. Nothing serious. No strings."

Aha! Nothing serious. No strings. That was his male
bachelor reflex kicking in, no doubt. She shook her
head to clear it. "There are a hundred reasons why
we shouldn't pursue this . . . this whatever-it-is."

He raised his eyebrows. "Really? I'd love to hear
them, 'cause I've been trying to convince myself of
that very thing and I'm coming up blank. Name
one."

Okay. One should be easy. There were easily a hundred. Or at least a dozen. So why the heck couldn't
she think of one? Probably because of the way he was
looking at her, his handsome face serious, a lock of
midnight hair falling across his brow. It lulled her
brain into a completely dormant state.

Her thought processes suddenly kicked in and relief washed over her. "Okay. Here's one. We have absolutely nothing in common."

"That's not true. We have a lot in common."

"Such as?"

His gaze roamed slowly over her from head to toe,
igniting small bonfires all over her skin. When their
eyes met again, his gleamed with mischief. "We both
have belly buttons."

A breath she hadn't realized she held whooshed
from her lungs. "Belly buttons? Oh, Brother."

His lips curved in a sexy half grin. "I'll show you
mine if you show me yours."

"I'll bet. Are we still talking about belly buttons?"

"Of course."

Her gaze unconsciously drifted down to his abdomen. She nearly swallowed her tongue when she saw
the unmistakable bulging evidence of his arousal.

Clearing her throat, she said, "It would appear you have an 'outie.' "

"Constantly. Ever since I met you."

Good grief. Now she *knew* they weren't talking about belly buttons anymore. She somehow managed to force her gaze away from his fascinating "outie." Gazing into his amused eyes, she tried to recall what on earth they'd been talking about. Oh, yes. The hundred reasons why they shouldn't pursue a relationship.

"Okay," she said. "Here's another one. I know all about guys like you." Ha. So there.

A frown appeared between his brows. He looked puzzled. "Guys like me? What's that supposed to mean?"

"You know. Good looking, er, accountant types. Oh, you might appear harmless, but you're all philanderers."

"I'm a lot of things, but I am *not* a stamp collector."

"Not a *philatelist*. A philanderer. Someone who engages in casual affairs."

"Excuse me?"

"Fickle-hearted. Love 'em and leave 'em. Wham, bam, thank you ma'am . . ." her words trailed off as she noted his expression. All signs of amusement had vanished. In fact, he looked genuinely hurt.

He grew still, his eyes serious and unflinching. "That's what you think of me? What have I done to make you think so badly of me?"

Nothing. Damn it, he'd been nothing but kind. And he scared her to death. He rekindled desires and needs she'd ruthlessly buried when her fiancé had dumped her. Worse, this man made her feel things she'd never felt before, and that was reason enough to run and hide.

She pushed her hair behind her ears and realized her hands were shaking. "I don't think badly of you. You're just too . . . too *everything*. Too handsome. Too nice. Too sexy." She clasped her sweaty palms together and shook her head. "A boyfriend is the last thing I need. Relationships and I don't get along."

"I'm not him," he said in a quiet voice.

"Who?"

"The guy who hurt you." He laid his hands on her shoulders and gently shook her. "Melanie, I'm not him."

"I know." To her chagrin, hot tears pushed at the back of her eyes. Drat. She refused to cry. It was out of the question.

"Do you want to tell me about it?" he asked. "It might make you feel better—clear the air."

She shrugged and forced away the tears. "There's not much to tell. I was engaged. The day before the wedding I stopped in at my fiancé Todd's apartment to surprise him with a gift." She paused and took a deep breath. "I surprised him all right. Him and Missy, my maid of honor. Doing the wild thing right on the kitchen floor."

A pained expression creased his face. "Ouch."

"That's exactly what Todd said when I belted him upside his head with my purse."

"I hope you gave him a lump."

A tiny smile touched the corners of her mouth. "Actually, I gave him a concussion, a fact which helped my pride but didn't do much for my broken heart. I lost my fiancé and my best friend in one fell swoop. Not to mention the humiliation involved in canceling a wedding with only a few hours' notice."

Chris gently drew her across the seat, into his arms, and settled her head against his shoulder. Melanie closed her eyes and sighed. He felt so good. He smelled so good. Like warm sunshine. His heart thumped against her cheek in a soothing, lulling rhythm. It would be so easy to get used to snuggling against him.

He dropped a kiss into her hair. "I'm sorry, Melanie. Sorry something so hurtful happened to you. But at least you didn't marry the jerk."

"No, I didn't," she said into his shirt. "But the experience made me careful. Very careful."

Leaning back, he placed his fingers under her chin, forcing her to look at him. The half smile tilting his mouth was at odds with the dead-serious look in his eyes. "I can promise you'll never find me boffing your best friend on the kitchen floor." He raised his hand. "Scout's honor."

"Chris, look—"

"I don't cheat, Melanie," he said quietly, all vestiges of his smile and humor gone. "I don't lie and I don't make promises I can't keep. I always try to be upfront with the women I date. I'm very attracted to you. I'd like to see where it leads. I'm not looking for a lifelong commitment. Just a date." He shrugged. "Who knows? Maybe we'll go on one date and end up hating each other."

Fat chance. Melanie had a sneaking suspicion that she'd end up falling hard and coming up empty again. Her stomach cramped at the thought.

"The point is," she said, "you've come along at a really bad time. I simply don't have *time* for you. I don't *want* to want you."

"Well, if it makes you feel any better, I don't want to want you either. So how about dinner tomorrow night?"

He drew her closer, until they were pressed intimately together. The heat of his body surrounded her, igniting flames in her newly awakened erogenous zones. Her body leapt to life with a ferocity that left her bordering on panic. She had to get away from him. Right now.

Pulling herself out of his arms, she grabbed her purse, scooted across the seat, and all but bolted from the car.

Chris turned off the engine and joined her on the driveway.

Feeling completely unhinged, she paced back and forth. "Uh-uh. This is too much, too soon. I can't do this." She stopped in front of him, grasping for any excuse that would save her from this devastating man who threatened the peaceful existence she'd carved out for herself. "I can't possibly go out with you. You're . . . you're an *accountant,* for crying out loud. I can't possibly date an accountant. Accountants are stodgy and boring. Nothing but conservative suits and ties. Numbers and flowcharts."

She nodded vigorously, desperately trying to convince him—and herself. "If I was looking for a man— which I'm not—but if I was, it certainly wouldn't be an *accountant.* It would be a Marlon Brando type." Yeah. Yeah. That's the ticket.

Doubt was written all over his face. "You're looking for a three-hundred-pound actor old enough to be your father?"

"No, of course not. I meant a young Marlon Brando. Like in that movie where he's on the motorcycle."

"So you want a motorcycle kind of guy?"

"Yeah. That's right. I've always wanted to be a biker chick." She spread her hands, palms up. "So you see? As tempting as you are, we'd never work this out.

You're all actuary tables and balance sheets, and I long for the open road, the wind in my hair, the asphalt beneath me. My motto is—it's motorcycle guys or no guys."

He nodded his head slowly, never taking his eyes off her. "I see."

He saw. Good. Now all she had to do was escape. Before her resolve crumbled to ashes. Holding out her hand, she said, "Thanks for everything. I had fun."

He shook her hand. When he tried to pull her closer, Melanie snatched her hand away. "Good-bye."

" 'Til we meet again," he corrected with the hint of a smile.

Not if I can help it. Melanie walked into the house, closed the door, and leaned back against it. She heard his car door slam and listened to the Mercedes drive away.

Thank goodness he was gone. She should be thrilled. The man was a hazard to the female population. Yup. She was happy as a clam at high tide. Happy as a flea on a hound dog.

She felt like crying.

SIX

"The only thing all that pacing is gonna give you is varicose veins," Nana said the next afternoon at the Pampered Palate, peering over her bifocals at Melanie. "Back and forth. Back and forth. It's like watchin' a dang tennis match. If you don't knock it off, I'm gonna need a chiropractor."

Melanie raked her hands through her hair. "I can't help it, Nana. The accountants will be here in an hour. There's so much riding on this independent review—the loan, the truck, Pampered Palate's future." She stopped and pressed her hand to her flopping stomach. "Do you realize that if all goes well, we could have our catering truck within two months?"

"A whole lot of good it'll do us if you're in the hospital," Nana stated. "Calm yourself. You said everything went fine at the bank this morning."

"It did," Melanie agreed, a rush of pleasure washing over her. "The loan officer was very impressed by the Pampered Palate and our plans for the future."

Noticing Nana's scowl, Melanie forced herself to sit down. She immediately started shredding a paper napkin emblazoned with the red and blue Pampered Palate logo.

"It's really happening, Nana," she said, elated and terrified at the same time. "It looks like our hard work is finally going to pay off." Nerves cramped her stomach and she groaned. "Jeez. I hope success isn't going to make me sick."

"Listen, honey, you've got to relax. Look how well you've done in only a few months." She patted Melanie's hand. "Those bankers will give you the loan."

"Only if we get a favorable review from the accountants."

Nana huffed out a breath. "Those accountants give us any trouble, I'll swat them upside their heads with a skillet."

For the first time in hours, Melanie managed a smile. "I appreciate it, Nana, but it probably won't help our cause if we're in the slammer for assault and battery."

Nana puckered her brow and nodded. "Hmmm. You're right. I guess we'd better settle for Plan B."

"Plan B?"

"Fresh-baked apple pie. With homemade vanilla ice cream." A big smile creased Nana's wrinkled face. "Like I always say, if you can't beat 'em, bribe 'em."

Melanie laughed. Everything was going to be okay. As always, Nana was there to keep her sane. "Sounds good to me."

"You're darn tootin'," Nana said. "As we're so fond of saying here at the Pampered Palate, let's get cookin'!"

Chris sat in his corner office and reached for the stack of financial statements piled on his mahogany desk. His morning had consisted of writing a proposal for a new client, a series of budget meetings, and lunch with a prospective new hire.

Turning his attention to the mountain of paperwork awaiting him, he pored over the balance sheets and income and cash flow statements, but he found it difficult to concentrate on the endless columns of figures.

The numbers blurred and ran together as images of Melanie flashed through his mind, distracting him, disrupting his train of thought. Her bright smile and infectious laugh. Those chocolatey eyes and full, kissable lips.

The incredible taste of those full, kissable lips.

Remembering their steamy kisses killed whatever small bit of concentration he had left. Tossing down his pencil in defeat, he decided he needed a strong cup of coffee. He was just about to head for the break room when Glenn Waxman, the senior partner, walked into his office and closed the door behind him.

Chris immediately noticed two things. One, Glenn held a manila folder in one hand. And two, Glenn had his other hand clapped over his mouth.

"What's up, Glenn?"

"Hmmphttpshm," replied Glenn through his fingers.

Chris laughed. "I might understand you better if you moved your hand."

"Hmmphttspm." Glenn removed his hand and curled back his upper lip.

His two front teeth were gone.

"What the hell happened to you?" Chris asked, staring at the gaping black hole in amazement. The always perfectly groomed Glenn Waxman looked like a full-grown second-grader.

"I lotht my crownth," Glenn said, his face puckered in a grimace. "I've got an emergenthy dentith appointment." He thrust the manila folder into Chris's hands. "Can you handle thith for me? Shouldn't take you more than an hour."

"Sure. No problem."

"Thankth. I owe ya one."

"How could I say no to a guy who sounds like Daffy Duck?"

"Ha, ha, ha. You're hythterical. Thee you tomorrow." Glenn clapped his hand over his mouth and left.

Postponing his coffee break for the moment, Chris opened the folder Glenn had given him. He froze the instant he saw the name at the top of the first page.

Melanie Gibson.

His attention riveted, he scanned Glenn's notes. Melanie was applying for a fifty-thousand-dollar loan to purchase a catering truck and had hired Waxman, Barnes, Wiffle, and Hodge to conduct the independent review required by the bank. Chris noted that the bank was one of his firm's clients.

So *that's* why the name *Pampered Palate* had seemed so familiar to him. He must have heard Glenn or one of the other partners talking about the upcoming review. As it wasn't his client, he wouldn't have paid particular attention.

Until now.

According to Glenn's scribbled notes, he needed to conduct an on-site inspection of the facilities and pick up the client's paperwork and books. Bob Harris, a junior accountant, would be handling the actual review. They had an appointment at the Pampered Palate at four o'clock.

Chris glanced at his watch. Ten past three. A slow smile eased over his face. He'd known he would see Melanie again—he'd had every intention of making sure that happened.

He just hadn't realized it would happen quite so soon.

At five minutes to four, Melanie paced around the Pampered Palate's kitchen like an expectant father in a maternity waiting room. The butterflies in her stomach had butterflies. She tried taking deep breaths, but she was afraid she would hyperventilate.

There's no reason to be nervous. Of course not. It's not like this was important or anything.

Nana laid a comforting hand on Melanie's arm. "Calm yourself. The apple pie is cooling, the ice cream is made, and the dinner rush won't start for another hour. It's not going to help if you faint on them."

Melanie smiled and laid her hand over Nana's. "I know. I just want everything to be perfect."

"Everything *is* perfect. Stop worrying. You'll get pimples."

"Goodness knows I don't need . . ." Her voice trailed off as the bell on the front door jingled. "Oh, boy. It's them." Squaring her shoulders, she drew a deep breath, beat back her panic, and left the kitchen.

Two tall men stood in the front room. One was handsome and unfamiliar.

The other one smiled at her and she all but swallowed her tongue.

Good grief, what was *he* doing here? She couldn't talk to him *now.* The accountants were coming!

And darn him for casually dropping by and reminding her how beautiful he was. It had been at least three minutes since she'd thought of him. How was she supposed to forget him if he kept on *showing up*?

Forcing a calm she definitely didn't feel, Melanie walked around the counter. Before she could utter a word, the unfamiliar man asked, "Are you Miss Gibson?"

At her nod he extended his hand. "I'm Bob Harris. From Waxman, Barnes, Wiffle, and Hodge. Chris tells me the two of you have already met."

Melanie wasn't sure what kind of expression she had on her face, but whatever it was, it prompted Bob Harris from Waxman, Barnes, Wiffle, and Hodge to add, "We're the accountants. I, er, believe you were expecting us?"

Melanie shook his hand, somehow remembering how to speak. "I had an appointment with Glenn Waxman."

When Chris extended his hand, Melanie shook it and tried to ignore the sizzle that snaked up her arm at his touch.

"Glenn had an emergency," Chris said, holding her hand just a bit longer than necessary. "He asked me to fill in for him today. Bob here will be doing the bulk of the work, and Glenn will review it."

"So the accounting firm you work for is—"

"Waxman, Barnes, Wiffle, and Hodge," Chris said. "Guardian Savings and Loan is our client."

"I see." Perfect. Just when she needed all her wits about her, she was faced with the one man who made her forget her own name.

Melanie decided her only defense was to not look at him. If she didn't see him, she wouldn't think about him. If she didn't think about him, she could concentrate on the task at hand. She therefore focused her attention on Bob Harris with the zeal of a scientist peering at brain cells through a microscope. "What do we do first?"

"Let's start with a tour of the facilities," Bob suggested with a friendly smile. He sniffed. "It sure smells great in here. Like apple pie."

"We just took one out of the oven," Melanie said, mentally blessing Nana as she led the way toward the kitchen. "Maybe you'd like a piece with some homemade vanilla ice cream before you leave?"

"Sounds great," said Bob.

The instant they entered the kitchen, Nana descended on them. "Well, if it isn't the hunk," she said, her face wreathed in a huge smile. She enveloped Chris in a bone-jarring hug, leaving floury hand prints on the back of his navy suit jacket.

"Nice to see you, Nana," Chris said, grinning.

"You, too, handsome." She jerked her head toward Bob. "You bring him along for me for a double date? He's kinda young, but that's okay. He's real cute. Great butt." She turned to Bob. "Want some pie, honey?"

The expression on Bob's face reminded Melanie of a driver's license photo—bewildered and dumbstruck. Choking back a laugh she said, "Nana, Chris and Bob are the accountants we've been expecting."

Nana looked crestfallen. "You mean no double date?"

Melanie shook her head. " 'Fraid not."

"Dang it." Nana shrugged in a philosophical manner. "Oh, well, I'd best get back to work. Let me know when you're ready for that pie."

Melanie led the two of them on a complete tour

of the spacious professional kitchen, explaining the daily operations.

"Each day starts off with our morning deliveries," she said. "Fresh bread and produce arrive daily; meat and fish usually twice a week. In addition to our regular menu, we offer two daily specials."

Indicating the huge freezer, she continued, "Some items, such as tomato sauce and soup stocks, are prepared ahead of time and frozen, but the bulk of our fare is made fresh every day. The morning is spent preparing for the lunch rush, and during the late-afternoon lull we get ready for dinner. We do a decent walk-in business, but corporate lunches and dinners are our specialty."

While she spoke, she noticed that Bob scribbled copious notes on a yellow legal pad, occasionally asking questions. Chris paid rapt attention but said nothing.

She dared a peek at him once, and her cheeks flamed when she discovered his gaze resting thoughtfully on her mouth. Although he stood a dozen feet away from her, it seemed as if he'd caressed her. He glanced up and their eyes met. The long, intense, heated look he gave her stopped her in midsentence.

Her mind emptied and a tremor sizzled through her. She couldn't have felt more scorched if she'd backed up into a 450-degree oven. Completely flustered, she turned away from him and focused her attention back on Bob.

Forty-five minutes later, Melanie said, "Well, that's it, gentlemen. Do you have any other questions?"

Bob shook his head. "No, I think I have everything I need. If you'll just give me your books and business records, I'll be finished."

Melanie pointed to a shopping bag bearing the Pampered Palate logo. "Everything's in there. Books, bills, receipts, corporate records, bank statements, the works."

Bob shot her a smile. "Great. You'll hear from us in two to three weeks. Now how about that pie and ice cream?"

By the time Melanie arrived home that evening, she was exhausted. Her unexpected meeting with Christopher Bishop had thrown her for a loop. She'd been nervous the entire time he was at the Pampered Palate, but at least Bob had done most of the talking. After barely surviving that sexy look Chris had thrown at her, she'd avoided looking at him.

He must have taken the hint because when they left, Chris had merely shaken her hand and smiled at her. Very businesslike, impersonal, and polite.

Melanie didn't know whether she was relieved or irritated.

Nana ambled off to bed with a hot toddy and a steamy romance novel, but Melanie's nerves were too frazzled for reading. She decided to indulge in a relaxing bubble bath.

Five minutes later, she sank up to her neck in a hot, gardenia-scented tub and heaved a blissful sigh. Ahhh. Just what the doctor ordered. Her tense muscles loosened and a small smile touched her lips. Now if she could just banish the image of Christopher Bishop from her mind, all would be right with the world.

No sooner had the thought entered her mind than the phone rang. Drat. It was one of the basic laws of physics: the moment a body is submerged in water, the telephone rings. *I'll let the answering machine get it.* The ringing stopped and she closed her eyes. Seconds later she heard a knock on the bathroom door.

"What is it, Nana?" Melanie asked.

Nana opened the door and walked in carrying the portable phone. Setting the instrument on the edge of the tub, she said, "It's for you." Before Melanie could utter a word, Nana left, closing the door behind her.

Great. Figures. Probably someone wanting to sell her insurance or a cemetery plot. She grabbed the receiver. "Hello?" she all but barked into the phone.

"I can't stop thinking about you," said a low, sexy voice.

Uh-oh. If this was someone selling cemetery plots, she could be in trouble. It's not good to have people looking for cadavers say they can't stop thinking about you.

But she knew it wasn't someone wanting to measure her for a crypt. It was *him,* and damn it, he was just as deadly.

The sudden heat engulfing her had nothing to do with her bathwater. Annoyed that he could affect her like this over the *phone,* she asked in a bored drawl, "Who is this?"

"It's Chris. I can't stop thinking about you," he repeated in a husky whisper that caused a jillion and one goose bumps to pop out on her overheated flesh. After a pause he asked, his voice sounding distinctly annoyed, "Who the hell did you think this was?"

Melanie was tempted to make up a name, any name, but she couldn't. There was no sense pretending. "I knew it was you."

"Good." He waited several heartbeats before continuing. "I have several things to say to you."

Melanie gripped the phone with her soapy fingers, half terrified, half delirious with anticipation. "I'm listening."

"First, I want you to know that the reason I didn't say much to you today was because I was only there as a favor to Glenn Waxman. He's the partner on your account. He'll be signing off on your review. I was just observing, making sure Bob got everything he needed."

"What difference does it make which partner does my review?" Melanie asked, confused.

"It matters. Glenn can do it. I can't. Conflict of interest."

"Conflict of interest? I don't understand."

He blew out a breath. "It would compromise my firm and your chances of getting your loan if I signed off on a review for someone I'm involved with. So you'll be dealing with Bob and Glenn from now on."

Melanie sat up so quickly, water sloshed over the side of the tub. "What do you mean, *involved*? You and I are *not* involved."

"Wanna bet? I am most definitely involved. And if you're honest with yourself, you'll admit you are, too."

"Am not."

"Are, too. I saw the way you were looking at me today."

"I wasn't looking at you!"

"Like hell. I caught you staring at me like you wanted to stick me between two slices of rye bread and have me for lunch."

Melanie's temper kicked in. Conceited dope. And boy, was he wrong. In truth, she'd been staring at him like she wanted to stick him between two slices of *sourdough* bread and have him for lunch. Shows what *he* knew.

"Well?" he asked, when the silence stretched on. "What do you have to say?"

"I'm taking the fifth."

"If you won't talk to me over the phone, I'm coming over."

"No!" Melanie gripped the receiver so tight her knuckles turned white. "Don't come over."

"Why not?"

"I'm in the bathtub."

She heard him take a deep breath, then exhale a groan, and she couldn't squelch the momentary zing of feminine satisfaction that washed over her.

"You're killing me, Melanie. You really are. In the bathtub. Jesus. Now I've got that picture in my mind. How the hell am I supposed to sleep tonight?"

He cut loose with a growl. "Listen, I only called to tell you that my strictly businesslike behavior today was to avoid any conflict of interest. And if you think we're not involved, you're nuts. Maybe you don't want it, and I certainly don't want it, but it's there, and it's not going away."

"It will if we ignore it."

"Not an option," he stated firmly. "I've been trying that since we met, and it doesn't work."

"This is ridiculous," Melanie said, pushing her damp hair out of her eyes. "If you hadn't taken Mr. Waxman's place tonight, we never would have seen each other again."

"Do you really believe that?" The soft, husky question raised the hairs on the back of her neck. Before she could even think of a reply, he continued, "We absolutely would have seen each other again, Melanie. I would have made sure of it."

It was a good thing she was sitting down, because the sexy undertone in his deep voice melted her insides like a flame to wax. If she wasn't careful she'd slip under the water and drown, a boneless, quivering mass of feminine flesh.

"You're not saying much," he said, "so I'll take that as a good sign. At least you're not arguing. So, on to the next thing. What are you doing Friday evening?"

"Friday evening? Why?" Good grief. Was that squeaky noise her voice? She coughed to clear her dust-dry throat.

"I'd like to have dinner with you."

"Dinner? You mean like a *date?"*

"That note of horror I hear in your voice is pretty deflating to my ego."

"We've been through this. I don't date. And even if I did, I don't want to date you."

"I don't want to date you either. Something we have in common. And since you don't date, I guess that means you don't have plans Friday night. I'll swing by and pick you up at eight."

"But—"

"I'll be out of town for the rest of the week, so you won't be able to reach me—just in case you're considering backing out."

"There's nothing to back out of. Listen, you can't fool me. I know your type. Smooth. Good-looking. Good-looking guys are nothing but trouble, and that makes you trouble with a capital *T.* "

"So you don't want to have dinner with me because—"

"You're too handsome. That's right."

"I have to say, I've never been turned down for that reason before."

A snort escaped her. "Ha. I bet you've never been turned down, period."

"Have, too."

"Really? When? Second grade?"

He chuckled. "No. Third grade."

"Any turndowns prior to puberty are null and void. Besides, if—what was her name? The one in third grade?"

"Betty Waterhouse."

"If Betty Waterhouse could see you now, she'd kick her own ass black and blue."

"I had a blind date a few months back who hated me," he said in a low, sexy, confiding tone that prickled her heated skin.

"Hated you? Why?"

"She doesn't like accountants. Bad experience with the IRS. She practically broke out in hives when I told her I'm a CPA."

Melanie's eyes narrowed. "You planning to audit me?"

"Only if you want me to."

His tone was so suggestive, she almost dropped the phone into the bathwater.

Before she could find her voice he continued, "C'mon, Mel Gibson. Whaddaya say? You. Me. Dinner. I can do ugly. Really. Totally grunge."

Melanie rolled her eyes. "Oh, sure. You probably look good when you wake up in the morning."

"Hmmm. There's one way to find out."

"Forget it. Besides, I thought accountants were nerdy guys with leaky pens in their shirt pockets who wore high-water pants, white socks with black shoes, and held their glasses together with safety pins. You're not an accountant. You're a menace to female hormones."

"No menace. No audit. Just dinner. Maybe a movie."

"You'll be ugly?"

"Totally gross. Promise."

A sigh escaped her. "Are you always this persistent?"

After a long pause he said, "No. Actually, I'm never this persistent. Friday night. Eight. Dress casual. 'Bye, Melanie."

The dial tone sounded in her ear. Melanie held the phone away from her and stared at it as if it were the Loch Ness monster come to life in her tub. Dazed and confused, she clicked the OFF button and carefully laid the instrument on the bathmat. She had a date. With Christopher Bishop. Friday night.

Sufferin' succotash, how had *that* happened?

Probably because I didn't open my mouth and say no. But Melanie had a feeling that Chris wouldn't have taken no for an answer anyway, a fact she should have found annoying but instead found utterly romantic. And exciting.

Nana stuck her head in the door. " 'Bout time you got off the phone. I was getting a crick in my neck from pressing my ear against the crack in the door."

Melanie buried her hands in her face. "You heard?"

"Only your side. What's the scoop?"

Melanie sighed heavily. "We have a date Friday night."

Nana stuck two fingers between her lips and let loose an ear-piercing whistle. "Praise the Lord! It's about time you came out of mourning over that two-timing gigolo Todd. Hot damn! A date with the hunk. I might even get me some great-grandchildren to spoil."

Melanie almost choked. "Nana! It's only a date. One date. That's it."

Nana regarded her steadily through very wise eyes. "If that's what you think, honey, then you'd better brace yourself, because one date is not what that young man has on his mind."

"I have no intention of getting involved," Melanie said with a sniff.

"Intentions, inschmentions," Nana said, shaking her head. "Your heart doesn't listen to intentions. His won't either." Leaning down, Nana patted Melanie's waterlogged hand. "Sweetie, don't close yourself off from someone who might bring you happiness just because your last beau was an idiot. Sometimes the least-expected path is the one that leads to the treasure." After uttering those sage words, Nana left the room, closing the door behind her.

Treasure. Phooey. Melanie pulled the plug and stepped out of the tub, wrapping herself in a thick pink towel. Christopher Bishop wasn't a treasure. He was a hazard. Granted he was sexy, yummy, and goose-bump-inspiring—but he was a hazard just the same.

And she had a date with him Friday night.

God help her, she couldn't wait.

SEVEN

The week passed by in a blur for Melanie. Each day at work was busier than the last, but in spite of the hectic demands on her time, she loved every minute of it.

And she hardly thought about Chris and their upcoming date at all.

Yup. Hardly at all.

Except every time she inhaled.

Thursday proved to be one of the busiest days in the Pampered Palate's brief history. Three midtown offices had made large lunch orders based on recommendations from other clients, a group of Japanese tourists wandered in, and an outdoor arts-and-crafts festival drew dozens of walk-ins.

Melanie peeled potatoes at lightning speed for her famous red potato and dill salad and kept one eye on the apple cobblers through the glass oven door. Nana was a veritable whirling dervish, flitting from the stove to the refrigerator to the oven without missing a beat.

If business kept up at this pace—and Melanie fervently hoped it would—she'd soon have to hire an assistant. Maybe two. Maybe she could even lure her parents down to Atlanta to help out. She knew her dad missed the daily hustle and bustle of the restaurant business. He'd sold his family-style eatery in New York several years ago, ready to enjoy his hard-earned retirement, and he had. For a while.

But when she'd spoken to him on the phone yesterday, she clearly detected boredom in his tone. "I'm tired of puttering around the house," James Gibson had grumbled in her ear, "and your mother is grousing about me being constantly underfoot. By gum, I know all the names of those young and restless people on the soap operas. I don't *want* to know about the trials and tribulations of Erica Kane and all her bold and beautiful children!"

Melanie smiled, recalling his disgruntled tone. She missed Mom and Dad and looked forward to their upcoming visit in September. Maybe when they came down, she'd be able to convince them to buy a retirement home in the area. She knew they weren't happy about the prospect of facing another New York winter. And she suspected that once Dad saw her new catering truck, he'd be eager to be a part of the action.

Finished with the potatoes, Melanie turned her attention to sautéing tender filets for the daily special, veal marsala. Nana was busy packing up orders of southern fried chicken and barbecued ribs, and Mike the delivery man was alternately loading the orders into his van and helping Nana. Voices from customers in the front of the store drifted back to Melanie. Someone laughed, and she heard Wendy's melodic Alabama drawl as she worked the cash register for the takeout orders.

If Melanie's hands hadn't been so occupied, she would have rewarded herself with a hearty pat on the back for hiring Wendy. Not only was the girl smart and a hard worker, but it seemed that half the male student population at Georgia Tech was in love with her and made it their business to drop by the Pampered Palate whenever she was working, which was most afternoons. Nothing like hungry college students to boost the sales.

On several occasions the entire football team had ordered lunch from "their girl" Wendy. Their large, athletic bodies had filled the small storefront to capacity, and Melanie had probably sold more chicken and biscuits those days than the Colonel himself. And Nana had had a grand old time with all that male testosterone crowded into the place. She'd patted her frizzy red hair and flirted like a schoolgirl.

Opening her gleaming professional oven, Melanie slipped out the apple cobblers and placed them on the counter to cool. With quiet concentration, she went about her tasks—stirring the minestrone, adjusting spices in the pasta sauce, basting a turkey breast, preparing thick ham sandwiches on homemade sourdough bread.

She was so busy, her mind so occupied with what she was doing, she almost didn't think about *him*.

Almost.

But even as she ladled savory minestrone into bright red-and-blue striped to-go containers, she wondered what Chris was doing. Was he thinking of her?

You dummy. He probably hasn't given you a second thought. Which would have been fine, but in the few days since she'd seen him, she'd given *him* a second thought. And a third, fourth, and fifth thought. Okay, a six thousandth thought, but who was counting?

She removed a succulent pork roast from the oven and cut generous slices, forcing herself to concentrate on the task at hand and not think about their dinner date tomorrow night.

She failed miserably.

Anticipation curled through her, and a vivid image of Chris popped into her mind; him capturing her lips in a long, slow, drugging kiss. His hands drifting down her body, caressing her, insinuating his warm fingers under her skirt. Then, as in all good fantasies, they were suddenly naked, their clothes mysteriously dissolving into thin air. He leaned over her and . . .

"Are you all right, Melanie?"

Melanie blinked. "Huh?"

Nana looked at her over her bifocals. "I asked if you're okay."

No, I'm losing my mind. I have sixty-three meals to prepare in the next seven minutes and I'm having a sex dream. "I'm fine. Why do you ask?"

"You groaned. Did you hurt yourself?"

Groaned? Swell. The confounded man wasn't even here and he was causing problems. He'd awakened her libido from its long hibernation, and no matter how hard she tried to beat her hormones back into submission, those darn hormones were winning. Hands down.

"I'm fine, Nana. I just had a dry spot on my throat." She cleared her throat several times for good measure and finished slicing the roast, praying her grandmother wouldn't notice the flush heating her face.

Nana noticed.

"You look flushed. Maybe you have a fever."

Nana looked genuinely concerned and Melanie smiled at her. "I'm not sick, Nana. Promise."

A knowing gleam sparkled in Nana's wise eyes, and Melanie suspected that a sly comment was about to be launched with the accuracy of a SCUD missile. Wendy, God bless her, chose that moment to pop into the kitchen and wave a lunch order at Melanie.

"Prepare yourselves," the perky redhead warned with a devilish grin. "The Georgia Tech basketball team just called in this mega order."

Melanie glanced at it and raised her brows. Holy cow! Basketball players ate even more than football players! She gave Wendy a thumbs up and wasted no time in starting to fill the orders.

Dinner proved no less hectic than lunch, and by the time Mike departed with the last batch of deliveries, Melanie's body ached with fatigue and her feet were ready to stage a mutiny.

But her weariness couldn't overshadow her exhilaration. If today was any indication, her business was on its way to succeeding, and if her loan was approved, she knew she could make the Pampered Palate a huge success. After growing up loving her father's restaurant, she'd always dreamed of owning her own eatery. And by God, she was determined to see her dream come true.

"Quite a day," Nana said, easing herself into an oak hard-back chair.

Melanie noted the telltale weary lines around Nana's eyes and her heart squeezed. She couldn't name a more vital, energetic woman than her grandmother, but Melanie worried that she'd overtax herself.

"You must be exhausted, Nana," Melanie said, pouring two frosty mugs of iced tea.

"More tired than a one-legged dog with a gaggle of fleas," Nana agreed, "but I enjoy every minute of it. Keeps me young and fit."

Mike stuck his head into the kitchen. "Last delivery

is done," he announced, his relief evident. "Either of you ladies need a ride home?"

"I'm going to stay a while and get some things ready for tomorrow," Melanie said. "Nana, you go home."

When Nana frowned and looked about to argue, Melanie added, "Please. If you don't rest, you won't have the stamina to go out with Bernie the next time he calls."

Standing so swiftly that she almost toppled her chair backwards, Nana said, "Let's go, Mikey."

After they left, Melanie locked the front and back doors and turned off the storefront lights. Alone in the kitchen, she breathed a contented sigh. She loved to spend time here after everyone had gone. While it was quiet, the kitchen had familiar noises all its own that she found soothing and comforting. The swish of the dishwasher, the gentle hum of the overhead fluorescent lights. The purr of the freezer. The occasional drip of the faucet.

She loved the gleaming copper pots, the shiny professional stainless-steel stove and ovens, the gleaming white countertops, the sparkling clean floor.

But most of all she loved the smells. The sweet scent of fresh apple pie, the lingering aroma of fried chicken. She breathed deeply and recognized the tang of lemon and the delicious fragrance of fresh basil. They brought back vivid, wonderful childhood memories of times spent baking at home with her mother, or helping at the restaurant, watching her dad flip juicy burgers and steaks while he entertained his workers with silly jokes.

Humming to herself, she methodically chopped dozens of onions, peppers, carrots, and celery stalks, sealing them in stay-fresh bags and storing them in the fridge. By doing these prep chores at night, her work the next day went much more smoothly. She then set about peeling another mountain of potatoes for tomorrow's vegetable of the day.

That task done, she decided to call it a night and clean up. She'd just shoved a handful of potato peels down the garbage disposal hole when she heard a knock at the back door.

Melanie looked at the clock. It was almost midnight. The knock sounded again, and a frisson of fear zipped down her spine. Was someone trying to break in? But what the heck kind of burglar knocked?

Not willing to take any chances, she reached for the phone, ready to call 911 and let the police figure out what kind of burglar knocked, but before she could even lift the receiver, a muffled but familiar male voice drifted through the door.

"Melanie? Are you in there? It's me, Chris."

Her hormones snapped to attention and her heart jumped. Suspecting she would have been safer with the burglar, Melanie hurriedly unlocked the door and opened it.

Oh, boy. It was Chris all right.

Standing in a bright pool of light from the security lamp mounted above the door, looking tired, rumpled, and sexy as sin. Dressed in a conservative navy blue suit, he looked good enough to eat. The top button of his wrinkled white shirt was undone, his paisley silk tie loosened and askew, his double-breasted jacket unbuttoned. The hint of a five o'clock shadow darkened his square jaw, and his mouth— whoa! Better not even look there!

She *wanted* to ask him to remove all his clothes and submit to a thorough physical examination. Instead, she pulled herself together and cocked a brow. "I appreciate punctuality as much as the next person, but according to my calculations"—she glanced over her shoulder at the clock—"you're about sixteen hours early for our date."

A slow, sexy grin quirked his lips. "I live by the rule that it's better to be sixteen hours early than one minute late."

She opened her mouth to reply, but before she could, he leaned forward and brushed his lips over hers in a warm, friendly kiss, effectively erasing every thought from her head.

"Nice to see you, Mel Gibson," he said, tweaking one of her curls. "Are you going to invite me in?"

Not on your life, her mind screamed.

"Of course," her lips said. She held the door wide and fumbled with the lock after he walked in. A subtle whiff of his woodsy cologne teased her nostrils and she clamped her lips together to squelch the feminine sigh of pleasure threatening to escape. And clamping her lips together came with the added bonus that it kept her from drooling.

By the time she turned to face him, he was comfortably sprawled in a chair, his long legs stretched out in front of him. She scooted around him cautiously, not getting too close for fear she'd be tempted to jump onto his lap.

The guy probably had some sort of Star Wars force field surrounding him. If she ventured too close, he'd suck her in and she'd never escape. To be safe, she headed for the sink and nervously crammed several more handfuls of potato peelings down the disposal hole.

"I thought you were out of town," she said, proud that her voice sounded so normal.

When he didn't reply, she looked over her shoulder at him and noticed his gaze was trained on her butt. Heat zinged through her like she'd been shot with a laser. She cleared her throat to attract his attention.

He looked up and winked at her. "Nice view."

"Ah, thanks. I thought you were out of town."

"I was. I finished my audit ahead of schedule and decided to catch a plane home tonight instead of waiting until morning. I was driving down Peachtree and saw the Dodge parked in the lot and thought maybe you were stranded here. Is the car running okay?"

"The best it has in a long time. Thanks to you."

"Do you always work this late?"

"Sometimes. It depends on how busy the day was. We set a new record today. It was our busiest lunch and dinner ever—and all in the same day."

A tired smile lit his face. "That's great. It sounds like the Pampered Palate is off and running."

"You betcha. Just try and catch me."

A devilish gleam lit his eyes. "Hmmm. Sounds interesting. Is that a dare?"

"No!" she all but shouted. "No," she repeated in a calmer tone. "Just an expression."

He rose and came to stand behind her. Leaning over her shoulder, he asked, "What are you doing?"

A legion of chills skittered down her spine when his warm breath brushed her ear. Thank goodness she was finished using her sharp knife—there was no way she could have concentrated with him so close. "Cleaning up some potato peels. I was just getting ready to leave."

"Great. I'll wait and walk you to your car. Protect you from any lurking bandits."

The only lurking bandit that worried her was the

one standing right behind her, his breath ruffling her hair, his body radiating sensual heat like a blast furnace.

Who exactly was supposed to protect her from *him*? He was more lethal than a loaded pistol.

Trying her best to ignore him, she turned on the water and flicked the disposal switch.

A weak *grrrrrr* sounded and nothing else. She tried it again. An even weaker *grrrrr* came out. On the third try, nothing.

"Problem?" Chris asked.

She shut off the faucet and glared at the dirty water in the sink, complete with floating potato peels, and squelched the urge to stick her tongue out at it.

"You could say that. The garbage disposal is clogged. I must have shoved in too many potato peels at once." She tipped her head back and huffed out an exasperated breath. "Just what I need. A big fat bill from a plumber. And I probably won't be able to get one here tomorrow before noon."

"No need to call a plumber," Chris said. "My mom does this same thing at least twice a year. As long as it's just a clog, I can fix it for you."

Hope bloomed in her chest. "You can? Really?"

"Sure. I'll have you fixed up in no time."

If she hadn't been convinced before this moment that he was the most attractive man who breathed air, this clinched the deal. Jeez, he was just like Superman. Gorgeous, and able to leap clogged garbage disposals in a single bound.

He shrugged out of his suit jacket and rolled up his shirtsleeves. Lowering himself to his knees, he stuck his head and shoulders into the cabinet under the sink, leaving Melanie an unobstructed view of what had to be the best male rear end since the dawn of man.

She wondered if he was wearing boxers again and found herself staring, engrossed in attempting to see through his summer wool trousers to solve the mystery. Boy, that Superman sure had a good thing with that X-ray vision. He'd be able to find out in a jiffy—

"Are you alive up there?" came Chris's muffled voice from inside the cabinet. "What the heck are you doing?"

Oogling your ass, trying to figure out what kind of Calvin's you're wearing. "Nothing."

"Has the water drained down yet?"

Melanie looked in the sink. "Yup. It's almost all gone." She had to hand it to him. For an accountant, he sure knew his way around kitchen appliances. He'd fixed that clog in nothing flat.

Chris backed out of the cabinet, sat back on his heels, and looked up at her. "What did you say?"

"I said it looks like you've fixed it." She reached over and hit the button.

The disposal erupted like Mount Vesuvius, spewing a geyser of dirty water and potato peels into the air.

Melanie jumped back, out of harm's way, but Chris wasn't so lucky.

She stared down at him and clapped her hands to her cheeks, her jaw slack with shock. "Oh. My. God."

Murky water dripped off his nose and earlobes. His shirt was plastered to his shoulders, his hair flattened to his head.

And he was dotted from head to toe with brown plops of potato peel.

Some of the mess had landed on the floor and the sink backsplash, but not much. Nearly all of it, the gunk from fifty potatoes, covered Chris.

Uh-oh. This is bad. They both remained frozen in a stunned tableau for several seconds, then, without uttering a word, Chris wiped his dripping forehead with the back of his hand. The water disappeared, but the brown flecks remained, as if they were pasted to him.

She had to say something, but God help her, she had no idea what. The poor guy looked like something that had been fished from a dumpster. If a genie had suddenly popped up and granted her one wish, she would have bypassed world peace and a million dollars and opted for another chance not to flick that damn switch.

Reaching out, she plucked a dish towel from the counter and handed it to him. "I'm so sorry, Chris. I . . . I guess you weren't quite finished with your repairs."

He wordlessly accepted the towel and wiped his sopping face with a stoic expression that increased her guilt triplefold. His clothing appeared ruined beyond all hope, and it was all her fault.

Now wait a darn minute, her inner voice said. It was actually all *his* fault. If he hadn't dropped by and gotten her all flustered, she wouldn't have overloaded the disposal. She suspected, however, that he wouldn't appreciate hearing that right now, so she kept that opinion to herself.

And blaming him was a weak argument anyway, and she knew it. It wasn't his fault she'd lost her mind the minute he walked in the door. He couldn't help it if the mere sight and smell of him sent her into a brain-numbing tizzy.

Squaring her shoulders, she knelt beside him and helped him brush off his once pristine white shirt. "I guess I'm in the doghouse, huh?"

"Actually," he said in a perfectly calm voice, "I've always understood that the doghouse is a place for men only." He flicked a potato peel from his bottom lip. "We might have to make an exception in your case." Glancing down at his ruined pants, he shook his head and muttered, "Another one bites the dust."

He was so calm, she couldn't tell if he was holding in raging anger or if he was just an incredibly good sport.

She prayed he was an incredibly good sport.

Plucking a blob of goop from his shirt, she said, "I'm really sorry about this. Of course I'll pay for your cleaning bill. . . ." Her voice trailed off as a particularly large peeling disengaged itself from his hair and flopped down, covering his left eye.

Before she could stop it, a giggle bubbled up in her throat, and she bit her lips to contain it.

One dark blue eye glared at her. "You're not *laughing*, are you?"

She shook her head, desperately fighting to control her amusement, but each passing second brought her closer to exploding.

"Because *laughing*," he said, pulling the peel off his eye, "would *not* be a good idea."

Giggles erupted from between her lips and, unable to contain the torrent, she gave in to her mirth. She stood, staggered to lean against the counter, and laughed until her sides ached.

"You . . . you look like Mr. Potato Head with brown measles," she gasped.

He was on his feet in an instant, looming over her. Bracing his spud-encrusted arms on either side of her, he all but growled, "Mr. Potato Head?"

She peeked up at him from under lowered lashes.

" 'Fraid so. Although in all fairness, he was sort of doofy-looking, and you're not."

"He was *very* doofy-looking."

"Yes. And you're not." Another giggle bubbled up and she coughed to cover it. "Except for right now, of course. Right now you're extremely doofy-looking."

"I'm delighted you think so. Personally, I don't find this all that amusing."

"Then you must have had your sense of humor surgically removed, because this is funny." Reaching out, she flicked a peel from his shoulder. "Trust me on this."

"You realize the timing of that request is not the best."

Unable to stop herself, she allowed her palm to drift over his wet shoulder and settle on his chest. His muscles jumped and his heart thudded against her fingertips. "I'm truly sorry, Chris. Forgive me?"

Chris looked down at her hand resting over his heart and sighed. The woman was an environmental hazard. He wanted to suggest that she consider looking for a nudist for her next boyfriend, since she was such hell on clothes. But since he wanted to fill the boyfriend shoes himself, he kept his mouth shut, not a difficult thing to do as the damn potato starch was starting to tighten his skin.

He should have been furious. Or at the very least angry. Or annoyed.

But when he looked into those big brown eyes, brimming with remorse, a dozen feelings swarmed through him, and not one of them resembled anger.

Desire? Yes. Anger? Not even close.

In fact, he actually found this episode pretty amusing. Of course, he wasn't about to tell *her* that.

Arranging his stiff face into a stern expression, he

said, "I suppose I can forgive you, provided you promise never to do such a thing again."

"You mean the flick-the-switch-before-the-repairs-are-done maneuver?"

"Precisely."

"I promise. I've learned my lesson. Yes, sirree. No more flicking for me. Ever."

He nodded slowly, considering her vow. "All right. But I insist we seal your promise with a kiss."

Mischief danced in her eyes. "Oh, my. I haven't kissed a Mr. Potato Head since I was five. As I recall, he was rather stiff-lipped and his nose poked me in the eye."

"Serves you right." Leaning forward, he touched his mouth to hers and his heart *zinged* into overdrive.

This is what he'd wanted to do from the moment he'd walked into her kitchen. Touch her. Taste her. Feel her.

The damn woman hadn't left his thoughts the entire time he'd been out of town. In fact, *she* was the reason he'd been able to come home early. He couldn't sleep for thinking about her. Her smile, her laugh, her kissable lips. So instead of restlessly tossing and turning in an empty bed, he'd worked every night until two or three in the morning, cutting an entire day off his trip.

Never had three days seemed like such an eternity.

But now he had her in his arms again. And he certainly wasn't going to allow a few potato peels to come between them.

Crushing her to him, he deepened their kiss.

By damn, he wasn't going to allow *anything* to come between them.

EIGHT

By Friday evening, Melanie had everything in perspective. Sort of.

So she had a date. And he was picking her up in five minutes. So what. Big deal. They'd have dinner, share a few laughs, end of story. One date, that was it. Nothing serious. Besides, he'd promised to be ugly. *Totally gross* were his exact words. Gross was good.

It didn't make any difference that he'd kissed her socks off last night in the Pampered Palate's kitchen. And who cared that he'd then helped her clean the potato mess off the floor and walls? What difference did it make that in spite of the disaster she'd caused, he'd proceeded to finish his repair job and unclog her garbage disposal?

So he was a nice guy. A nice, fun, smart, sexy, gorgeous guy whose kisses could melt brain cells into puddles and who had the patience of a saint. Whoop-dee-doo. Lot of guys were just like that. Probably. Just because *she* didn't know any of them didn't mean they weren't out there. Somewhere.

After dressing in a pair of lightweight turquoise pants and a matching sleeveless cotton blouse, she slipped on her Keds and laughed aloud at herself for making such a big to-do over nothing. She'd just finished spritzing on her favorite cologne when the doorbell rang.

Perfectly calm, she walked down the stairs, giving herself a last-minute pep talk, like a coach encouraging his team before the big game.

"He's just a guy like any other guy. Probably leaves dirty socks, damp towels, and empty pizza boxes on the floor. His kitchen cabinets are no doubt full of sugar-frosted cereals and Spaghetti-O's. Undoubtedly mixes last week's Chinese takeout with scrambled eggs and calls it Egg-Foo Breakfast. So snap out of it, Melanie! This is just a date. He's just a *man.*"

She pulled open the door and froze.

Just a man.

Good grief, and what a man.

She took one look at him and all her resolve trickled away like sand drifting through an hourglass.

He stood on her porch, a tall, dark, lethal hunk of manhood dressed in snug Levis faded in all the right places. A baby blue Polo shirt stretched across his chest, accentuating his shoulders and strong arms and bringing out the color of his eyes. A sprinkling of dark, intriguing chest hair peeped above the top button on his shirt. Wildly windblown ebony hair, a sexy half smile, and the subtle scent of his woodsy cologne completed the picture. The single long-stemmed red rose he held didn't hurt either.

What the heck had happened to ugly and totally gross?

Melanie gulped. She was a goner.

She would have said hello, invited him in, *something,* but it seemed she had suddenly forgotten how to swallow. And talk. Her hormones, however, were annoyingly vocal. *Zippity doo dah,* they sang, strutting their little hormone tushies.

He handed her the rose. "Hi."

She brought the bud to her nose and inhaled its sweet, heady fragrance. *We love roses,* her hormones said.

Okay. She'd say hi as soon as she remembered how to speak English. Resisting an urge to pound her chest with her fists á la Tarzan and shout, "Me woman, you man, let's mate," she managed to say, "Hi."

"You look great, Mel Gibson," he said in a soft, velvety voice that brought to mind long, slow, deep kisses.

She cleared her throat and somehow managed to smile at him. *Good. That's good. A smile. Now talk.* "Thanks. You look nice, too." Melanie almost groaned at herself. *Nice?* That was such an understatement, it fell into the realm of a blatant lie. "Thanks for the rose. They're my favorite."

"You're welcome." Reaching out, he tugged gently on one of her curls. "You ready to go?"

"Yup." Thank goodness she remembered how to speak. Now if she kept her eyes closed so she didn't see him, and stopped breathing so she couldn't smell him, she just might survive the evening.

He peeked around her into the foyer. "Where's Nana?"

Melanie smiled. "She and Bernie went to the latest James Bond flick. She said not to wait up and not to call the cops if she wasn't home until morning."

"Sounds like fun. I'm happy for them."

"Me, too." Remembering her manners, Melanie asked, "Do you want to come in? Have a drink before we go?"

He shook his head. "No thanks. We need to leave. It'll be dark soon."

"So?"

"So, I want to get where we're going before there's no light left. Let's go."

Melanie ran inside long enough to put her rose in water, then grabbed her purse and locked the door. She was halfway down the porch when she halted. "Where's your car?"

He grabbed her hand and tugged her along. "Home."

"Home?" Allowing him to lead her, they walked past her Dodge, which sat in the driveway. When she saw what was parked behind the Dodge, she halted.

She peered at the huge black and chrome machine and felt her stomach roll down to her feet. "Wha . . . what's *that*?"

"What does it look like?"

She stared, slack-jawed. Uh-oh. This smelled like big trouble. "It *looks* like a motorcycle."

"Not just a motorcycle," he said with a wide grin. "A Harley Davidson."

"This is *yours*?"

"Sure is. Had it ever since college." He slapped a shiny black helmet into her hands and swung one leg over the leather seat. "Let's go."

She gaped at him, then at the monstrous gleaming steel machine nestled between his long legs. Sweat popped out on her forehead.

"Go?" she asked in a weak voice.

"Yeah. Go. You know, the open road, the wind in your hair, the asphalt beneath your feet."

Melanie puckered her lips. It really irked her when someone tossed her own words back at her. And verbatim, no less. What did he have, a photographic memory?

She plastered a false smile on her face. "As appealing as that sounds, I, ah, I'm afraid I can't. Maybe some other time. Why don't we take the Dodge?" She handed him back the helmet. He leaned over and plopped it on her head.

"Better buckle that up." He chucked her under the chin and grinned. "It's the law."

Melanie stood rooted to the spot and watched with mounting trepidation as he released the kickstand and backed the motorcycle down to the street. He strapped on his helmet, then turned to where she still stood on the driveway.

"Hey, you're lookin' kinda green, Mel Gibson. What's up?"

With as much dignity as she could muster, Melanie walked over to him. So she'd lied. So what. Lying wasn't a crime. She stood next to the motorcycle. Holy smokes. He looked totally sexy sitting astride all that steel and chrome. She almost swallowed her tongue.

"I'm not green," she reported in her haughtiest, queen of England demeanor. "I simply don't want to ride on that . . . thing."

He raised his brows. "Why not?"

"I'll, uh, get helmet hair. Bugs in my teeth. A sore butt. Besides, I try to avoid things with a negative fun/risk ratio. You know, three minutes on a motorcycle, eight months in the hospital."

His smile grew broader. "Chicken."

Melanie drew herself up. "I am not chicken."

He leaned forward until they were nose-to-nose. "Then prove it, Miss I-don't-want-a-boring-account-ant-I-want-a-motorcycle-kind-of-guy. Correct me if I'm wrong, but I believe your exact words were 'My motto is—it's either motorcycle guys or no guys.' "

She shot him a dirty look. "Hasn't anybody ever

told you it's impolite to throw people's words back at them? You might piss someone off."

"Hasn't anybody ever told you to be careful what you wish for? You might just get it."

Yeah, she'd heard it. Blah, blah, blah. She'd always hoped it would apply to winning the lottery. She made one last desperate attempt to save herself. "Nana would be worried sick if she knew I was on that . . . thing."

"Ha. Ten bucks says Nana would love to go for ride on this 'thing.' "

Darn it, he was right. A lump of real fear lodged in Melanie's throat. She'd never even been close to a motorcycle before. No doors, no seat belts, no nothin'. It gave her the willies.

"Look," she said, giving up all pretense at bravery, "I lied. I don't want a motorcycle guy. Wind in my hair gives me split ends and I'm allergic to asphalt." She swallowed the rest of her pride. "I just can't get on that thing. I'm not ready to die. There are too many things I still want to do."

He leaned his forearms on the handlebars and regarded her with interest. "Such as?"

"Such as . . . go canoeing. Play in a tennis tournament. Teach a cooking class. Try a martini. Bake the chocolate cake I found the recipe for in yesterday's newspaper. Skinny-dip. Lots of stuff."

"Great. I'll help you with five out of six. Let's go."

"Five out of six?"

"I'll take you canoeing, be your partner in a tennis match, and you can teach me how to cook something. I make a great martini and"—his grin turned wolfish—"I'll arrange for the skinny-dipping any time you say. You're on your own with the cake."

Melanie couldn't smother the laugh that escaped

her. She shook her finger at him. "If Nana knew how you were talking to me, she'd take a rolling pin to you."

"Good. We'll use it to make your cake. Now I'm six for six." He held out his hand. "C'mon, Melanie. Climb on. Take a chance. Do something wild."

"Hey, I do plenty of wild things. Lots of 'em. Wild is my middle name."

He crossed his arms over his chest and regarded her with amusement. "Oh, really? What's the last wild thing you did?"

She shuffled her feet. "Uh, well, yesterday I hand-washed a rayon shirt that said dry clean only."

He hooted out a laugh. "You're a regular Evel Knevel."

"Ha, ha, ha. I once put bubble bath in the Jacuzzi—"

"Now that's more like it."

She sent him a withering look. "I was twelve."

He made a *tsking* sound and shook his head. "That's pathetic. Absolutely pitiful. Boy, are you lucky I came along to save your sorry butt."

"It's my sorry butt I'm attempting to save by not getting on that thing."

A warm, teasing, utterly sexy expression entered his eyes. Melanie felt the pull of that look and groaned. "Don't look at me like that," she protested, knowing she was going down for the third time with no lifeboat in sight. "Time out. No fair."

"C'mon, Mel. Ride with me." He leaned forward and brushed his mouth over hers. Their helmets bumped. "I promise you'll like it."

Riding on a Harley with the sexiest guy east of the Rockies, arms wrapped around him, pressed into his body. Oh, yeah. She'd probably like it no end.

That was exactly what she was afraid of.

And if the motorcycle didn't kill her, the overdose of potent male sexuality no doubt would.

She took a deep breath.

Oh, well. What the heck.

Everybody's gotta go sometime.

NINE

They'd been on the road for a good fifteen minutes before Chris felt the death grip she had around his waist loosen a bit. The sun was just slipping beneath the horizon, bathing the sky with a palette of pinks and oranges. He cruised down the road, feeling the tension of the past several hectic weeks ease from his body and mind. There was nothing like a motorcycle ride to relax a person.

And there was nothing like a warm female body pressing against his back, hugging his waist, to remind him that not *every* part of his body was relaxed. He smiled, remembering the look of utter stupefaction on her face when she'd first seen his Harley.

"You okay back there?" he shouted.

He felt her helmet unjam itself from between his shoulder blades and knew she'd lifted her head at last.

"Prop your chin on my shoulder," he urged loudly. "I promise you'll love it."

It took her a minute, but she finally settled her chin on his shoulder.

"I don't have to open my eyes, do I?" she yelled.

"If you don't, you'll miss the most beautiful sunset you've ever seen," he yelled back.

They drove on in silence, along a tree-lined, winding road that ran parallel to the Chattahoochee River. Chris smiled when he felt her rigid body slowly relax. By the time he parked in front of his condo, he suspected she'd changed her mind about motorcycles.

He turned off the ignition and looked behind him. "Well?"

She pulled off her helmet and shook her head, spreading a flurry of curls that settled like a halo around her face. Her eyes were bright and her cheeks flushed pink.

"That was awesome," she said, laughing. "Incredible."

He grinned. "I hate to say I told you so . . ."

"Oh, go ahead and say it. You were right, I was wrong. You're a big macho motorcycle hunk and I was a wuss." She swung her leg around and slid off, then practically danced around the bike in her excitement. "What a feeling. Like flying. Like nothing I've ever done before."

"Glad you liked it."

"Yes, sir," she enthused, patting the Harley, "I've gotta get me one of these babies." She looked at him and asked in a dead-serious tone, "How do you think I'd look in one of those black leather biker-chick outfits?"

The thought of her dressed in black leather gave him palpitations and made his knees sweat. He removed his helmet and hung it by its strap on the handlebars. "Come here."

Her eyes narrowed and a knowing, provocative, totally sexy smile curved her lips. She sauntered over to him, hips swaying. It was all he could do to remember to breath. Inhale, exhale. Inhale, exhale.

She stopped when she stood directly in front of

him. Reaching out, she walked her fingers up the front of his shirt.

"You'd better not be thinking about trying anything funny, big boy," she whispered in a husky drawl that tightened his groin and raised his temperature ten degrees. "I'm a real badass, bitchin', Harley babe now."

"Oh, yeah?" he challenged. "Prove it."

"All right." She gracefully swung her leg over and straddled the leather seat, facing him. Then she looped her arms around his neck and wrapped her long legs around his waist. "How's this?"

Chris hoped his tongue wasn't hanging out. It took every ounce of his rapidly deteriorating concentration to keep his feet planted on the ground so the Harley didn't keel over.

She leaned forward and gently nipped the side of his neck with her teeth. "Am I doing okay?"

A shaky laugh escaped him. "Yeah. You're a real badass." His skin suddenly felt too tight. Like it had shrunk a couple of sizes in the last two minutes. But there was no way he was going to bypass this opportunity.

Hauling her up even tighter against him, he said, "I hope you know CPR."

Her tongue flicked out and brushed his earlobe. His eyes glazed over.

"CPR?" she whispered. "Why's that?"

"Because I'm about to have a heart attack," he said, his voice a low growl. Fisting his hand in her hair, he dragged her mouth to meet his in a kiss that left him shaking.

He didn't know why this woman affected him the way she did, but he was apparently helpless to stop it. He hadn't wanted this, but this was the hand he'd been dealt, and by God he was going to play it.

No longer gentle, his tongue demanded entrance to her mouth, plundering the silky interior, claiming it as his own. She tasted like sugar and cinnamon and she smelled like flowers. His hands caressed her impatiently, kneading her back, then coming forward to cup the soft fullness of her breasts. He stroked his thumbs over her nipples and groaned when they peaked into hardened points.

God, he wanted her. So badly he couldn't think straight. So much he'd forgotten they were in the parking lot. Good thing it was nearly dark and no one was around. He was in no condition to make apologies to his neighbors or give explanations to an arresting officer. He had to get off this bike, out of this parking lot, and into the privacy of his condo before he exploded. He was so hard he didn't know if he'd ever be able to walk again.

"Chris," she murmured against his neck. "Chris, we have to stop . . . while we still can. Please. This isn't the time . . . or the place."

He heard her words through a steamy haze of passion. He lifted his head, breathing hard. Sweat dripped down his spine and his heart pounded so hard he wondered if he really was having a heart attack.

She stared at him, her brown eyes huge and dazed. Her hair was a mess thanks to a combination of the helmet and his plundering hands. Her lips were moist and swollen from his kisses. Reddish abrasions marked her cheeks and neck where his five o'clock stubble had rubbed her. The tip of her tongue peeked out as she wet her lips.

"My God," she whispered in a breathless tone. She

eased herself away from him and slid off the bike on legs that were clearly unsteady. Chris made no move to stop her. Indeed, he decided it was best that she move away from him before he simply let nature take its course.

Drawing a deep breath, he gripped the handlebars and forced himself to calm down. Whatever had just possessed him, he was pleading temporary insanity. At the moment he wasn't sure if he wanted to drag her off and make love to her until they both passed out, or run away from her and whatever potent spell she'd cast on him as fast as his shaky legs could carry him.

Havoc. That's what this woman wreaked. Havoc. With his senses, his mind, his body. He'd only met her a week ago, and his life was turned upside down. A week ago he'd wanted nothing more than his bachelor freedom. Now he wanted Melanie. And nothing else.

She touched his arm. "You okay?" she asked in a small voice. "You're a million miles away."

He tried to smile and failed. He wanted to say he was fine, but that would have been an outright lie.

"To be perfectly honest," he said, plunging unsteady fingers through his hair, "I'm a bit shaken."

"I know what you mean." She wrapped her arms around herself. He knew she couldn't be cold. It had to be two hundred degrees outside. "I'm sorry about that, Chris. I guess I just got caught up in the moment." She raised questioning eyes to his. "How about you?"

"Caught up, yes. Sorry, no."

"I think it might be best if . . ." Her words trailed off and a frown formed between her brows. "Where are we?"

"My place." Forcing a calmness he was far from feeling, he locked the bike, set the kickstand, then swung his leg over the leather seat. "I hope you're hungry." At her blank stare he added, "I'm making dinner."

"You're cooking me dinner?"

He took her hand and pulled her toward his front door. "That a problem?"

He actually heard her gulp. He smiled, glad she wasn't calm while he was like Elvis—all shook up.

"No problem," she said. "I'm just surprised. What's on the menu?"

"Steak, potatoes, salad. And my famous martinis. Real bachelor-guy stuff."

"I thought bachelor-guy stuff was moldy bologna, stale potato chips, and beer."

"That was last night. Tonight, we feast." He unlocked his door and pushed it open with a flourish. "Welcome to my humble abode. I haven't had much time or inclination to decorate, but all the essentials are covered."

"Essentials?" she asked, craning her neck.

"Beer in the fridge; towels in the bathroom; gym equipment in the dining room; stereo, TV, VCR, recliner in the den." He led her into the den and indicated a tan leather sectional. "Make yourself at home. That's the most comfortable sofa on earth. I'm just going to get the steaks going. I'll be right back." Before heading into the kitchen, he flicked on the stereo. The smooth sounds of Eric Clapton played softly through the speakers.

Melanie took advantage of his absence to look around. The den was spacious, with one wall a series of sliding doors that led onto a roomy deck. Soft track lighting highlighted the gleaming hardwood floors, and a plush sea-foam green and cream Oriental rug lay in front of the marble fireplace.

She wandered past a huge whitewashed oak entertainment center chock full of complicated-looking stereo equipment and a TV. Built-in bookshelves flanked the fireplace, and Melanie perused his selection of books. Lots of accounting texts. The latest Grisham novel alongside a pictorial history of New Orleans. Several volumes concerning cars and motorcycles and, most surprising, a book of poetry.

She counted over a dozen framed photos of his family placed on the shelves. One photo in particular caught her attention. She picked it up and studied a teenage Chris standing next to a very handsome man who looked exactly like him. They grinned identical smiles into the camera.

"That's my dad," he said, entering the room. He set two drinks down on the glass coffee table. "It's my favorite picture. My mom took it just a week before he died."

Melanie turned to him, and her heart flipped over. He was gazing at the photo with such a sad look on his handsome face, she felt like crying. Not knowing what else to say she whispered, "I'm sorry."

His face cleared and a half smile touched his lips. "Yeah. Me, too. He was a great guy."

After setting the photo back on the shelf, he led her to the sofa. Once they were seated he handed her a drink.

She sniffed it and her eyes fogged up. "Yikes. What is this?"

"It's the best vodka martini you'll ever have."

Raising her brows, she repeated, "Martini?"

"I seem to recall you saying you wanted to have one before you died."

"This may come as a shock to you, but I'm not planning to kick the bucket anytime soon."

"No time like the present," he said, clinking the edge of his skinny, triangular-shaped glass to hers. "Try it."

Melanie took a tentative sip. The alcohol was icy cold and powerfully potent.

"Well?" he asked, watching her closely.

"I like it. Kinda tastes like freezing-cold lighter fluid."

He laughed. "You can no longer say you've never tried a martini." He leaned back and stretched out his Levis-clad legs. "I thought we'd start on the other stuff tomorrow."

"What other stuff?"

"Canoeing. Tennis. Cooking lessons. Baking." He shot her an exaggerated leer. "Skinny-dipping."

"Whoa," she said, alarmed by the chain reaction of chaos his words started in her stomach. Skinny-dipping meant Chris naked, and she'd already vowed not to say those two words in the same sentence. The mere thought of him naked made her toss back a hefty swig of her drink. "Those are lifetime goals. If I knock them all off in one weekend, what will I have to live for?"

He leaned forward and dropped a warm, teasing, heart-accelerating kiss on her lips. "I'm sure we can come up with something," he said against her mouth.

Before Melanie could jolt her vocal chords into replying, he stood and said, "The steaks need to be turned. Would you like to set the table?"

"Sure." She followed him into the kitchen, and raised her brows. This was definitely not the month-old-linguine-encrusted room she'd envisioned. Sparkling white cabinets contrasted with dark blue granite countertops. The white ceramic tile floor gleamed with a spotless shine. A large window overlooked the deck, where steam escaped from a gas grill.

"Very nice," Melanie remarked, turning around in a circle. "Very manly, not filled with girlie gew-gaws. And clean, too." She nodded her approval. "I like it."

"Thanks. Dishes are in the top-left cabinet. I'll get the steaks."

Ten minutes later Melanie sat across from him in the small breakfast room at a round, glass-topped table. When she eyed her steak with trepidation, he laughed. "You're not about to be poisoned," he promised. "Steak is the only thing I know how to cook, and after lots of practice, I'm good at it."

Thus assured, Melanie sampled a bite, then smiled. "This is very good."

"Coming from a gourmet cook, I'm flattered, but the note of surprise in your voice is a bit deflating."

"I'm not surprised. Well, maybe a little," she conceded. "I guess I had a stereotypical view of bachelors—can't cook, live in green fungus-filled squalor, spray Lysol on dirty clothes rather than do the laundry." She waved her fork around. "I must admit, I'm impressed."

"Wait 'til you taste dessert."

Melanie looked at him, at the twinkling gleam in his eyes, and almost choked on her salad. She wasn't sure what dessert was, but based on that devilish look in his eyes, she had a feeling it was going to scare her to death. And that she would love it. She gulped down the rest of her drink and held out her glass for another.

After dinner they sat on the deck, sharing a cushiony blue-and-white striped patio loveseat. Melanie leaned her head back and sipped her third martini. By the time she was halfway finished with it she realized that those suckers tasted pretty damn good—in fact, they were the most delicious thing she'd ever tasted.

Of course, they were kinda strong, a fact that came to her attention when Chris asked her a question. She turned her head to look at him and noticed her vision arrived several seconds later.

He narrowed his eyes at her. "You okay?"

She fought a powerful urge to giggle. "Certainly."

Leaning over, he peered at her in the darkness. "Uh-oh. That third martini was probably not a good idea."

"Nonsense. I can hold my liquor as well as you."

"I've only had one."

She glared at him. "One?"

"I'm driving," he said in a mild tone.

"You know, that's one of the things I like about you," she said, slapping her palm against his thigh. "You're very responsible."

He took her hand and raised her fingers to his lips. "I'm glad to hear there are things about me you like, 'cause there's a whole lot I like about you."

The warm, inviting look in his eyes made her tingle all over. "Really?" she asked. "Like what?"

"Everything. Your smile, your laugh, your sense of humor. You're smart, beautiful, funny, kind, and you make the best cookies I've ever eaten." He traced his tongue down the center of her palm and she almost slithered bonelessly off the chair in response.

"Not to mention," he continued in a husky voice, "that you're incredibly sexy."

Wow, wow, holy cow. Melanie finished off her icy drink with a long, deep glug, hoping to cool the fire his words had lit. One more compliment like that and she was going to go up in a puff of smoke.

He squeezed her hand. "You said there were things you liked about me?"

She huffed out a breath. "Ohhhh yeaaahhh. There's a whole big bunch of stuff I like about you."

He brushed his mouth across her palm. "I'm listening."

Melanie stared at him, her head swimming. Jeez, it was hot. Didn't he have air-conditioning? Oh, they were outside.

"I uh, like your smile," she said. "The way you treat your family. The way you treat Nana." He flicked out his tongue against her wrist and a legion of goose bumps chilled her flesh. "The way you treat me," she finished with a sigh.

He drew her index finger into the warm silk of his mouth and Melanie almost swooned. "I, umm, I like that, too." She rested her head on the cushion. "Whew! Is it *hot* out here, or is it just me?"

He took her empty glass and set it on the deck, then leaned forward until his lips touched her ear. "It's definitely not just you," he whispered. "Let's go inside."

Standing, he held out his hand and pulled her to her feet.

A giggle erupted from her. "Holy smokes. Who's moving the floor?"

Chris wrapped a strong arm around her waist and led her through the sliding glass doors. Just as they entered the kitchen, Melanie stumbled. She clung to his shoulders and said, "Whoopsie-doo! Hey, I left something outside."

"What's that?"

"My knees." Holding on to him, she shook one

leg, then the other. "My knees are gone." She touched her face. "My eyebrows, too."

"Oh, boy. That third martini was *definitely* a mistake."

"Nonsense. I feel swell. In a numb, tingly sort of way. I'm not sure about the numb, but the tingly is definitely all your fault."

Feeling wonderfully free and uninhibited, and unable to remember why she shouldn't, Melanie stood on tiptoe and kissed his neck. "Yum. You smell good." She pressed herself against him, running a series of tiny kisses up his jaw. "Would you, by any chance, be dessert?"

A choking sound came from his throat. "Melanie . . ."

She gently bit his earlobe. "Hmmmm?"

"Let's get you in the car. I think I'd better take you home."

Home? No, she didn't want to go home. She wanted to stay right here. Where they could get comfortable and he could put out the fire he'd started inside her.

But if he wanted to go to her place, that was okay. Nana would be out all night with Bernie.

Too languid to argue, Melanie gathered her purse and let Chris lead her to the Mercedes. She spent the fifteen-minute drive to her house in a hazy daydream, imagining making love to Chris.

She wanted him. There was no point in denying it any longer. It had been so long since she'd wanted a man . . . since a man had wanted her. She'd fought this attraction, but she was ready to admit defeat.

Without warning, an idea popped into her mind with such clarity, she imagined a lightbulb bursting to life above her head. Since she didn't want a relationship, she'd just use him for sex!

What a perfect plan! Why hadn't she thought of that in the first place? He wasn't interested in a long-term relationship, so as long as she remembered the rules—no strings, no commitments, no emotional attachments—she wouldn't risk a broken heart. They'd just enjoy hot, feverish sex. *Am I a genius or what?*

When he pulled up in front of her house, he said, "C'mon, princess. We're home." He walked her to the porch, his arm wrapped firmly around her waist. By the time they stood in front of the door, Melanie's heart was pounding. If he didn't kiss her in the next ten seconds, she was going to jump him.

"Do you have your key?" he asked in an amused tone.

"Key? Of course I have my key." She stared at him, waiting for him to kiss her. A good minute went by. Nothing.

A smile quirked his lips. "Do you need help finding it?"

"Finding what?"

"Your key."

"Shertainly not." Melanie dug around in her purse and came up with the key. "Ta-da!"

Chris took it and opened the door. The moment they stepped into the darkened foyer, Melanie turned, pushed the door closed, and wrapped her arms around his neck. "Are you going to kiss me, or what?"

A strangled sound passed his lips. "I'm going home. Now. While I still can."

Melanie slowly pulled his Polo shirt from his jeans. "I don't want you to leave," she whispered. "I want to touch you. I want your hands on me." She pushed her hands under his shirt and ran her palms up his smooth back. "I want to make love with you."

Groaning, he tunneled his fingers through her hair and looked into her eyes. "Melanie. Jeez. You're killing me." He dropped his head until their foreheads touched. "This is so ironic. You've finally said the words I've wanted to hear, and you probably won't remember saying them in the morning."

Melanie leaned back and glared at him. "Are you insinuating that I'm tipsy?"

"Does the expression 'three sheets to the wind' mean anything to you?"

"I am *not* three sheets to the wind."

"You're right. You're *four* sheets to the wind. Completely snookered."

Insulted, she drew herself up. "I've never been snookered in my life." A sudden wave of dizziness washed over her. *"Snockered,* maybe. Snookered never."

"Oh, yeah? How are your knees?"

She concentrated for a moment. "Missing in action."

"Eyebrows?"

"Gone." She hiccuped. "But not forgotten."

He sighed and cupped her face between his hands. "Listen to me, Melanie. When we make love, I want you to remember every single second. I want you completely aware every time I touch you. Everywhere I touch you. As much as I'm literally aching to stay here and take you up on your offer, I can't. Tonight is not the night."

Melanie stared at him—both of him—and frowned. "In other words, you're leaving."

"Yeah. But I'll be back."

"When?"

"Tomorrow morning. Ten o'clock. Wait, better make it eleven. You're going to need the extra hour's sleep."

"What are we doing tomorrow?"

He kissed the tip of her nose and opened the door. "Canoeing. Better rest up. And you might want to take a couple of aspirin."

"Canoeing? Aspirin? What do you mean?"

"Canoeing because it's on the things-to-do-before-you-die list, and aspirin for your headache. Get some sleep. I'll see you tomorrow." He left, closing the door behind him.

Melanie started for the stairs, lurching a bit. Damn it, how was a person supposed to walk when the floor kept shifting? She huffed out a breath and held on to the banister.

Canoeing? She didn't want to go canoeing. Didn't know the first thing about it. And what was that about aspirin? What headache?

By the time she'd staggered into her bedroom and undressed, her temples were pounding like the hammers of hell.

Oh. *That* headache.

TEN

Chris stopped at the bakery for cinnamon rolls on his way to Melanie's the next morning. The place was packed, as it always was on weekend mornings. He pulled a paper number from the machine and glanced at it. Forty-eight. A lighted sign indicated number thirty-two was being served. That was the problem with this bakery—they made the best doughnuts and pastries in Atlanta and everyone knew it.

Resigned to the lengthy wait, he snagged a copy of the morning newspaper from the stack by the door and skimmed the headlines. He was halfway through the sports page when a snippet of conversation from the people behind him caught his attention.

One of them said "Pampered Palate."

Discreetly turning his head, Chris saw two men about his own age, one dressed in running shorts and an Atlanta Braves T-shirt, the other wearing a ratty sweatsuit. Both sported sweat-flattened hair and the faint aroma of gym socks.

"My client is scheduled to close on the property early next month," Running Shorts said. "Mark my words, it's going to be the hottest eatery in Atlanta once it's up and running."

"What kind of food?" asked Ratty Sweatsuit.

"A combination of Italian and Mexican. Eclectic decor, live music, patio bar. They're calling it Spaghetti Loco and believe me, there's nothing else like it."

"Sounds great. When's it scheduled to open?" asked Ratty Sweatsuit.

"In about six months."

"Your client isn't worried about the established restaurant right across the street?"

Running Shorts chuckled. "The Pampered Palate? Hell no. That's not even a restaurant. They're a small takeout place. We'll put them out of business within a year."

"Hey, don't do that," Ratty Sweatsuit protested. "I order from there at least once a week. The food's good, and the owner's not bad either."

"Yeah?" Running Shorts dropped his voice, and Chris leaned back to catch his words. "Hot body?"

"Very."

"You gettin' any?"

"Not yet," Ratty said, "but she's definitely on my 'list of things to do.'" They both chuckled.

Chris fisted the newspaper into a tight ball and attempted to hold his temper in check. Hot jealousy and outrage slammed into him at the thought of that creep ogling Melanie. It was all he could do not to drag the bastard outside and firmly disabuse him of his amorous plans, then shove his "things to do list" down his throat.

If Ratty Sweatsuit thinks he'll get within fifty feet of my woman, he's in for a big surprise. Turning fully around, Chris glared at the two men, memorizing their faces. If he ever saw either one of them anywhere near

Melanie, he'd have to hurt them. And Ratty was just going to have to start ordering lunch from Taco Bell.

Running Shorts jerked his head toward the counter. "You're next," he said to Chris, clearly oblivious to the fact that he was on the receiving end of a dark, angry stare.

After one last killer look, Chris placed his order, paid, and left before he gave into the temptation to do bodily harm and ended up in jail on assault charges.

Seated in the parking lot in the Mercedes, he gripped the steering wheel until his knuckles turned white. *God damn it!* He couldn't recall the last time he'd felt so unsettled and frustrated.

The idea of Ratty Sweats, or *any* guy, dating Melanie—touching her, kissing her, *making love* to her, tied his insides into hard knots and made him want to break things. He'd never experienced such hot, pulsing, jealous anger before, and he didn't like it. Not one damn bit.

This caring about a woman business was a major pain in the ass. He'd be much better off sticking to his carefree bachelor plan and dating a string of beauties. And that's exactly what he was going to do.

As soon as he got Melanie out of his system.

A couple of weeks of no-strings-attached fun and games, and they'd amiably part company. His inner voice yelled that that might not be as easy as it sounded, but Chris ruthlessly squashed the pesky voice.

After several minutes, he regained his composure and started the car. Muttering to himself about kicking some sweatsuit ass, he was halfway to Melanie's house before the other part of Ratty and Running's conversation worked its way back into his mind.

A new restaurant was scheduled to open right across the street from the Pampered Palate.

The ramifications of that information hit him like a bucket of cold water. Did Melanie know about this?

But more important, did the *bank* know? The fact that a competitor was opening so close by could and probably *would* influence the bank's decision on granting Melanie her loan. It was definitely information that should be disclosed in his company's independent review.

If the bank didn't already know . . . Chris groaned at the thought. If they didn't know, he'd have to tell them. Or at least inform Glenn so *he* could tell the loan officer.

Damn it! Technically, he supposed he could keep quiet about it. Who would ever know what he'd overheard? But his conscience would chew at him, even though it was a gray area.

Maybe the bank already knew. Was it possible Glenn or Bob Harris had found out and were already going to include the info about the new restaurant in their review? Or perhaps Melanie knew and had told Glenn and the bank. Maybe Chris's firm or the bank would investigate the empty stores to find out what kind of businesses were planning to rent them.

He wouldn't know all the facts until he spoke to Glenn on Monday. He briefly considered calling him at home but recalled that Glenn was away for the weekend. In the meantime, he'd ask Melanie a few discreet questions. If she already knew and had disclosed the info, there was no problem. If she didn't know . . . he pushed the disturbing thought aside.

And prayed he wasn't going to ruin her chances of getting her loan.

***

Chris rang Melanie's doorbell at exactly eleven o'clock, and Nana threw open the door.

"Well! If it isn't the hunk!" she said, her face wreathed in smiles. "And you brought those yummy doughnuts again." She looked him up and down over her bifocals. "Jiminy Cricket. You're a looker for sure."

Chris laughed. "Same goes, Nana."

She patted her bright red hair and blushed. "Now don't you go flirtin' with me, young man. I've got a beau of my own."

"Bernie's a lucky man."

"You're darn tootin'," Nana agreed with a wink. "Come on in. There's coffee brewing, and I just took a batch of double chocolate chunk cookies out of the oven."

Chris rubbed his hand over his stomach. "I love you, Nana."

Following Nana into the kitchen, Chris made himself at home in one of the chintz-covered chairs. He really liked this house, he decided, accepting a yellow ceramic mug filled with aromatic coffee. And he especially liked the women who lived in it.

He scooped a cookie from the serving tray. "Where's Melanie?"

"She'll be along. I heard the shower running earlier. Did you have fun last night?"

Chris bit into the cookie and moaned in ecstasy. He felt like an eight-year-old, sitting at the table after school, munching on home-baked cookies for an afternoon snack. "Last night was great. Melanie loved the motorcycle."

Nana raised her brows. "Motorcycle?"

"Didn't she tell you?"

"No. I, er, only arrived home two hours ago."

The bright pink blush creeping over Nana's cheeks amused him. So did the wicked gleam in her eye. "Nana! You devil."

She chuckled. "Ain't it the truth? Now, what's this about a motorcycle?"

Chris told Nana about Melanie's inaugural bike ride—leaving out the part where her granddaughter had all but seduced him in the parking lot. He'd just finished when Melanie walked into the kitchen.

"Good morning," Nana said, eyeing her granddaughter up and down.

Melanie mumbled something unintelligible and headed straight for the coffeepot.

Nana raised her brows and picked up her mug. "I'm outta here, kids. I'm gonna take me a nice long, hot bath. Bernie's taking me to Chili's for the early-bird special, then we're heading back to his place to watch the Braves game and drink martinis."

"Take my advice, Nana," Melanie said, easing herself into a chair. "Don't drink martinis. Ever."

"So that's why you're looking so peaked." Nana fixed her gaze on Chris. "Did you get my granddaughter drunk, young man?"

Chris lifted his palms in surrender. "No, ma'am. She did it all by herself."

She eyed him with interest. "You take advantage of her weakened condition?"

"Nope." A smile tugged at his lips. "She tried her darndest to seduce me, but I wouldn't let her. I did the honorable thing and hauled her tipsy butt back home. The effort almost killed me."

Melanie glared at both of them, her hands wrapped around her coffee mug like it was a lifeline.

"Would you two stop talking about me as if I'm not here?"

Nana hooted out a laugh. "Oohh, she's a prickly one this morning." She patted Chris's shoulder. "Good luck, young man. You're gonna need it." Waving her fingers at them, she left.

Chris stretched out his legs, helped himself to another cookie, and watched Melanie sip her coffee with her eyes closed. Damned if she wasn't adorable, even if she was kinda grumpy.

He wanted to ask her about the vacant store across from the Pampered Palate but decided to wait until he could casually toss his questions into the conversation. He wasn't about to spoil their day when there might not be anything to worry about.

She didn't speak until she'd poured herself a second cup of coffee. Then she cleared her throat.

"Ah . . . about last night." She looked at him with those big brown eyes and his insides squeezed together. "I think I may have had one too many martinis."

He watched, fascinated, as a peachy blush suffused her entire face. "How do you feel?"

She huffed out a breath. "Actually, I feel pretty good. Good grief, I slept like someone hit me on the head with a hammer. I woke up with a headache, but I took some aspirin and it's almost gone." She twisted her fingers together, then raised her gaze to his. "What I'm really feeling is embarrassed."

"Why?"

She stared at him as if he was nuts. "*Why?* How can you even ask? I threw myself at you. And if that's not bad enough, you turned me down. How humiliating is *that?*"

If she hadn't looked so distraught, Chris would

have laughed. She thought he'd turned her down? Crazy woman. He stood and drew her to her feet. Tipping up her chin, he forced her to look at him.

"You have it all wrong, Melanie. I didn't turn you down. All I did was postpone the inevitable." He lowered his head and kissed her softly. She tasted like cookies.

She drew back, her eyes as round as saucers. "You mean you think we're going to . . ." Her voice trailed off.

"Absolutely. Don't you?"

"I don't think that's a good idea."

"It's a *great* idea. But even if it wasn't, it's still going to happen."

"How do you know?"

He looked down into her warm, chocolatey, confused eyes and fell a little farther into the black abyss of emotional commitment yawning in front of him. "Because I can't seem to stop it. There's something between us, and I can't walk away from it. Much as I'd like to, I can't."

"I can."

He searched her eyes and knew she wasn't telling the truth. "Liar," he said softly.

A small smile lifted her lips. "Well, I can try."

"Forget it. It won't work. Believe me. I know." He dropped a quick kiss on her nose. "Now, I suggest we enjoy one more cup of coffee before heading out on our canoeing expedition."

She groaned. "In other words, let's put *this* embarrassing episode behind us so we can move on to other, more potentially embarrassing episodes."

"You nailed it."

"Great. I guess I'd better tell you I know diddly-squat about canoeing."

"Don't worry. You're in good hands. We'll have a lot of fun."

She eyed him with clear suspicion. "Define fun."

He laughed. "Trust me on this."

An hour later, Melanie was fervently wishing she hadn't trusted him on this.

She stood at the end of the floating dock and pointed down, a sinking feeling in her stomach. "What is *that*?"

"That," Chris said, his voice filled with suppressed laughter, "is a canoe."

"Canoe, my ass. It's nothing but a carved-out, six-foot cigar." She planted her hands on her hips. "If you think I'm getting in that skinny excuse for a boat, you're out of your mind."

Chris cocked a brow at her. "*You* said canoeing was something you wanted to do. So here we are, at beautiful Lake Lanier, a canoe rented and at our disposal for the next hour." He crossed his arms over his chest. "So what's the problem?"

Melanie could tell he was trying not to laugh at her. Raising her chin, she said, "When I said *canoeing*, I was speaking strictly metaphorically."

His lips quirked. "Oh, really?"

"Of course. When I said I wanted to go *canoeing*, I *meant* I wanted to go on a Caribbean cruise." She nodded vigorously, knowing she was beat but willing to try one last, desperate attempt to save herself. "Clearly you're much too literal-minded to appreciate the finer points of symbolism. Canoe. Cruise. Both boat words that start with c. It's really rather interesting how—"

"Yeah, it's fascinating. We'll talk about a cruise some other time. Right now we're going canoeing."

Drat. The guy had a one-track mind. Melanie looked out at the sparkling lake. More than a dozen canoes dotted the calm waters nearby. Farther out she could see speedboats and wave runners racing over the small waves. A shaded picnic area stood off to the left, and several families were taking advantage of the facilities, setting out their coolers, lighting the charcoal grills.

She glanced down at the pencil-thin craft tied to the end of the dock and sighed. Next time she rattled off a list of things she wanted to do before she died, she was going to make damn sure she replaced "canoeing" with "three months in Tahiti."

Drawing a resolute breath, she said, "All right. Hoist the anchor, *el capitán.*"

"Atta girl," Chris said with a big grin. "Just sit still and you'll do great. You're gonna love this."

Melanie somehow doubted that, but she was willing to give it a go.

Besides, how hard could it be to drive a canoe?

Ten minutes later, Melanie knew exactly how hard it was.

Pretty damn hard.

Holding Chris's hand, she gingerly stepped into the canoe. Using extreme caution, she sat down while Chris, who still stood on the dock, untied the craft from the aluminum cleat.

Once her butt was settled on the hard wooden seat, Melanie breathed a sigh of relief. This wasn't so bad, she decided, clutching the sides of the craft. In fact, it was sorta fun.

Until she sneezed.

One minute she was sitting in the canoe, the next she was underwater.

She came up, sputtering, pushing her hair from her eyes. "What the hell did you do that for?" she yelled at Chris, who stood on the dock clutching his sides and roaring with laughter.

"I didn't do anything," he said, shaking his head. "I told you to sit still. Canoes are very tippy."

"Tippy? All I did was *sneeze!"*

"You must have sneezed too hard. Don't worry. You'll get used to it. It just takes practice."

"Yeah. Practice," she muttered, swimming to the dock. "That's just what I want to do."

Disgruntled, Melanie climbed the wooden ladder and stomped to the end of the dock. Water dripped from her body and squished from her Nikes. While Chris pulled the rope attached to the canoe and righted the craft, she squeezed water from her clothes.

He shot her a grin. "Wanna give it another try?"

"Might as well. I'm certainly not worried about getting wet." She sizzled a baleful glare at the offending canoe. "Anyway, I refuse to let this excuse for kindling beat me. I am woman. Hear me roar."

"That's my girl." Once again he handed her down into the canoe.

The instant he let go of her, she felt the damn canoe slipping out from under her feet. It was like trying to stand on wet ice. At least this time she was ready when she hit the water. She surfaced and, ignoring the fact that he stood on the dock laughing his ass off, swam to the ladder, pulled herself up, and squished over to him.

"Wanna quit?" he asked, an infuriating grin on his face. His *dry* face.

"Absolutely not," Melanie said between gritted teeth. "This has become a quest."

He reached out and touched the skin under her eye. "I think you need to invest in waterproof mascara. You look like a pirate."

Melanie planted her hands on her wet hips, tapped her soggy Nike, and glared at him.

Holding his hands up in surrender, he said, "Whoa! A *cute* pirate. A *very, very* cute pirate. The cutest. Really."

"Pirate, huh? Ask me where my buccaneers are."

"Okay. Where are your buccaneers?"

She waggled her brows at him. "Under my buccan' hat."

He threw back his head and laughed. "Ready to try it again, matey?"

"Sure." She eyed him up and down. "But this time *you* get in first."

Chris paddled the canoe and covertly observed Melanie through the dark lenses of his Ray-Bans. She was nearly dry and sat with her eyes closed, her face turned up to the sun. He noted with amusement that she sat perfectly still, clutching the edges of the canoe with a white-knuckled grip.

His gaze slid over her and his stomach tightened. Her hair curled in wild profusion around her face, the sun shooting the brown locks with shafts of reddish fire. Her skin glowed with the sheen of some kind of sunscreen that made her smell like a delicious combination of coconut and pineapple. She reminded him of one of those tropical drinks with the paper umbrellas—sweet, cool, and scrumptious.

His gaze drifted downward, taking in her long, slim legs. She'd left her soggy Nikes on the dock to dry, and now her pink-tipped toes peeked at him. Even her feet were cute. Chris shook his head. Damn, he had it bad.

And the fact that she was such a good sport about getting dunked in the lake made him like her even more. Every other woman he knew would have pitched a hissy fit in a similar situation.

But not Melanie. Nope, she'd just taken it in stride, wrung the water out of her clothes, pushed her hair out of her eyes, and grown determined to beat the canoe at its own game.

That unassuming, unfussy side of her appealed to him more than any perfectly made-up, exquisitely groomed woman ever had. A mental image of her, disheveled from a bout of frantic lovemaking, flashed in his mind and he had to stifle a groan. He decided to get a conversation going before he melted into a sweaty puddle.

"Has Glenn called you about your review?" he asked in a casual tone, gliding the craft slowly through the calm water.

"No, but Bob Harris said it would take about two or three weeks. I'm praying it goes well. This loan means everything to me."

I know. "I noticed two vacant storefronts across the street from the Pampered Palate. Any idea what's going in them?"

"One is going to be a liquor store. I don't know about the other one."

Chris's stomach clenched. She didn't know.

He considered telling her but decided to wait until

after he'd talked things through with Glenn. There was no point in destroying her weekend, and he knew the news would do just that. And he refused to ruin their time together with speculation over something that might not be a problem at all. At least he hoped it wouldn't, although his pesky inner voice told him differently. Firmly pushing his concerns away, he asked, "So what do you think of canoeing?"

She pursed her lips. "It's fun. I like the ride, the breeze, being out on the lake. Of course, being *in* the lake was not quite so much fun." She eyed his dry shorts with a pointed glare.

"Have you noticed," she continued in a reflective tone, "that every time we see each other we end up wet? We met in the rain, swam in the pool at the cookout, and now this." She glanced down at her wrinkled shorts and shirt. "And between your suits and my shorts, one of us always seems to end up with ruined clothes."

Chris nodded slowly. "Now that you mention it, yes. We've definitely developed a pattern."

"Seems so." Her gaze drifted down to his dry socks and sneakers before returning to his face. "Of course, *you* missed out on today's water portion of the entertainment. You being on the dock and all."

"I know better than to get into a canoe with a novice."

"Ah. So you set me up. You knew I would end up in the lake the minute I stepped into this dug-out log."

"I had a pretty good idea, yeah."

"Hmmm."

He caught the impish grin spreading over her face. He knew trouble when he saw it.

"You realize," she said in a casual tone, "that no

matter how fast you paddle this tub you'll never make it back to the dock dry."

He dug the paddle in, trying not to laugh. "I can try."

Her smile widened, deepening her dimples, and Chris's heart thumped. She looked so damned adorable, challenging him, her eyes filled with laughter, a piece of seaweed stuck to her shirt.

I'm falling in love with her. God help me, I'm falling in love with her.

Stunned by the enormity of the revelation, he barely noticed when she yelled, "Banzai!" and tipped the canoe, dumping them both into the lake.

Melanie surfaced and shook her hair out of her eyes. Chris came up next to her, sputtering. He pushed his hair back with his hands and Melanie gulped. Good grief. How the heck did he manage to look so sexy? She was sure she looked like two miles of bad road.

He settled his dripping sunglasses on top of his head. "You dunked me," he said, standing up. The water lapped at his chest. Sunlight bounced off his tanned, bare shoulders, and droplets glistened on the thatch of dark chest hair visible above the water.

Why, oh why, had the blasted man taken off his shirt? To torture her? Those firm muscles under golden skin had bunched and flexed every time he dug the oar into the water. Jeez. The guy was more tempting than chocolate. Than double, triple chocolate with whipped cream and a cherry on top. *What am I? Made of stone?*

She forced her hands to remain at her sides—not an easy task when her fingers literally itched to reach out and touch him. "Dunk you? Damn straight. You put me back in that tippy little sucker and I'll do it again. I've decided I'm not canoe-inclined. I'm definitely a cruise ship sort of girl."

He grabbed her arms and hauled her up against him. Melanie caught her breath as she bumped into the hard wall of his bare chest, and her pulse speeded up to triple time when she looked at his face. His eyelashes were spiky from the water, and his eyes darkened with that look she was not only coming to know, but to anticipate with bated breath. That look he got just before he destroyed her with his kiss.

She wrapped her arms around his neck and waited to be wrecked.

He lowered his head and kissed her with such slow, long, deep perfection, she could practically feel steam rising from her skin. The stunning contrast of the cool lake water, the hot sun, and the hard man pressing against her soft curves did her in. She knew exactly where this was leading, and it had nothing to do with martinis.

Running his fingers through her wet hair, he whispered her name against her mouth. "Melanie . . ."

Lost in a passionate haze, she answered, "Chris . . ."

"The canoe is sneaking away."

It took a moment for his words to sink in. She finally lifted her head and looked behind her. The upside-down canoe floated a good hundred yards away. The paddle was nowhere to be seen.

He walked her the short distance to the dock and helped her climb up. "I'll be right back," he promised, pushing off with a splash.

While he was rescuing the canoe and returning it to the rental booth, Melanie busied herself setting up their picnic lunch. She needed an activity, *any* activity, to keep her mind occupied and off *that*. Because it was so hot, she opted for a blanket under a shady willow rather than one of the redwood tables in the sun. The last thing she needed was more heat.

When Chris joined her, she handed him a frosty lemonade and watched him polish it off in a series of long swallows. Good grief. Even drinking lemonade, he was beautiful.

He flopped down on the blanket and helped himself to a sandwich. Melanie nibbled on her turkey club, trying to define the fluttering in her stomach. That same half-thrilling, half-terrifying sensation she experienced every time she looked at him. Every time she thought of him. She squeezed her eyes shut, praying it wasn't what she suspected but knowing it was.

"What's up, Mel Gibson?" he asked in a teasing tone. "You look so serious."

Melanie opened her eyes. He was sprawled on his side on the blanket, propped up on one elbow, studying her.

Serious. Yes. That's what I am. Seriously crazy about you. She stared at him, at his handsome face, the lock of dark hair falling across his brow, and knew she was more than crazy about him.

She was falling in love with him.

Good grief, how had *that* happened?

Okay, maybe it was because he was the most gorgeous man on earth. But Melanie shook her head and took an absent bite of her sandwich. His looks might have attracted her at first, but it was so much more than that.

He was kind. And thoughtful. He bought Barbie dolls for his niece and was sweet to his mother. He chatted with Nana and was going out of his way to do the crazy things she'd said she wanted to do before she kicked off.

Feeling a tingling warmth on her leg, she looked down and saw his hand resting on her knee.

"Is something wrong, Melanie?" he asked, sitting up, his voice filled with concern. "Are you okay?"

No. And it's all your fault, you gorgeous, sexy man, you. You have me all tied up in knots. I've got knots on my knots.

"I'm fine. Just sleepy, I guess. Too much sun, too much lake, too much food." *Too much man.* "All those dunks in the water left me kinda sore."

"I know just what you need. Lie down on your stomach."

Uh-oh. Being in a prone position while Chris was in the vicinity had "bad idea" written all over it. She glanced around. While the picnic crowds had thinned out, they weren't exactly alone. She was safe enough. Probably. "Lie down? Why?"

"Back rub. Guaranteed to cure what ails you." When she hesitated, he made a *tsking* sound. "Come on. This won't hurt. Just relax."

Relax? Fat chance. But before she could protest, Melanie found herself lying face down on the blanket, with Chris's palms skimming lightly over her back.

He increased the pressure, massaging her muscles with an expertise that left her purring like a kitten within seconds. He worked his way from her shoulders to the small of her back, kneading until she felt as loose and relaxed as a pile of watery Jell-o. When he finally stopped, she heaved out a loud, blissful sigh.

"Incredible," she moaned, rolling over onto her back. "Absolutely incredi—"

His mouth descended on hers, cutting off her trib-

ute to his massage skills. He deepened the kiss, dancing his tongue with hers, and every relaxed part of
her jumped back to life with a screaming roar. Wrapping her arms around his neck, she arched up against
him, breathing his name.

He slanted his mouth over hers again and again,
his fingers tangling in her hair, his upper body pressing her into the blanket. Just when she thought she
was going to liquify into mush, he abruptly sat up.

Prone and breathless, Melanie watched him scrub
unsteady hands down his face. Then he stood and
hauled her to her feet. Yanking up the blanket and
the picnic basket, he grabbed her hand and pulled
her along.

"Where are we going?" she panted, half from passion, half from the exertion of keeping up with his
long-legged strides.

"Home."

Disappointment flooded her. Darn him for being
so noble. "Oh."

When they reached the Mercedes, he tossed the
blanket and basket into the trunk, then regarded her
with dead-serious dark blue eyes.

"*My* home. Right now. As fast as I can get us there.
We're going to finish this, and here is not the place.
If you have any objections to that plan, I suggest you
speak now or forever hold your peace."

Melanie's insides turned to goo. Objections? To
making love with this incredible man? Did she have
STUPID stamped on her face? Her previous hesitation
and reluctance had turned into impatient need and
anticipation.

But there was something she had to tell him first—
something he needed to know up front.

Taking a deep breath, she blurted out, "I don't

have any objections, but I have to warn you, I'm no good at . . . well, at *that.*"

A frown appeared between his brows. *"That?"*

"Sex." A shaky laugh escaped her. "I just thought you should know. If you want to change your mind, I completely understand." *Please God, don't let him change his mind.*

He stared at her as if she was speaking a foreign language. "What the hell are you talking about? Why would you say something like that?"

"Because it's true. My ex-fiancé, Todd, was not impressed with my . . . er, performance." She ticked off items on her fingers. "He said I was too uptight, too unimaginative, and basically kind of cold. Oh, and I almost forgot—boring. At least that was his justification for sleeping with my best friend."

Something flashed in his eyes. A muscle ticked in his jaw. Several seconds passed before he replied in a low voice, "We've already established that your ex-fiancé was a jerk. Surely no one else has ever said something like that to you."

Melanie studied the scuffed toes of her Nikes. She might have experienced a more humiliating conversation in her life, but she couldn't recall it right now.

He touched his fingers under her chin and forced her to look up at him. His eyes were dark and a frown bunched his brow. "Melanie?"

To her utter consternation, hot tears filled her eyes. A look of amazed understanding dawned on his face. Uttering a groan, he pulled her against him.

"Are you telling me there hasn't been anyone else?" he asked, stroking her hair.

Melanie nodded, completely mortified. She never should have started this. Could humiliation be a cause of death? She hoped not, or she'd be buried in the ground in no time.

"Todd was the only one," she whispered. Oh, well. She'd told him. Let the chips fall where they may.

He leaned back. "Look at me."

When she did, she saw that his eyes were serious, but a small smile tugged at the corner of his mouth. "Do you know what you need?" he asked, tucking her hair behind her ear.

"A psychiatric consultation?"

"Nope." A sexy, devastating smile eased over his face. "You need a second opinion."

Melanie looked up at him, at that devilish yet tender expression, and her heart nearly flew out of her chest.

When she remained silent he continued, "Important matters always require a second opinion." He dropped a kiss on her nose. "Just call me Dr. Chris."

Melanie bit her bottom lip. "I wouldn't want to disappoint you—"

"Don't," he said, his voice suddenly harsh, his eyes flashing. "I don't want to hear you say that." He cupped her face in his hands. "You and I are going to make beautiful love together. The only worry I have is that the waiting may kill me."

Whatever lingering doubts Melanie might have had vanished in a heartbeat when he kissed her—a long, slow kiss filled with unmistakable passion, desire, and longing.

Resting his brow against hers, he said in a husky voice, "I want you so badly I can barely think straight." He leaned back and searched her eyes. "Do you want me?"

Melanie knew if she said no, her nose would grow three feet à la Pinocchio.

"Yes," she whispered, her heart pounding, praying she wasn't making a mistake. "I want you."

"Thank God," he breathed against her lips. "Let's go."

ELEVEN

By the time Chris parked the Mercedes in front of his condo, he'd managed to get his emotions under control. Barely. Every time he thought of Melanie's words, of how she thought she stunk at sex, he wanted to break something—and that jerk Todd's face was at the top of the list. *God help that bastard if I ever meet him.*

It infuriated him that someone could steal her self-confidence in such a cruel way. Anybody who thought Melanie was unimaginative, boring, and cold had to be an idiot. There was no doubt in Chris's mind that he and Melanie would make beautiful love together.

But first he was going to undo whatever damage Todd-the-jackass had done.

When they arrived at the condo, he held her hand and led her inside. As soon as the door closed behind them, he took her in his arms and kissed her long and deep. He hadn't necessarily meant to fall on her the minute they arrived, but he couldn't seem to keep his hands off her.

Luckily Melanie apparently suffered from the same problem. The instant their lips touched, she wrapped her arms around his neck and pressed herself against him.

Chris slipped his tongue into her silky, warm mouth and moaned. No woman had ever tasted this good, this sweet. This right. Without breaking their kiss, he scooped her up in his arms and carried her to his bedroom, where he gently set her on her feet.

She looked up at him, her eyes glazed and droopy. "You're a great kisser," she said in a breathy voice that raised his blood pressure to a dangerous level.

"Because of you," Chris murmured, running his hands up and down her back. "You have the most beautiful mouth. It inspires me." To prove his statement, he gently traced her full bottom lip with the tip of his tongue.

"And your neck," he continued, running his lips down the long, slim column, "makes me crazy. Especially here." He brushed his fingertips over the hollow at the base of her throat. "I can see your pulse beating." He laid her hand against his chest. "It's pounding almost as hard as mine."

Their gazes locked. When Chris read the uncertainty in her eyes, he made a mental vow to banish that look forever. He had to show her how deeply she affected him.

Deciding the best way for her to gain confidence was to encourage her to be free with him, he said, "Undress me."

Her eyes grew round. "What?"

He looked at her steadily, letting his eyes convey his desire, willing her to see his need. "Undress me." When she hesitated, he toed off his Reeboks and pulled off his socks. "I started. You finish."

Reaching out tentative hands, she pulled his Polo shirt from his shorts. He helped her pull it over his head, then she dropped it on the floor.

"Touch me, Melanie," he said in a low voice. "Put

your hands on me. Feel how much I want you. Don't be afraid."

Chris felt her momentary hesitancy, but she slid her hands up his chest, tunneling her fingers through the hair, lightly grazing his nipples. A long, low, heartfelt moan of pleasure flowed from him.

"Do you like that?" she asked, smoothing her hands over him again.

"God, yes. Don't stop."

Never taking his eyes off her, he easily sensed the surge of feminine power sweeping through her, encouraging her, making her bold. Every time he moaned, her confidence clearly grew. He could almost hear her thinking, *Maybe I'm not so bad at this after all.*

She continued her explorations, running her hands over his chest and back, and Chris found it more and more difficult to stand still. It seemed everywhere she touched, his flesh burned. When she leaned down and kissed his chest, he swore softly, and when her tongue flicked over his nipple he growled low in his throat.

Forcing his hands to remain at his sides, he gritted his teeth in an agony of pleasure when she unzipped his fly. Dipping her hands beneath his waistband, she lowered his shorts and boxers down his hips in one smooth motion. He kicked them off and stood before her, completely naked and painfully aroused.

He watched her gaze wander over him. Desire flared in her eyes, and her cheeks flushed crimson. She stretched out her hand and gently brushed her fingertips over the tip of his arousal.

He sucked in a breath and closed his eyes.

She continued to explore, touching him tentatively, then more boldly. It took all his willpower to remain still, but when she wrapped her fingers around him and gently squeezed his erection, he knew he couldn't take any more.

He reached out and grasped her wrist. "No more," he managed to say, "or this will be over before it's begun."

Before she could reply, he took over, plunging his fingers into her hair. Her head dropped limply back on her neck, and he took immediate advantage. His lips skimmed hot kisses along her jaw while his fingers worked the buttons on her cotton blouse free. When the last button was unfastened, he slowly pushed the material open.

His breath caught. She was incredible, her full breasts encased in a skimpy bit of cream-colored lace. Watching her all the while, he removed her shirt and bra, dropping both to the floor.

"You're beautiful, Melanie," he murmured, trailing his fingertips over the swell of her breasts. A breath shuddered from her, and her nipples hardened into tight peaks at his feathery touch. Bending his head, he brushed his tongue over one distended peak, then the other.

She gasped, and Chris reveled in the breathy sound. With infinite care, he caressed her breasts with his mouth, kneading her shoulders and back with his hands. Slowly he worked her shorts and panties down until she stood bare before him.

His gaze slowly skimmed over her from head to foot. She was truly a vision. A blushing, long-limbed, beautiful vision. It required all his strength not to fall on his knees before her.

He held out his hand and she slipped hers into it without hesitation. Entwining their fingers, he led

her the few steps to his bed, praying he'd somehow
find the strength to go slow with her.

Melanie laid back on the navy and maroon comforter, thankful to be off her feet before her knees
gave out. Chris followed her down, lying on his side
next to her. She looked into his eyes and her heart
nearly stopped at the intensity of his gaze. Unmistakable desire and need burned in the dark blue depths.

No one, not Todd, *no one* had ever looked at her
like that. Like she was the most desirable, beautiful
woman in the world. Like he would die if he didn't
have her.

He brought her hand to his mouth and kissed her
fingers one by one. His firm lips, his warm breath
caressed her skin, leaving a trail of fire in their wake.
He'd barely touched her, yet her heart pounded as
if she'd just run a marathon.

When he lowered his mouth to hers, Melanie
sighed his name and arched against him. While their
lips and tongues played lazily, she reveled in the long-
forgotten feeling of a man's hands on her, and the
unfamiliar, mind-blowing sensation of him arousing
every inch of her. It had been so long since a man
had touched her, and Todd's idea of foreplay had
been thirty seconds of petting.

Not so with Christopher Bishop.

He lavished attention on her, starting with her lips
and working his way slowly down her body, touching
her everywhere, his knowledgeable fingers and
mouth making her crazy.

"This," he whispered, gently touching the beauty
mark next to her navel with his lips, "is exquisite."

Melanie fisted her hands on the comforter when

he dipped his head lower, his warm breath and clever fingers toying with the curls between her thighs. When his mouth closed over her heated flesh, she threw her head back and cried out, her insides coiling tighter than a spring.

Slipping his hands beneath her bottom, he lifted her, his lips and tongue caressing her to wildness. Unable to control herself, Melanie moved against him, moaning, mindless.

Intense orgasmic waves crashed into her for an endless moment, throbbing through her, touching every pore in her body. When the spasms finally subsided, she shuddered, breathless, boneless, and utterly fulfilled.

Lost in a dreamy haze, she felt his weight shift and heard the unmistakable sound of a condom packet tearing. Several seconds later, he settled himself between her thighs. A blissful sigh escaped her lips.

"Open your eyes, Melanie."

She struggled to lift her heavy lids. It felt as if someone had glued cement bags to her lashes. When she finally succeeded, she saw the most beautiful eyes she'd ever seen staring down at her, tenderness and desire glowing in their heated depths.

Without taking his eyes off her, he slipped inside her with one long, heartfelt stroke. He remained perfectly still for several heartbeats, his weight braced on his forearms, his hands tangled in her hair.

And then he began to move, slowly at first, then more powerfully, watching her face, his expression intense. Melanie arched against him, running her hands over his back, down to his buttocks, urging him deeper. The force built inside her again, growing, growing, until she felt as if she were dynamite and he'd lit the match to detonate her.

When the explosion came, she moaned his name, falling over the edge into a previously unknown sensual oblivion that for an endless moment erased everything from her mind but the liquid throbbing of her body and the man inside her.

She was still quivering when Chris groaned and plunged into her one last time, pulsing inside her, his face buried in her hair. She wrapped her arms and legs around him and held on tight, listening to him whisper her name over and over like a prayer.

A good five minutes passed before Chris finally gathered the strength to lift his head. When he did, he found himself looking down into languid, dreamy, chocolate eyes. A spurt of masculine satisfaction washed over him as he noted her tangled hair and the satisfied smile lurking around the corners of her kiss-swollen lips.

Mine, a deep, primitive inner-man voice claimed. *This woman is mine.* He half expected to feel panic at the thought, but only deep contentment washed through him.

And I am hers, continued his inner voice. Chris braced himself for bachelor panic, but none came. Again, only warmth and happiness flowed through him at the thought. *I am hers, she is mine.*

God, that felt good. He wasn't quite sure how love had managed to sneak up on him, but it had. There was no point denying that he'd fallen, and fallen hard. Fallen? Hell, he was splattered all over the sidewalk. His bachelor days were sinking below the horizon like the setting sun.

He shook his head in amazement. Done in by a set of big brown eyes, a tangle of curls, and the sweetest smile ever created. Not to mention the gentlest hands, and the kindest heart.

Just then, one of those gentle hands brushed his cheek. He turned his face and kissed her palm.

"You were right," she said in a breathy voice that sparked interest in his recovering private parts.

"Of course I was," he replied with exaggerated male smugness. "What was I right about?"

"You said we'd have great sex." She closed her eyes and stretched like a contented cat. "We did."

A frown tugged between his brows. Sex? Like hell. Irritation bubbled up inside him. He said nothing, just waited until she opened her eyes. When she did, he watched her expression grow wary as she read the discontent he knew showed on his face.

"Oh," she said in a small voice. "Maybe the sex wasn't as good as I thought."

"We need to get something straight right now, Melanie. I never said we would have great *sex*. I said we would make beautiful *love* together. And we did. What we just shared was not sex," he said, enunciating his words very carefully, so she would not misunderstand. "We just *made love*. Believe me, there's a big difference."

Her eyes grew round; then to his chagrin, they filled with tears. His annoyance instantly evaporated, replaced by that panicky sensation only female tears could induce. Rolling them onto their sides, he gathered her into his arms and held her close.

"Hey, don't cry. Really. Please don't cry."

She sniffled against his chest. "I'm not crying."

Wet tears hit his chest and he groaned. "Don't do that, Melanie. Stop. I mean it. Tears kill me." He tried to pry her chin up, but she just burrowed deeper into his chest, soaking his skin with her tears.

Giving up, he patted her back, praying she'd turn off the waterworks soon. He didn't know what the hell he'd said or done to bring on the flood, but he was damn sorry about it.

Ten torturous minutes passed before her sobs tapered off into juicy hiccups. He spent those ten minutes alternately stroking her hair and cursing himself for hurting her. When she finally lifted her tear-streaked face, he cupped her face in his hands.

"I'm sorry," he whispered. "Whatever I said or did to make you feel so bad, I'm sorry. I swear I didn't mean it."

Her damp eyes widened, and to his amazement, she laughed.

He shook his head. "Now you're *laughing?* Women! If I live to be a hundred, I'll never understand them. Groaning in passion one minute, crying their eyes out the next, then laughing." He watched her, wary, wondering what was next.

"I think," he said carefully, "I know what made you groan. Would you care to fill me in on what made you cry and why you're laughing now?"

She reached out and stroked his face, her eyes filled with tenderness. "You," she whispered. "*You* made me groan by the incredible ways you touched me—ways no one else ever has. *You* made me cry—but they were happy tears. Emotional tears. Because of how you made me feel.

"And *you,*" she continued, "made me laugh because you were so sweet and concerned that you'd done something wrong, when you'd done everything so right." She gently kissed him. "So wonderfully, totally, completely right."

Relief swept through him. He brushed back her tangled hair. "I have one request, okay?"

She waggled her eyebrows at him suggestively. "Only one?"

He chuckled. "All right, maybe two. Hmmm. Maybe two dozen. But definitely one."

Running her hand down his chest, she tickled his navel and whispered, "Your wish is my command."

Chris sucked in a breath. "No more tears," he said, his concentration deteriorating at an alarming rate. "Next time you're happy, please smile. Don't cry."

She leaned forward and nibbled on his earlobe. "That sounds simple enough." She breathed into his ear and a chill raced down his spine, snapping his arousal to immediate attention.

Leaning back in the circle of his arms, she looked at him, her eyes filled with mischief.

"Is that your *only* request?" she asked, arching a single brow.

"Absolutely not." He rolled them until she sat astride him. Looking up at her, her beautiful, flushed face and soft, warm eyes, his heart clenched. Fisting his hand in her hair, he dragged her head down and kissed her hard.

"Are you ready for request number two?" he asked against her lips.

"Are you kidding?" She moved against him and his eyes glazed over. "I can't wait for request number two. Or three or four."

A slow smile lifted his lips.

He couldn't wait to see what she thought of requests five and six.

TWELVE

Melanie lay back on the rumpled sheets and covered her eyes with a limp forearm. Chris lay next to her, equally breathless.

"I read somewhere," she said when she could speak again, "that every time you make love, you burn about a hundred and fifty calories." Turning her head, she looked at him, sprawled out in satiated, naked male glory. "There's about three thousand calories in a pound. You're the math whiz. How much weight have we lost?"

He didn't move. "About forty-two pounds each."

Melanie would have laughed if she'd had the strength. She peeked at the clock. Seven forty-five A.M. They'd been at it the entire night.

"Good grief," she said. "I thought making love all night long was something that only happened in the movies."

"Clearly that is a misconception."

"Clearly," she agreed. "Well, one of us is going to have to get up and find us something to eat and drink before we shrivel up and die of starvation and dehydration."

He still didn't move. "Yeah, I guess one of us is going to have to do that."

The husky note of utter exhaustion in his voice amused her. Summoning up what little energy she had left, Melanie rolled onto her side, propped her head up on her palm, and gazed down at her lover.

Her lover.

Those two simple words echoed over and over in her mind, inundating her with a kaleidoscope of feelings she'd never before experienced. She'd spent the night with Chris, *her lover,* doing things she'd never done before. Her previous experiences with what's-his-name had always left her feeling awkward and clumsy.

But not with Chris.

She'd lost count of how many times they'd made love, but the multitude of discarded foil packets scattered on the comforter let her know that it was quite a few. And each had proven more incredible than the last.

But they hadn't only made love. They'd talked and laughed, explored and discovered. Until last night she'd honestly thought sex consisted of thirty seconds of optional foreplay, several minutes of moaning, followed by eight hours of sleep. Chris had certainly disabused her of *that* notion.

By the time they'd reached "request number three," all Melanie's previous inhibitions had faded into oblivion. The words *shy* and *retiring* no longer resided in her vocabulary.

And Chris certainly didn't seem to mind. In fact, he'd encouraged her to take the initiative, and she had. Several times. Much to their mutual pleasure.

Her gaze drifted over him and she sighed with deep contentment. Christopher Bishop had to be the sexiest man on the planet. Lying next to her, gorgeous, naked, one arm flung over his eyes, the other upraised to pillow his head, he was the most incredible man she'd ever seen. And in the lover department—well, the man was definitely a ten. More like an eleven. Okay, he was a 2,435.

Now *here* was a candidate for cloning, she decided, her gaze drifting down, over his muscle-ridged abdomen, lingering momentarily on his relaxed but still impressive manhood, then continuing down over his long, strong legs. Why the hell waste time cloning *sheep* when there were guys like Chris around? What a waste of medical science.

Her emotions had bubbled to the surface several times during the night, but she'd ruthlessly beaten them back. This was an affair. A temporary arrangement with no regrets. Yet one emotion had refused to be bludgeoned into submission. This man, *her lover,* who was as beautiful on the inside as he was on the outside, had made her feel something she'd never thought she'd feel again toward any man.

Trust.

She trusted him. Completely. When their affair ended, she could at least thank him for restoring her faith in the male species. He'd proven beyond all doubt that not all men were like Todd.

She wanted to reach out and touch him, but his deep, even breathing suggested that he'd dozed off. Besides, the mundane—mainly the need for food and drink—was intruding. Moving carefully so as not to wake him, Melanie scooted to the edge of the bed. She stood, stretched, and suppressed a groan.

Muscles she hadn't made use of in a long time tingled. A warm tenderness throbbed between her legs, and when she recalled the reason, a blush washed over her entire body. It amazed her that she still *could* blush. Heaven knew she didn't have any modesty left.

Instead of bothering with the wrinkled, lumpy mess that constituted her clothes, she opened Chris's closet and pulled out one of his dress shirts. Slipping it on, she made her way to the kitchen. The first thing she did was call home so Nana wouldn't worry. The answering machine picked up, which meant Nana was no doubt with Bernie. After leaving a message saying where she was and not to expect her anytime soon, Melanie opened the refrigerator.

True to bachelor form, there wasn't a whole lot on the shelves, but at least nothing appeared to fall into the science-experiment category. Humming softly, she set about preparing breakfast, her hands automatically chopping peppers and whisking eggs while her mind and her heart commenced a heated argument with each other.

Well, that was certainly a great evening, her mind commented. *Great idea, using him for sex. Couldn't have picked a better lover. Hey, heart! You stayed in the other room, right?*

Her heart pumped with indignation. *No, I did not stay in the other room. I was right there, the whole time. Falling more and more in l—*

Whoa! Hold it right there! mind interrupted. *Don't even think of saying that. We had a deal. This is my gig. You're not supposed to be involved.*

Too bad, said heart. *I'm involved. Big time.*

Mind rolled its eyes. *Oh, that's just great. Well, I suggest you UN-involve yourself. Right now. Before you get hurt. Chris is a great guy, but you know he's not looking to settle down. He wants to lead the bachelor life. Besides, look what happened the last time you got all mushy. You broke into a*

*thousand pieces. Why don't you just take a nice, relaxing
vacation and leave Chris to me.*

Heart shook its head. *It's too late.*

No! Mind yelled. *It's never too late. You don't want a
serious relationship anyway. I'm not going to let you ruin
my fun! Go away!*

I wish I could, said heart. *Dear God, I wish I could.*

Pull yourself together and just do it.

I'll try.

Atta girl.

Strong arms encircled her waist from behind, jerking her from her reverie.

"It sure smells good in here," Chris said, nuzzling
the back of her neck with warm lips. "Whatcha'
cookin'?"

A parade of tingles marched down her spine.
"Your cupboard was sort of bare—"

"I *am* a bachelor, you know," he broke in, kissing
the sensitive skin behind her ear.

Mind stuck out its tongue at heart and said, *Nah,
nah, told ya.*

Melanie shook her head to shut mind up. "What
we have here is my version of *huevos rancheros.*"

"Wow. I love it when you talk French."

Melanie giggled. "That was Spanish."

He turned her around and laid one of those toe-
curling, knee-weakening, slow, deep kisses on her.

"How long before breakfast is ready?" he asked,
nibbling on her bottom lip.

"Why?"

He rubbed himself against her and Melanie realized he was naked. And fully aroused.

"Why do you think?" he asked.

Laughter bubbled up in her throat. "You can't be
serious."

He leaned back and looked pointedly downward. "Do I look like I'm joking?" He started unbuttoning her shirt.

Melanie peeked down and gulped. Holy smokes. He *was* serious. "I thought you were hungry."

The shirt hit the floor. He bent his head and fastened his lips on her nipple. "I'm starved," he murmured.

The spatula slipped from Melanie's fingers and clattered on the ceramic tile floor. She somehow had the presence of mind to reach behind her and turn down the stove before he scooped her up and carried her back to the bedroom and gently deposited her on the rumpled sheets.

"I woke up and you were gone," he said, kneeling between her splayed thighs. He ran a single finger between her breasts down to her navel. "I missed you."

Melanie watched him, her heart speeding up as his finger continued on its lazy journey and played with the sensitive skin of her inner thighs.

"I thought you wanted breakfast," she murmured, hot desire pooling low in her body.

"I do. Later." He trailed his fingers up her thigh and tangled themselves in the curls at the apex. "Right now I want you."

"Oh, well, all right," Melanie managed to say, her eyes drifting closed when he caressed the moist, swollen flesh between her legs. "If you insist."

Thirty minutes later, once again clad in Chris's dress shirt, Melanie poked at the congealed mess in the frying pan.

"How do you like your eggs?" she called. "Black or brown?"

Chris walked into the kitchen, dressed in a clean T-shirt, a pair of navy shorts, and his Reeboks. He looked over her shoulder and whistled.

"Yuck," he said, shaking his head. "That looks like stuff you scrape off tires. Good thing I'm heading out to grab us some grub."

Melanie cocked a brow at him. "This would have been a perfectly respectable breakfast if certain people hadn't distracted the cook."

He patted her behind. "Couldn't help it. The cook was mighty distracting."

Melanie turned and found herself face to face with him. Dark stubble shaded his jaw, and his hair looked as if someone—namely her—had been running her fingers through it. He looked incredibly sexy and slightly rumpled, as if he'd just rolled out of bed, which, of course, was precisely the case.

"I think," she said, wrapping her arms around his neck, "that *you* are just easily distracted."

"Funny thing is, I'm usually not."

"Could have fooled me. As far as I can tell, you get aroused by a strong breeze. Not that I'm complaining."

He cupped her face with his hands, his gaze long and searching. "I get the impression," he said, a frown forming between his brows, "that you think what happened between us last night is a normal and frequent occurrence for me."

"Isn't it?" Melanie shook her head in disbelief at her own question. She held up her hands. "No, never mind. I don't want to know. It's none of my business anyway."

"None of your business?" he repeated, an incredulous note in his tone. "Oh, boy. Listen, we are going to talk about this. But later. I'm in serious need of sustenance. Why don't you put on some coffee while I'm gone." He dropped a kiss on her nose. "I'll be right back."

"I'll be right here."

A slow smile curved his lips. "Then it seems I have you right where I want you." He grabbed his keys and left, whistling slightly off key.

Standing in his kitchen, Melanie heard the front door click shut.

He was gone.

But definitely not forgotten.

When Chris walked into his condo half an hour later, he was greeted by the heady aroma of fresh brewed coffee, the soft sounds of Elton John on the stereo, and the woman of his dreams wearing his favorite dress shirt, setting his table.

He stood in the doorway leading into his kitchen, feasting his eyes on the sight of Melanie giving his counter a swipe with a sponge. From the top of her curly head to her bare feet, she looked disheveled and well loved.

And by God, that's what she was.

Well loved.

She satisfied him more completely, fulfilled him more absolutely than any woman ever had.

The thing that surprised him was how calm he felt about loving her. He'd always thought he'd panic at the first sign of falling in love—find himself in a frenzy to escape and cling to his freedom.

But not with Melanie. He knew without a doubt that she was "the one." The one he wanted to spend his life with, wake up next to every morning, live with, love with, and share everything with. His plan hadn't been to find "the one" for another few years, but what the hell, he was flexible.

Now all he had to do was convince *her.*

She was understandably gun-shy of relationships, and he didn't want to scare her off. Yet, his pesky inner voice yelled that persuading her to continue their relationship would be damned hard to do if he screwed up her chances of getting her loan.

He firmly told his pesky inner voice to shut up.

"That was a great breakfast," Melanie said, leaning back and patting her full stomach. "Best cheese danish I've ever eaten."

Chris winked at her. "You should try my cinnamon buns."

She laughed. "I thought I already had."

"Are we still talking about breakfast?"

"Beats me." Melanie pointed to the unpacked grocery bag on the counter. "What's in there?"

Chris stretched out his legs and sipped his coffee. "Cake stuff."

"What do you mean, 'cake stuff'?"

"Stuff to make a cake. It's on your things-I-want-to-do-before-I-die list. Besides, you're a gourmet cook. You should know what cake stuff is."

Curious, Melanie peeked in the bag. There were three boxes inside. She reached in and pulled out a box of Duncan Hines chocolate cake mix. The next box yielded a mix for fluffy fudge frosting. She pulled out the last box and choked back a laugh.

"Condoms?" she asked, raising her brows. "What do condoms have to do with making cakes?"

He grabbed her hand and pulled her onto his lap. "We have to do *something* while the cake is in the oven," he said, nuzzling her neck.

"The cake only has to bake for thirty-five minutes. This is a package of thirty-six condoms."

"So we'll have one left over," he said against her lips.

Melanie laughed. "Maybe we should try to pace ourselves."

"No can do. In case you can't tell, I want you again."

"I can tell, and I must say I'm amazed. And flattered." She wrapped her arms around his neck and kissed his stubbly jaw. "Don't you ever get tired?"

"If you'd asked me that question last week, I would have said yes. Today, the answer is no. It appears that you are to me what spinach is to Popeye." He nibbled on her neck. "One taste of you and I have the strength of a thousand men."

"A *thousand* men? I think you're gonna need some more condoms, Popeye."

"Now you're talkin'" he said, chuckling. "But first we shower. Then we bake. Then . . . well, we'll have to see." He shot her an exaggerated leer. "I have a feeling we'll find *something* to do."

Melanie laughed at his expression and tried to ignore her racing pulse. Again she had to force herself to remember that this was an interlude. An affair. No commitments, no promises. She had to enjoy it while it lasted, then let it go. No more relationships for her. No way. Just fun and games.

Now all she had to do was convince her heart.

In an effort to control the emotions simmering on the surface, she asked, "Shower? Us? You mean like, together?"

"Absolutely." He wrapped his arms around her and stood. "Never let it be said that I haven't done my part in the global water conservation effort." He walked toward the bathroom, kissing her all the while.

"Besides," he added when they reached their destination, "we have to do something to keep up with our tradition of getting wet every time we're together."

"I've never done anything like this," Melanie murmured, watching him turn on the water spray.

The intense, burning look he sent her melted her insides to the consistency of maple syrup. He unbuttoned her shirt and slipped it off her shoulders. "You have no idea how glad I am to hear that." Opening the shower door, he held out his hand to her. "Come with me."

"Hmmm. Now there's a phrase that's ripe with possibilities," Melanie said, managing to keep her tone light in spite of the ever growing tightness in her throat. Her heart and mind were battling it out again in the Olympic love-versus-lust war. She had a sinking feeling that heart was going to win.

She slipped her hand into his and stepped into the shower.

Oh, well. Let the Games begin.

THIRTEEN

"You look great," Chris said several hours later, leaning back to survey his handiwork. Melanie lay in the middle of his bed, naked except for several well-placed swirls of fluffy fudge frosting. "Fabulous, if I may say so myself."

"This is *not* how you decorate a cake," she insisted, squirming as he continued to "paint" her abdomen. "I've read dozens of cookbooks, and I've never seen instructions like this. If Betty Crocker even *suspected* what you're doing with that frosting, she'd fall down in a dead faint.

He drew a heart around her navel. "Who?"

"Never mind. And this may come as a shock," she added in a breathless voice, "but baking is normally done in the *kitchen*. Not the bedroom."

"This is not baking," Chris countered, dipping his finger into the glass bowl he held and spreading another dab of chocolate icing on Melanie's nipple. "This is decorating. We burned the cake. I wouldn't think of wasting all this great frosting." He leaned forward and sampled the delectable treat he'd just made.

"Delicious," he pronounced.

Melanie leaned up on her elbows. *"We* did not

burn the cake," she informed him in a haughty tone that made Chris smile. *"You* burned the cake."

"Only because you wouldn't let me take it out of the oven when the timer went off."

"Wouldn't let you! How do you figure that?"

"You were on top," he reminded her in a calm tone. He suppressed a laugh at the bright red blush creeping up her cheeks. "I couldn't move."

She shot him a dirty look. "Oh. Well, you could have moved if you'd wanted to."

"Ah, but I didn't want to," he said, spreading a thin layer of icing on her bottom lip. "I was very happy where I was."

He watched her eyes darken with remembrance of their earlier lovemaking, and his heart squeezed tight in his chest. There it was again—that warm rush of love sweeping over him. It washed through him, nearly stealing his breath and leaving a lump in his throat that he had to struggle to swallow around.

Even though she hadn't said so, he knew she was feeling the same things he was. She had to be. He could see it in her eyes every time she looked at him, feel it in her touch, taste it in her kiss. He wondered how she would react if he told her he loved her.

You idiot. She'd run like a scared rabbit. And that was the last thing he wanted. It was too soon.

Besides, how do you tell a woman something like that? Just blurt it out? *Damned if I know.* He'd never told a woman he loved her—except his mother and sisters, and they didn't count.

Do you just tell her? Open your mouth and let the words flop out? Yeah. Let 'em flop out. Simple was best.

But he had to wait until she was ready. He'd give her another week. Nodding to himself, he decided that was fair. She could have one more week to realize they were meant to be together. Then he'd tell her that he loved her, she'd tell him the same thing, and that would be that.

A sobering thought burst through his reverie. *What if she doesn't love me?* A shudder ran through him, and he swatted the disturbing idea aside.

She does. She has to. And if she doesn't yet, she will. I'm not going to marry someone who doesn't love me. Since I'm going to marry her, she just has to love me. Period. That's the bottom line. End of discussion.

He was about to dip his finger into the frosting again when his hand froze. *Did I just think what I think I thought?*

Sure did, buddy, his inner voice replied. *You just thought the dreaded M word.*

Marriage. He was thinking about marriage.

Lifelong commitment. House in the suburbs. Kids. He sat perfectly still, waiting for panic to seize him. Only panic never came.

Instead, a warmth unlike anything he'd ever felt suffused him. Like bachelors everywhere, he'd always avoided the M word like it harbored E. coli. The thought of spending the *rest of his life* with one woman gave him hives.

But not anymore. Not since he'd met Melanie. In fact—

"Are you okay?" Her voice penetrated his musings.

He looked at her, feeling dazed. "Huh?"

She snapped her fingers in front of his face. "I asked if you're okay. You look like a piano just fell on your head."

He laughed and wondered just what his expression looked like. "Squashed and half an inch high?"

"No. Kinda shocked, surprised, and"—she peered

at him—"green around the gills." She grabbed the bowl of frosting from him and set it on the nightstand. "You've eaten enough of that. You're obviously suffering from sugar-induced dementia."

A slow smile eased over his face. He leaned over her and licked her bottom lip. "On the contrary, I haven't had nearly enough."

She leaned back and sighed. "You'll get a tummy ache."

"It's not my tummy that's aching."

"Think of all those cavities."

"I have a great dental plan," he whispered against her lips. "Any more arguments?"

She arched against him. "Would there be any point?"

"Nope."

"Very well. Carry on."

He settled himself between her thighs. "Okay. If you insist."

At ten o'clock Sunday evening, Melanie sat in the Mercedes, her thoughts in turmoil. They would arrive at her house in less than five minutes, and she had no idea what to say to the man with whom she'd just spent the last thirty-six hours. Naked.

An offhand "Thanks, it's been great" didn't really seem appropriate, but neither did "I love you madly, please don't make me go home."

In fact, Chris had asked her to stay, but Melanie had somehow found the strength to say no. After spending only one night in his arms, she was addicted to the feel of him. The taste of him. If she stayed another night, her heart would suffer a fatal attack of the love-sickies.

Oh, who am I kidding? She already had the love-sickies so bad she was ready for the intensive care unit.

And boy, have I done it this time. Falling head-over-heels, ass-over-backwards in love. And with a confirmed bachelor, no less. That was certainly brilliant.

She looked out the window and cursed her stupidity at letting her hormones get her into this mess. It was entirely their fault. She should have shot those suckers dead the minute they started acting up. Bang! Death, followed by a hormone funeral and a brief period of mourning. Then back to her orderly life.

But nooooo. She had to meet Mr. Gorgeous. One look at him and all her plans had hopped out the window and plunged forty stories to their demise.

She sneaked a peek at him from the corner of her eyes. There he sat, calm, cool, collected, humming off-key to the radio, while she was suffering. He'd probably already forgotten about their time together. No doubt the minute he left her, he'd forget her name. She bet he'd come up with some excuse to not see her for the rest of the week, then conveniently "forget" to ever call her again.

Well, that was fine. Who needed him anyway? They'd spent their time together, now it was finished. She'd go on with her life, he with his. Two ships that pass in the night, make love several times—okay, several *dozen* times—then say *adios.*

She needed to nip this now. She knew firsthand where falling in love left a person—in a big, dark, painful hole with your skin ripped off. It had taken her a long time to climb out of that dungeon once before, and she didn't ever want to do it again.

She'd had her fun; now it was time to end it.

Before it was really too late.

"You're a million miles away, Mel Gibson."

She blinked at the sound of his voice and realized they were parked in front of her house. The porch lamps blazed cheerfully and the kitchen light glowed, announcing Nana's presence.

Melanie stared at him, unable to look away. She wanted to say something, *anything,* but she couldn't force any sound past the lump lodged in her throat. God help her, she didn't want to go inside and leave him. But she needed to end this before he did and left her in tatters.

He touched her cheek with a single, gentle finger. "I'm sort of at a loss for words," he said, a sheepish smile tilting one corner of his mouth.

Melanie swallowed. "Yeah. Me, too." *Say good-bye. Say have a nice life. Get out of the car.* Her mouth and feet refused to cooperate with her brain. She remained silent and motionless.

Taking her hands, he entwined their fingers. "This was the most incredible weekend of my life," he said in that soft, husky voice that sent chills up her spine.

Melanie nodded. She wanted to agree with him, but she couldn't speak. Tears were on their way, and it took all her concentration to hold them at bay.

"I'm leaving on a business trip tomorrow afternoon," he said, "and I won't get back until late Friday night." He squeezed her hands. "How about I pick you up Saturday morning and take you out for breakfast?"

"Chris, I—"

"I want you to spend the night again. The whole weekend." A sexy grin touched his lips. "We still have some skinny-dipping to do."

"I can't." There. She'd said it.

"Why not?"

Good question. "I, ah, can't sleep over."

"Sleeping wasn't exactly what I had in mind."

The tears hovering close to the surface threatened to spill over. Sure, that was fine. He had nothing to lose. A few weeks of sexual fun and games, then he'd move on to the next woman.

And that was the way it was supposed to be for her, but her heart was involved, damn it. Even though she'd firmly ordered it not to, her heart had jumped into love faster than ice melted in July.

"Listen," she said, "last night was fun, but—"

"No *buts*. As I recall, you owe me a cooking lesson. You're not trying to welsh on your promise, are you?"

"I never promised—"

"Because I deal with promise-welshers very harshly." His tongue traced a warm path up her palm, and a legion of pleasurable tingles skittered up her arm. "You'd find yourself on the receiving end of a severe tongue-lashing."

"Oh, my." Clearly his definition of a tongue-lashing was not the one that appeared in Webster's Dictionary. The mere thought evaporated her concentration like a puddle in the Sahara.

"And then there's the matter of the tennis match you want to play," he murmured against her palm. "How's your game?"

"Ah, quite good. Why?"

"There's a guy at work I wouldn't mind trouncing on the court. You up for the challenge?"

She looked into his dark blue eyes—eyes that somehow managed to be teasing and serious at the same time—and knew she couldn't refuse. Not when her hormones and every bone in her traitorous body had joined forces with her heart and ganged up on her. She didn't stand a chance.

Adopting what she prayed was a casual smile, she said, "You've got yourself a tennis match. And since I'd never let it be said that I'm a promise-welsher, I'll teach you how to cook something. Any requests?"

A half smile curved his lips. "Lots of them."

"I meant for our cooking lesson."

"Oh. Anything, as long as it's not complicated. You have a very bad effect on my ability to concentrate." Cupping her face between his palms, he kissed her long and deep, until she could barely recall what planet she lived on. "See what I mean?" he whispered against her lips. "I can't remember what we were just talking about."

"Tennis lesson. Cooking match," she whispered back. Whew. What a relief. He didn't affect her concentration at all.

Not one little bit.

On Monday afternoon, Chris sat on a Chicago-bound jet and tried to focus on the spreadsheet illuminated on his laptop screen. But his mind refused to cooperate.

All he could think about was his early morning conversation with Glenn Waxman about the vacant store across from Pampered Palate, and how that conversation would ultimately affect Melanie's loan.

Glenn hadn't known about the proposed restaurant. Chris squeezed his eyes shut and stifled a groan. *Well, he knows now, thanks to me.* In fact, Glenn had been very grateful for the information, explaining that if the review had gone to the bank missing such pertinent facts, the firm would have looked foolish.

Chris had pointed out that since he'd merely overheard the conversation, there was always the chance the info was incorrect. Glenn had promised to verify the facts before adding them to the review.

It won't matter. She'll still get the loan.

But no matter how hard he tried to convince himself, a sick ball of dread cramped his stomach and refused to budge. Glenn had said the review should be finished by the end of the week, which meant Melanie would hear from the bank by the middle of next week.

Since she'd only worry, he decided there was no point in telling her what he'd done until Glenn had verified the information and she knew the bank's decision. *We're only talking about a few days. By remaining quiet, I'll save her from getting an ulcer.* After she heard from the bank, he'd tell her. If the loan was approved, he had nothing to worry to about.

If it wasn't, he'd simply explain why he'd done what he had.

And pray he didn't lose her in the process.

When the doorbell rang at nine A.M. Saturday morning, Melanie inhaled a calming breath and forced herself to walk slowly down the stairs. She knew Chris stood on the other side of the door, and she didn't want to appear overly anxious.

Not that she *was* overly anxious to see him. Not a bit. After all, she'd just seen him five days ago. She huffed out a breath. Had it only been five days? It had felt like five years. Five long, dreary years in solitary confinement.

Get a grip, Melanie. Hadn't he called twice from Chicago? Yeah, but both calls had been brief, and they had left her aching for him. For his touch, his arms around her, his kiss—

Tossing in the towel, she ran down the last few steps and threw open the door.

Before she could even say hello, his arms were around her, his lips crushing hers, his tongue seeking entrance to her mouth. Every cell in her body melted and sighed, *welcome home.*

Nipping tiny kisses along her jaw, he said, "Boy, I'm sure glad it wasn't Nana who opened the door."

A breathless laugh escaped Melanie. "A kiss like that and poor Nana would pass out. I'm feeling a bit faint myself."

The sexy grin she loved eased over his face and her pulse jumped. "Faint, huh?" He dropped a kiss onto her nose. "That sounds very promising, but you'd better buck up 'cause we're playing tennis in forty-five minutes."

"Forty-five minutes! I thought we had a breakfast date. I'm starving." *I want to stay here and kiss you. All day.*

"Change of plans. We can grab a bagel and coffee on the way to the courts." His gaze roamed over her cherry red shorts and matching tank top. "You look great, but you might want to change into your tennis gear." He glanced at his watch. "Not to rush you, but you have about three minutes. We're playing another partner in my firm, Dave Webber, and his girlfriend-of-the-moment, whose name escapes me. Dave's beaten me the last three times we've played and he's pretty insufferable about it. I really want to wump him today."

Disgruntled, Melanie led him into the house. He leaned against the door and she stomped up the stairs, muttering under her breath.

Darn man. Who did he think he was, kissing her like that then calmly announcing tennis plans as if he hadn't just rocked her world? And how the heck was she supposed to "wump" anybody at tennis if she didn't eat breakfast first? Why should she—

"Melanie?"

She turned and gazed down at him, standing at the bottom of the stairs, his expression serious, looking more beautiful than any man had a right to. "Yes?"

"I missed you."

Her annoyance evaporated instantly. She'd missed him, too. Constantly. Of course, it wasn't necessary that *he* know that. Mimicking his earlier words, she said, "That sounds promising, but I need to buck up. There's a tennis match to play, you know."

It took Melanie all of two minutes to agree with Chris that Dave Webber was indeed insufferable about his previous victories on the tennis court. Dave's girlfriend, Jenni, sported an innocent smile and a killer forehand. Not good indications for a wumping.

The first set began with Dave, Melanie, then Jenni all holding serve. Chris's first serve landed in the net, as did his second one, resulting in a double fault. He switched court sides, and promptly double faulted away another point.

Melanie switched courts again and looked back at him from her position near the net. "You okay?"

He frowned and nodded. And promptly double faulted again.

Melanie walked back to the baseline. "What's wrong?" she asked in an undertone. "Are you nervous? You served beautifully in the warm-up."

"I'm not nervous," he said in a distinctly annoyed voice.

She raised her brows at his tone. "Then what's with you? You said you wanted to beat this guy, and I don't blame you. He's totally obnoxious. May I remind you that the idea is to hit the ball *over* the net? That expression 'nothing but net' is for basketball, not tennis."

"I know that."

"Could have fooled me. If you're not nervous, then what's wrong?"

"Your ass."

She stared at him. *"Excuse me?"*

"Your ass. That damn short tennis skirt. Those long legs staring me right in the face. You look incredible. I can't concentrate. Every time I try to serve, I see you up at the net, half bent over, and I lose it."

"As much as I appreciate the compliment about my, er, ass, we have a whole match to play here. If you can pull yourself together, we can hand this guy the thrashing he deserves."

"Okay." He eyed her legs. "Would you consider slipping on a pair of sweatpants?"

"Have you lost your mind? It's ninety degrees out here!"

"Are we playing tennis or chatting?" Dave called from the other side of the net.

Chris shot him a glare. "We're strategizing. Give us a minute." He turned back to Melanie. "All right. No sweatpants. But I need some kind of incentive."

Melanie narrowed her eyes. "Like what?"

A wolfish grin curved his lips. "What do I get if I win?"

"What do you want?"

"You. Just you."

She tightened her grip on her tennis racket to keep it from slithering from her boneless fingers. Forcibly banishing all thoughts of *that* from her mind, she said, "Based on your game so far, I don't have much to worry about. Okay, you're on."

Walking back to her position at the net, Melanie prepared for Chris's next serve. Seconds later the ball zoomed by her ear with gale-force strength for an ace. He went on to serve another ace, then another, and then one more to even the score at deuce. She and Chris won the next two points to take the game.

Tossing her a wink, he said, "See? I just needed a little incentive."

They battled it out for another two hours, but finally Melanie and Chris won in three sets. The instant after everyone shook hands, Chris scooped up the tennis gear in one hand, grabbed Melanie's arm with the other, shouted good-bye, and literally dragged her off the courts.

"Whoa!" Melanie protested, jogging to keep up with him. "Where's the fire?"

He stopped abruptly and kissed her with an intensity that blew the bottoms off her Nikes. With his body pressed hard against hers, he asked, "Feel the fire?"

Oh, yeah. She felt it, all right. All the way down to her smoldering toes. Mutely, she nodded.

"Then let's go. 'Cause as much as I love you *in* that skimpy skirt, I can't wait to get you *out* of it."

Again Melanie simply nodded. Who the heck was she to argue with logic like that?

The fifteen-minute ride to his condo was an exercise in agony for Chris. God, he couldn't wait to get his hands on her. Touch her soft skin, feel her pressed against him. He'd missed her so damn much, he'd wanted to fall on her the moment he'd seen her, but he knew he couldn't or they'd never make it to the tennis courts. Now the match was over, and she was all his. Thank God.

But for how long?

Glenn had told him that an eatery called Spaghetti Loco was indeed scheduled to open across the street from the Pampered Palate. That information had been included in the review, and Chris suspected it would sway the bank's decision concerning Melanie's loan. Would he lose her if the bank turned her down?

No. Damn it, he wouldn't allow that to happen.

Needing to touch her, he held her hand the entire way home, and the instant the condo door closed behind them, he pulled her to him, kissing her with a heated desperation unlike anything he'd ever felt before. His hungry lips trailed a hot path down her neck while his restless hands slid up her thighs, under her skirt.

"I don't think we're going to make it to the bedroom," he whispered against her mouth. He slipped his fingers into the waistband of her tennis panties and slid them down over her hips.

"I don't think we're going to make it out of the foyer," Melanie agreed in a breathless voice, her fingers busily working on his shorts.

"How do you feel about the floor?" he asked, pulling her top from her skirt.

"Works for me."

"This floor is damn hard," Melanie moaned fifteen minutes later. "I feel a killer cramp coming on."

Chris, lying flat on his back next to her on the hardwood, grimaced in clear agreement. "Next time let's at least try and make it to the sofa, okay?"

"Agreed. At the very least you need a rug in here. I just want to know which one of us is going to get up and call the paramedics for the other one."

A chuckle rumbled from him. "Hey, we kicked some serious butt on the tennis courts. Thanks for helping me put Dave in his place. I'm going to rename you Martina Navratilova."

"Thank you, Jimmy Connors." Melanie raised herself on one elbow and gazed down at him. He looked happy and tired, but unless she was mistaken, and it appeared obvious she wasn't, he was well on his way toward full-blown arousal again. A half-laugh, half-groan escaped her. Looking pointedly at his groin, she asked, "Good grief, is that what I think it is?"

Lifting his head off the floor, Chris looked down at himself. "I'm afraid so." Moaning, he rolled to his feet then helped her up. Brushing her hair out of her eyes, he said, "C'mon, Martina. Let's wander into the bedroom and you can finish paying off your debt of honor. Then, in keeping with our getting-wet-on-every-date tradition, we'll take a shower. After that you can teach me how to cook. How does that sound?"

Melanie's heart squeezed. How did that sound? "It sounds like heaven."

They didn't get around to their cooking lesson until late Sunday afternoon.

Dressed in shorts and her favorite *Kiss the Cook* T-shirt, Melanie forced herself to concentrate on the lesson, but it was darn hard to do when her pupil kept nuzzling her neck.

"Behave yourself," she scolded in her best school-marm voice. "What kind of student are you?"

"I'm just following directions," Chris said. He brushed his fingertips over her breasts. "It clearly says right here to kiss the cook."

"If you don't knock it off, I'll have to take this shirt off."

"Great! Boy, this cooking sure is fun!"

Melanie grabbed a wooden spoon and held it poised like a sword. "Don't make me get rough with you."

He waggled his brows. "This gets better and better."

Planting her hands on her hips, she said, "Back off. Cooking is serious business. No fooling around until we're done."

"Then let's hurry up and get done 'cause fooling around sounds like a hell of a lot more fun than cooking. Carry on, fearless chef."

"That's better." She nodded toward the ingredients she'd lined up on Chris's kitchen counter. "If you only know how to make one thing," she said in a businesslike tone, "then this is the thing you should know how to make."

Chris looked at the assembled items. "What are we making?"

"I call it 'The Only Sauce You'll Ever Need.' You can use it for dozens of things, it's very simple to prepare, and you don't have to use exact amounts of any of the ingredients."

"Sounds good to me. The only things I know how to make are steak, potatoes, and martinis."

"Not anymore. The first thing you do is coarsely

chop about a dozen plum tomatoes." She demonstrated, using deft strokes of a sharp knife.

"That looks easy."

"Then we're in good shape because that's the hardest part." She continued her lesson, adding chopped onions, minced garlic, olive oil, chopped fresh basil, and salt and pepper to the bowl of tomatoes. "That's it," she said, stirring the ingredients with a wooden spoon.

"You're kidding."

"Nope. It's so easy, it's almost laughable."

Chris peered into the bowl. "What do you do with it?"

For an answer, Melanie opened a bag of Mexican-style tostado chips. Dunking one into the sauce, she held it up to his lips.

He bit and chewed. "Hey, that's great."

She nodded. "It makes a fabulous salsa. At the Pampered Palate we call it 'Italian Salsa' because of the basil. If you slice and toast Italian bread and pour this sauce over it, you'll have a delicious *bruschetta* appetizer. For a main course, heat the sauce, toss it into a bowl of pasta and sprinkle on Parmesan cheese and you're all set. It's also great on salads instead of dressing, and it turns an ordinary omelette into a masterpiece."

"I can see why you call it 'The Only Sauce You'll Ever Need.' "

She handed him a recipe card with the Pampered Palate's logo printed in the corner. "I guarantee you'll impress whoever you make this for." The instant the words left her mouth, she regretted them. *Stupid, stupid!* How long before he stood in his kitchen, preparing *her* recipe while nuzzling some other woman's neck?

She wanted him to say something like "I'll never make this for anyone but you." Instead, he dipped another chip and said, "I'll be the most impressive guy in town. Thanks, Mel."

Clenching her hands, she fought the spurt of hot jealousy shooting through her. *Get a grip, Melanie!* Affairs end. Sooner or later, she and Chris would part ways. He'd move on to the next woman, continuing his bachelor lifestyle, while she . . . while she what?

Focused on her business? Yes. But while she easily envisioned Chris entertaining a different supermodel type every night, she couldn't imagine herself with any other man.

And that's when she knew that in order to save herself from a shattered heart, she needed to end this affair.

Just end it. A clean break. The longer this went on, the more impossible picking up the pieces would become. She did *not* want to be in love, and by damn, she was going to get herself *out* of love. Right now. Even if the effort killed her.

And she suspected it would do just that.

FOURTEEN

Melanie prepared herself during the ride back to her house. As soon as Chris parked the car, she'd recite her breezy "Thanks, it's been great, have a nice life" speech, then skip into the house. Easy as pie.

It was the heartache she knew lurked around the corner that scared her silly.

Chris parked the Mercedes in her driveway. Before she could speak, he asked, "What's troubling you, Mel Gibson? You're awfully quiet."

Clasping her clammy hands together, Melanie drew a resolute breath. "Chris, we need to talk."

He frowned and nodded. "Yes, I guess we do."

His serious tone sent a shiver down Melanie's spine. Women everywhere knew that tone. It was the it's-been-fun-but-now-it's-over tone. The I'll-call-you-but-he-doesn't voice.

So he would end it. She should have been thrilled. It saved her the awkwardness of doing the deed. Yippee.

Her heart felt like she'd ripped it out with a rusty pitchfork. Damn it! This love crap really stunk.

Chris reached out and touched her hand. "Our . . . *relationship* hasn't really gone the way I expected it to."

Pasting what she hoped was a devil-may-care expression on her face, Melanie nodded. Refusing to show the slightest sign of hurt, she braced herself for his next words. The words that would break her heart.

"I love you, Melanie."

Melanie actually felt the blood drain from her face. Every red cell she owned gushed downward until there was nothing left in her head except the echo of his words.

I love you, Melanie. I love you.

She had no idea how long she stared at him, speechless, but she figured it must have been a while, because his expression turned to concern.

"Are you okay?" he asked.

What the hell kind of question was that? Okay? *No!* How dare he say something like that to her! She loved him, but *she didn't want to!*

And she certainly didn't want him to fall in love with her. She knew where love led, and she was never walking down that rocky path again. This was supposed to be an *affair.* Nothing more. He couldn't possibly love her. It was just his overworked hormones talking.

"Chris—"

Once again he forestalled her words by placing a finger over her lips. "You don't have to say anything," he said in a quiet voice. "I didn't tell you so you'd feel obligated to say it back. I only told you because I have to fly to LA tomorrow morning and I didn't want to go away for three days and not have you know how I felt." He kissed her hand. "So don't panic, okay?"

Panic set in. *Ohmigod.* That didn't sound like hormones talking. Full-fledged, stark-raving, cold-sweat, heart-pounding panic gripped her and wouldn't let go.

"I have to go," she said, pulling her hands loose. "Look. There's Nana at the door. She's probably wondering what the heck we're doing out here."

"You spent the weekend at my house. I think she knows what we're doing."

"Still, it's time for me to leave." She grabbed her purse and opened the car door.

"I'll walk you in."

"No!" She took a deep breath and tried to remain calm. "You should go."

"Okay. I'll call you tomorrow from LA." When he leaned over to kiss her, Melanie brushed his cheek with her lips. Quick.

"Good. Gotta run. 'Bye." She hopped out of the car and sprinted across the lawn as if the devil himself pursued her. Pausing on the porch, she waved and smiled, then went into the house. She slammed the door, then leaned back against it and tried to catch her breath.

"Where's the hunk?" Nana asked.

"Gone."

"He must be some kisser. You're flushed and all out of breath."

Melanie opened her eyes and wiped the back of her hand across her overheated forehead. "I ran into the house."

"Seems to me you've got to be nuts to run away from a man like that." She peered at Melanie over the tops of her bifocals. "You want to talk about it?"

Hot tears filled Melanie's eyes. "No."

"He do something to upset you? 'Cause if he did, even though I like him and he's a hunk and all, I'll pound that sucker into the ground."

Tears dribbled down Melanie's cheeks. "He said he loves me."

Nana rolled her eyes. "Good night nurse! I guess I'd better get my rifle and shoot him dead, that no-good scoundrel. What nerve."

"I'm serious, Nana. He said he loves me."

"Then it seems to me you should be tap dancing on the roof, not standing there with big tears rolling down your face."

"But I don't *want* him to love me!" Melanie wailed.

"Horse feathers. Of course you do. What woman in her right mind wouldn't want a man like that? If I were a couple years younger, I'd wrestle you for him."

A sob escaped Melanie.

Nana immediately sobered. "Good grief, honey," she said, taking Melanie's hand. "I guess this is serious. You come on into the kitchen and I'll make you a nice cup of tea."

Melanie allowed herself to be led. She composed herself while Nana brewed chamomile tea. After taking a few sips, Melanie felt a little better.

"Now, what's got you so tied up in knots?" Nana demanded, settling in the chair opposite Melanie.

"I don't know where to begin," Melanie said with a sigh.

"How about at the beginning."

"The beginning? Okay. I knew that man was trouble the moment I laid eyes on him," Melanie stated with an emphatic nod.

"Trouble like he just got out of jail and we should hide the family silver?"

"No. Trouble like the silver's safe, but my heart isn't."

Nana stirred sugar into her tea. "And that's bad because . . . ?"

"Because I've clearly lost my mind." Melanie stood and paced around the kitchen, ticking reasons off on her fingers. "I had no intention of getting involved. I don't have time for him. I've been in love. Love stinks. It hurts. I don't like it."

"Melanie. Are you in love with Chris?"

Melanie stopped pacing and plunged her fingers through her hair. "Yes. But I don't *want* to be. How can I make it go away, Nana?"

Her grandmother laughed. "It's love, honey, not the flu."

"Feels just as bad," Melanie grumbled, flopping back into her chair.

"Now let me see if I understand this," Nana said. "You love Chris, and Chris loves you—"

"He *says* he loves me," Melanie broke in.

Nana raised her eyebrows. "You don't believe him?"

That brought Melanie up short. "Yes. No. I . . . I don't know. Todd said he loved me, and look what happened."

"You listen to me, young lady," Nana said, her eyes snapping. "That Todd was nothing but a horse's ass. From all I've seen, Chris is a fine, decent, honest young man. He doesn't strike me as the sort of fella who would tell a girl he loved her if he didn't mean it.

"But," she continued, her voice firm, "even if he was a crumb-bum, he wouldn't deserve to be compared to that imbecile Todd who was the flotsam below pond scum."

"But we barely know each other," Melanie said, shaking her head.

"You've spent the last two weekends with him," Nana observed archly. "Seems to me you should know each other pretty well."

Heat flooded Melanie's face. "Not well enough to be in love."

"Honey, how long do you think it takes to fall in love? A month? A year? Three years?"

"I don't know. I don't trust myself. I thought I was in love before. I can't make that mistake again."

Nana reached across the table and squeezed her hand. "I'll tell you how long it takes to fall in love. It only takes a moment." A faraway look came into her eyes. "I took one look at your Grandpa Will and knew he was the man for me. Luckily, he felt the same way. We'd only known each other three weeks when we got hitched." Her expression cleared. "The only time there's a problem is when you love someone who doesn't love you back. That doesn't appear to be the case."

Hope dawned in Melanie's chest. "You mean, you think he might really love me?"

"If he's half as smart as I think he is, I'm sure he does. He said so, didn't he?"

"And you don't think it's too soon?"

"How long did it take you to fall for him?"

A slow smile tilted Melanie's lips. "Only a moment."

"So don't you think the same thing could happen to him?"

"But he told me that he'd waited a long time to lead a bachelor life."

"Honey, a man who's determined to remain a bachelor doesn't tell a woman he loves her. It appears he's changed his mind. The question is, what are you going to do about it?" Nana regarded her steadily from wise eyes. "If you're really set on not being involved, you need to tell him. It wouldn't be fair to lead him on.

"But," she added, patting Melanie's hand, "if you decide to come out of your self-imposed exile and give love another chance—this time with a *real* man instead of a lying scuzzbucket—then you need to stop your cryin' and start celebrating. You've found yourself one helluva guy."

"I'm scared, Nana," Melanie whispered, wishing she wasn't.

" 'Course you are. You should be. But don't throw love away just because it came calling and you weren't ready. Love is ornery. It likes to wait until you least expect it, then it jumps up and bites you right on your unsuspecting ass. I always thought love was like childbirth. It hurts like hell, but in the end it's worth it."

Melanie took a deep breath and pressed a hand to her stomach. She was in love. And it was okay. In fact, it was wonderful! Chris was kind, honest, and loving. He would never betray her the way Todd had. Hadn't she already realized that she trusted Chris completely? Love didn't mean she had to give up anything. Only share. And sharing with Chris was something to look forward to, not dread.

She cringed, recalling how she'd panicked and practically run away from him. He must have thought she was loony. She wanted to call him and tell him she loved him, but she didn't want to tell him over the phone. She glanced at the clock. It was almost midnight. Too late to drive over. And he was going out of town tomorrow.

Darn it, she'd have to wait until Wednesday night to tell him.

But that was okay.

What could possibly go wrong between now and then?

Chris drove back to his condo, his thoughts in a whirl. For the first time in his life, he'd told a woman he loved her, and what happened? She'd looked like she swallowed a bug.

Damn it, he hadn't expected her to fall at his feet and declare undying devotion, but it would have been nice, or at least encouraging, if she hadn't bolted like a frightened deer. He'd been debating whether or not to tell her about the information he'd given Glenn, but her hasty departure had prevented him from broaching the subject.

According to Glenn, the bank wouldn't make its decision before Thursday, and Chris was scheduled to arrive back in Atlanta Wednesday evening. He certainly didn't want to tell Melanie over the phone.

I'm worrying needlessly. The bank will approve her loan. When I get back from LA, I'll tell her everything and we'll laugh about it. Besides, if the bank said it wouldn't make its decision before Thursday, that no doubt meant they'd decide sometime next week, or the week after.

Considerably cheered, Chris pulled into his parking space. What could possibly go wrong between now and Wednesday?

FIFTEEN

He *had* to talk to her. Right away.

But the gods were conspiring against him.

Chris glanced at his watch for the hundredth time and frowned. His flight to Los Angeles was boarding and he needed to speak to Melanie before he left. He'd called the Pampered Palate half a dozen times, but he kept getting a busy signal. That was good for business but not good for him.

He'd already left two messages on her answering machine at home. His flight was announced over the loud speaker.

Damn.

He *had* to talk to her, had to explain before she heard it from someone else.

Glenn had promised not to call Melanie until to-morrow morning with the news, which was fine—but not if Chris couldn't talk to her first. Damn it, he should have told her last night, but she'd left him in such a hurry, he hadn't had a chance. Not to mention that he'd been so caught up in telling her that he loved her, he hadn't mentioned that her loan might be kaput because of him.

Now he *knew* the loan was kaput, and he had to tell her. Jesus, when the hell did banks start doing things *ahead* of schedule? The loan officer had called Glenn at eight A.M. to deliver the regretful news that Miss Gibson's loan was denied. Glenn had sprung the news on him as he was racing out of the office to drive to the airport. And to make matters worse, Glenn also announced Chris's trip to Los Angeles needed to be extended to meet with another client and now he had to remain on the West Coast until Friday.

His stomach clenched at the thought of telling her over the phone, but it was all he could manage. Impatiently dropping coins into the pay phone, he cursed himself for not bringing his cell phone. He almost cheered out loud when he didn't hear a busy signal.

"Pampered Palate, Gourmet to Go," came Nana's gravelly voice over the line.

Relief washed through him. "Nana, it's Chris. Is Melanie there?"

"Hiya, handsome," Nana said, and Chris had a mental picture of her patting her bright red hair. "Mel just left. She's helping out with the last of the deliveries. It's been a zoo here."

Chris swore silently. "I have to talk to her, Nana. Will you tell her I'll call her tonight?"

"She won't be home tonight," Nana stated. "We have tickets to the Braves game. We're heading over to Turner Field as soon as she gets back."

"Final boarding call, Flight 423 to Los Angeles."

Chris raked his free hand through his hair. "Nana, please write down this phone number." He pulled his itinerary out of his briefcase and rattled off the number for the Los Angeles Marriott. "Ask her to call me tonight."

"We'll be getting home late," Nana said.

"It doesn't matter what time it is. Please tell her to call me. Tonight."

"Okay, honey. I'll tell her."

Chris said thanks, hung up, and sprinted for the gate.

He settled into his seat and laid his head back and closed his eyes. His stomach churned and his head pounded.

He had to talk to her before Glenn did.

The phone rang.

Chris rolled over and groaned. What the hell time was it? Peeking out of one eye, he grabbed the receiver.

"Melanie?"

A mechanical voice greeted him. "Good morning. The time is seven A.M. This is your requested wake-up call."

Chris's eyes popped open and he sat up straight. One look at the beside clock confirmed that it was indeed seven in the morning.

She hadn't called him.

He jammed down the receiver. "Damn, damn, damn!"

What the hell time was it in Atlanta? He shook his head to clear it of sleep. Ten A.M. He had to call Melanie right away. He was just reaching for the phone when it rang. He grabbed it.

"Hello?"

"You bastard."

Chris squeezed his eyes shut. God *damn* it. He was too late.

"Melanie. Let me explain—"

"I'd like to see you try," came her furious voice. He heard her tears and anger and cringed, knowing that she blamed him.

"I tried to call you," he said, "to talk to you before I left."

"That was damn big of you."

"Why didn't you call me last night?"

"The game went into extra innings. By the time we got home, it was late. I didn't think it would matter if I waited until morning to call you."

Her bitter laugh sizzled through the phone wire. "I couldn't call you until now because I've been on the phone for the last hour. First with the bank, then with Glenn Waxman. But I guess you know all about that. After all, you're the reason my bank loan was turned down."

"Melanie, listen to me. This whole thing was an accident. I overheard this guy saying that one of his clients had just signed the lease on the empty store across the street from the Pampered Palate and they planned to open a new restaurant."

"So?" she asked in that same cold, furious voice.

Chris scrubbed his free hand down his face. "So I had to tell Glenn."

"Why?"

"Because I felt it was pertinent to the review. I hated to tell him, but I felt it would have been unethical for me not to."

"So you knew when you told him that he would add it to the independent review? You realized it might mean the kiss of death to my bank loan?"

Chris blew out a breath. "Yes. And yes."

"Did you absolutely *have* to tell him, or was it a gray area?"

He knew he was sunk. "Technically, it's a gray area, but—"

"I see," she broke in, her voice changing from cold to frigid. "And when exactly did you overhear this conversation?"

He pinched the bridge of his nose. "The morning we went canoeing."

She was silent for so long, he wondered if she'd just put down the phone and walked away. When she finally spoke and he heard the icy hurt in her voice, he almost wished she had.

"In other words, right after you found out that my loan was as good as gone, you took me to bed. Without ever mentioning it."

"Melanie—"

"But of course you didn't mention it. You knew how upset and concerned I'd be. Certainly not in the mood for sex, and that would have royally screwed up your plans. And how convenient that you didn't bother to say anything about it over the next two weeks. *That's* what hurts most of all. Damn it, I *hate* being lied to!"

"I never lied to you. I was going to tell you—"

"But you didn't."

"I had every intention of telling you once the bank made its decision. And yes, I knew you'd be concerned and I didn't want to worry you needlessly. I was hoping as much as you that the loan would be approved."

"That's big of you. Really. Did it ever occur to you that I might be interested in the fact that another eatery was opening across the street?"

"You wouldn't have been able to do anything

about it for those two weeks, Melanie, except pace the floor."

"I'm not a child who requires coddling, and I resent you treating me that way."

"I wasn't coddling. I was just trying to spare you unnecessary anguish."

"Well, I don't need to be spared." A bitter laugh rang in his ear. "You said you loved me. I shudder to think how you'd treat someone you hated. I was so worried that you'd turn out to be another Todd, and look at what happened. You make Todd look like a prince."

Chris's anger kicked in. "Damn it, Melanie, stop comparing me to that guy. I'm nothing like him."

"You're right. You're much worse. All he did was break my heart and bruise my pride." Her voice broke. "You've done that *and* robbed me of my dreams, too. I hope you're happy. Good-bye, Chris."

Before he could say another word, the dial tone sounded in his ear. There was no mistaking the note of chilling finality in her voice when she said good-bye. Muttering an oath, he slammed the receiver back on the cradle.

She hoped he was happy?

No, he wasn't happy.

In fact, he was completely miserable. And pissed-off, too. He realized she was angry, but damn it, why couldn't she give him the benefit of the doubt? And how was he supposed to fix things when he was three thousand miles away from home for three more days? There was too much time and distance before he could talk to Melanie and make her understand.

He dropped his head into his hands and groaned. Damn it, he should have told her immediately. Told her that if this bank turned her down, she could reapply at another bank.

But he knew the futility of that. The information was now disclosed in the independent review, and every bank would require that document. It was unlikely that any lending institution would be any more willing to part with their money than the first bank was.

He flopped back onto the bed and groaned. Cripes, what a mess. The one woman he wanted thought he was sludge. Thought he was worse than that loser Todd.

Damn, that really pissed him off. Todd, the dirtbag, had screwed up by being a dishonest, lying coward. *I, on the other hand, screwed up by being honest and forthcoming. Doesn't that count for anything?*

But the realization of what he'd actually done suddenly hit him like a punch in the gut.

He hadn't been honest with Melanie. He'd been honest with Glenn.

His good intentions aside, he'd royally screwed up. Now the jackpot question was: How the hell could he fix this mess?

In desperate need of caffeine, he called room service, ordered a full pot of coffee, and showered while he waited. He was almost dressed and on his third cup of java when inspiration struck with the force of a lightning bolt.

A slow smile spread across his face as he mentally reviewed the ingenious—if he did say so himself—plan that hit him like a cement bag in the head.

It will work! It had to.

It was his only chance.

He ordered up another pot of coffee, then called to postpone his morning meeting until after lunch.

Then he booted up his laptop, plugged in his portable printer, and set to work.

Five hours, four dozen e-mails, and countless phone calls later, Chris blew out a breath and looked at the papers stacked in front of him. All that remained was to fax them to Glenn. After that, it was out of Chris's hands.

He'd done all he could.

He prayed to God it was enough.

SIXTEEN

Melanie sat at the butcher-block table in the Pampered Palate's kitchen, staring into her empty coffee cup. Another hectic dinner rush was over. All she had to do was turn on the dishwasher and lock up.

She didn't think she had the strength to do it.

Burying her face in her hands, she groaned. What day was it? Thursday? Was it only two days since her world had fallen apart?

It felt like a lifetime.

She'd had no idea she could hurt so bad. Yeah, she knew all about pain, thanks to Todd, but she'd found out that Todd had only been a warm-up to the excruciating agony she would suffer at the hands of Christopher Bishop. Once again she was left with a broken heart.

Only this time her soul was shattered as well.

She didn't bother to look up when she heard Nana scrape out the chair opposite her. At least she had Nana. Nana would never betray her. Nana would always be with her, be on her side. She hadn't told her grandmother about Chris's part in the loan fiasco—only that they weren't getting the money.

"How long are you planning to mope?" Nana asked.

Melanie raised her head and peered across the table through gritty eyes. "I don't know. Why?"

" 'Cause I'm gettin' tired of it." Nana's lips thinned with clear annoyance. "When I think of the time you're wasting sitting around with a long face, it makes me mad. I haven't got that kind of time to waste. I'm an old person. Jiminy Cricket, I'm so old I don't even buy green bananas. I've mourned with you for two days, but I'm done. Starting now. I'd suggest you wipe that mopey look off your face and get happy."

Tears filled Melanie's eyes. Get happy? She didn't think she'd ever be happy again.

Damn it, how many times was she going to allow herself to be annihilated before she learned her lesson? Well, never again. She was through with men. All of them. Forever. They were nothing but heartbreaking betrayers. She wondered what the requirements were to become a nun.

"You have to pull yourself together," Nana said in a clipped, no-nonsense tone. "Not getting the bank loan isn't the end of the world. We'll try another bank. And if that doesn't work, we'll figure out something else."

"It's not just the loan, Nana," Melanie said quietly, brushing away a tear with the back of her hand.

"Then I'm confused. What's got you in such a funk if not the loan?"

Melanie shook her head and looked down at her lap.

After a moment of silence Nana asked, "Okay, let me guess. It has to do with your young man."

Melanie's heart pinched. "He's not my young man."

"Does *he* know that?"

"He does now."

Nana huffed out a breath and made a *tsking* sound. "So you gave him his walking papers. Why? Two days ago you told me you loved him. And he loved you."

"Things changed."

A look of disbelief entered Nana's eyes. "All right. If you didn't want him, and you let him go, then why aren't you happy? Unless you think you made a mistake."

A wave of weary defeat rolled over Melanie. She simply hurt all over. "I didn't make a mistake, Nana. He betrayed me."

A myriad of emotions flashed over her grandmother's face. Surprise, skepticism, confusion, anger.

"Are you sure, honey?" Nana finally asked, reaching out to squeeze Melanie's hand.

Melanie nodded. "Positive. He admitted it."

Nana whistled softly. "Well, I'll be a son of a gun. If he admitted it, then there's no doubt, but I have to say I'm surprised. And mighty disappointed. I never would have pegged him for a cheater."

"He didn't cheat on me, Nana."

"He didn't? Then what the blue blazes did he do to betray you?"

Melanie took a deep breath and told Nana the whole story. When she finished, she felt better. At least now Nana would commiserate with her. Maybe they'd bake a batch of double fudge brownies when they got home. Yeah. She needed chocolate. Brownies covered with Edy's Grand Gourmet Rocky Road ice cream. Hershey's Kisses on the side. Death by chocolate. Suicide by cellulite.

She needed to languish in a huge dose of her grandmother's love, warmth, and support. But when she looked at Nana, her grandmother's expression made her draw back in surprise.

Nana didn't look loving, warm, or supportive.

Nana looked royally pissed.

"It's a sorry day," Nana said in a disgusted tone, "when a grandmother has to call her own granddaughter a horse's patoot, but that's what you are."

Melanie blinked, stunned. Nana had never spoken to her like this. "Why are you angry? What did I do?"

"Doesn't it strike you as ironic that you dumped Todd, with good reason, because he was a lying, cheating, unethical crumb-bum, and now you've dumped Chris because he's honest, upstanding, and ethical?"

"But . . . but . . . he didn't tell me about the other restaurant. Because of him we didn't get the loan."

"Phooey. He didn't tell you the minute he found out because he didn't want you working yourself into a frazzle. That sounds thoughtful to me. We didn't get the loan because we're a new business and another business the bank sees as direct competition is opening across the street. It's a simple case of the bank not wanting to take a risk."

"But the bank only knows about the other eatery because of Chris."

"So? You're going to condemn the guy for doing the right thing? And what makes you so sure one of those other accountant fellas or bankers wouldn't have found out anyway?"

"Technically, Chris didn't have to tell—"

"Maybe from a *legal* standpoint, but what about *his* ethical side? You're angry at him for not compromising his principles? Good Lord, Melanie, your last man didn't even *have* principles."

Melanie was starting to feel about two inches tall. "But I asked him if he *had* to tell—"

"So it was a gray area," Nana broke in. "Big deal. It obviously wasn't a gray area to *him*. Clearly it would have compromised his integrity to remain silent. Seems to me that's a man worth having." She looked at Melanie over her bifocals. "And you're a horse's patoot."

"But Nana, he . . . made love to me, knowing that he was going to place my loan in jeopardy. He didn't tell me. He knew for *two weeks* and never said a word."

"You make it sound like he knew for two *years*. No doubt he planned to tell you after the bank made its decision."

"That's what he *said.*"

"And you honestly don't believe him?" Nana blew out a breath. "Honey, he made a mistake. He tried to do the right thing and he screwed up. He can't help screwing things up—he's a male and it comes with the territory. Believe me, if a man like that made love to me, I'd certainly give him the benefit of the doubt. Did you?"

Melanie sat stock-still, realization dawning in her. A sick, queasy feeling settled in her gut. He hadn't meant to hurt her. He'd tried to help her. She'd just been so shocked and disappointed, she'd lashed out.

And lost him.

Clapping her hand to her forehead, she wailed, "Oh, Nana! What have I done?"

Nana *humpphed.* "Now that's better. Shame on you for blaming that sweet boy. Appears you have a lot to make up for."

"I was pretty harsh on him." She recalled their phone conversation and cringed. "He might not forgive me."

"You won't know unless you try. Chances are he's feeling as bad as you. Why don't you call him?"

Before Melanie could answer, the phone rang. It was after closing, but she reached for the instrument, hoping it might be Chris.

"Pampered Palate, Gourmet to Go."

"Is Miss Gibson there, please?" asked a vaguely familiar male voice.

"Speaking. Who's calling?"

"This is Vince Peters from Guardian Savings and Loan. I'm glad I caught you before you left for the evening."

The loan officer. The one who'd turned down her loan. Not exactly her favorite guy, but Melanie suppressed an urge to hang up on him.

"What can I do for you, Mr. Peters?"

"I'm calling with good news, Miss Gibson. In light of the additional information provided to me by Waxman, Barnes, Wiffle, and Hodge, and after carefully reevaluating your application, we've decided to approve your loan."

Melanie felt her jaw drop open and her eyes pop wide. They probably made a *boing* sound.

"I beg your pardon? I thought the additional information caused you to *turn down* the loan."

Mr. Peters chuckled. "I mean the *additional* additional information. The loan has been approved."

Melanie was glad she was sitting. Otherwise she would have fallen down with an unladylike splat.

"What information is that?" she asked in a weak voice.

"Why, the information about the dozens of private catering jobs you have scheduled over the next twelve months. I must say, Miss Gibson, when Mr. Waxman faxed me these job orders, it changed the entire complexion of your loan application. Obviously, the Pampered Palate is doing very well and growing fast in the private catering arena. Under those circumstances, Guardian Savings and Loan is happy to assist you. If you'll stop by the bank tomorrow morning, we'll sign the necessary papers. Is that satisfactory?"

Melanie jarred herself out of her stupor. "Yes, Mr. Peters. That's fine."

"Excellent. See you tomorrow. Good-bye."

" 'Bye." Melanie slowly replaced the receiver.

Apparently she looked as dazed as she felt because Nana said, "By the look on your face, I'm guessing that was Ed McMahon telling you you're a Publisher's Clearing House winner."

Melanie blew out a long, slow, calming breath. "Even better. That was Mr. Peters from the bank. My loan was approved."

Nana's eyes bugged out. "I thought you said—"

"I did. But he changed his mind." She jumped up and twirled around. "He changed his mind!"

Nana scratched her head and frowned. "That's great, honey. But did he say why?"

Melanie stopped spinning. "He said something about the dozens of catering jobs we have scheduled for the next twelve months."

"What catering jobs?"

Melanie came back to earth with a thump. Good grief, if this was some kind of mistake and Mr. Peters was going to take away the loan, she was going to scream.

"I don't know," Melanie said, "but I'm calling Glenn Waxman. He's the one who told the bank about them."

She dialed Glenn's number, hoping he'd be working late so she wouldn't have to wait until morning for the answers she wanted.

"Glenn Waxman," came a masculine voice.

"Glenn, Melanie Gibson here. I just heard from Mr. Peters at the bank. He said my loan was approved."

"Hey! Congratulations. I'm happy for you."

"He said he changed his mind based on additional information you gave him. Something about future catering jobs?"

"Well, yes. I simply told him about them and faxed him copies of the work orders."

As much as she wanted to remain silent, take her loan, and slink away, Melanie couldn't. Even if it meant losing the loan, she couldn't accept it under false pretenses.

"Glenn, I have to be honest with you. I have no idea what you're talking about. *What* catering jobs?"

She heard him shuffling papers around. "Let me see," he said. "There's the anniversary party for Mr. Walter Rich and his wife the first weekend in September, a birthday party for Mrs. Lorna Bishop the second weekend in September, a baby shower—"

"Did you say Lorna Bishop?"

"Yes. That's Chris's mother. There're twenty-seven orders in all. Chris faxed them to me from LA this morning."

Once again, Melanie gave thanks that she was sitting. What on earth had Chris done? Guilt hit her like a brick to the back of the head. Good grief. Clearly he felt so bad that she'd lost the loan, he'd made up some elaborate story about her having catering jobs lined up.

She felt awful. Horrible. He'd compromised himself to save her. She loved him for it, but she couldn't let him do it.

"Glenn, there's been a mistake. I know nothing—"

"There's no mistake, Melanie. I spoke to half the people on these job orders—hell, I *know* half the people on these orders. In fact, I *am* one. You're booked up the first Saturday in December for my daughter's sweet sixteen. These are legitimate catering jobs. You should start receiving deposit checks within the next couple of days. If you stop by the office tomorrow morning, I'll give you my copies."

"Uh, okay. I'll be there."

"Great. See ya then. 'Bye."

" 'Bye." Melanie hung up and stared at Nana. "You're not going to believe this," she said.

"Sure I will. I'm a gullible old lady. I'll believe anything."

Melanie repeated her conversation with Glenn.

"Well," said Nana, a smug look on her face. "How do you like that? Your Chris is not only a hunk, he's a hero, too. Swooped right in and saved his damsel in distress. What do you say about that?"

"Say? What can I possibly say? That I'm a dope and completely misjudged the most wonderful man I've ever met?"

"That's a pretty good start," Nana said with brutal frankness.

"Do you think he'll forgive me?"

Nana thought for a few seconds, then answered, "Seems to me a man who would go to all the trouble of booking two-dozen catering gigs is a man truly in love. I'd say chances are he'll forgive you." A small smile tugged at the corners of her mouth. "Of course, if he's as smart as I think he is, he'll make you suffer a bit first, so you'd better be prepared."

A shiver of anticipation zinged through Melanie at the thought of "suffering" at Chris's hands. "Hmmm. Yeah. Got any suggestions?"

"The best defense is always—"

"A great offense?"

"That's right. And take it from someone who's been around the block a few times, a woman's best offense is sexy lingerie. Those sweatpants you wear to bed don't qualify."

A plan—a fiendish plan—took root in Melanie's mind. "I have an idea, Nana."

"I knew you would, honey."

"Wanna help?"

"Does it involve hog-tyin' that handsome sucker?"

Melanie chuckled. "Something like that."

"Count me in, babe. Count me in."

SEVENTEEN

Chris unlocked his condo door Friday night and dropped his suitcase in the foyer. Closing the door, he leaned his back against it and closed his eyes.

God, he was tired.

And miserable.

But at least he was home, even if, thanks to his delayed flight, it was after midnight.

Pushing off from the door, he walked into the kitchen and checked his answering machine. No messages. *Everybody's worried sick about me.*

He'd hoped Melanie might have left him a message. Of course, he'd hoped she would call him in LA, but she hadn't. Then he'd hoped she might meet him at the Atlanta airport, but again, she hadn't.

He knew her loan had been approved. He'd spoken to Glenn Waxman, who'd filled him in on his conversation with Melanie.

So even though she'd gotten her loan, she still hadn't called. Obviously she was still angry with him.

Well, damn it, she was just going to have to get over it. He loved her too much to lose her. Now that there weren't three thousand miles between them, they would talk face to face and straighten things out.

If she refused to listen to reason, he'd just Velcro her stubborn ass to the sofa until she changed her mind.

That settled, he headed toward his bedroom, loosening his tie on the way. He opened the bedroom door and froze.

Dozens of candles in every size, shape, and color, covered his furniture, bathing the room with soft, flickering light. A trail of fragrant flower petals led from the doorway toward the adjoining master bath.

As if in a trance, he followed the trail to the bathroom door, which stood slightly ajar. He gently pushed the door open.

He actually felt his jaw drop. Thank God it was attached to his face, or it would have fallen on the floor, taking his teeth with it.

More candles adorned the counter and surrounded the bathtub. Melanie reclined in the tub, surrounded by a mountain of fluffy bubbles. Her hair was piled on her head with several corkscrew tendrils surrounding her face. A bottle of champagne rested in an ice bucket on the floor with two crystal glasses next to it.

"It's about time you got home," she murmured in a low, sexy voice.

He had to swallow to moisten his bone-dry throat. "My, ah, flight was delayed."

"I know. I called the airline."

Because his collar suddenly felt too tight, he ran his finger around the neck to loosen it a bit. A fragrant puff of steam filled his nostrils, rendering him almost light-headed.

He cleared his throat. "Not that I'm complaining, but what are you doing here?"

A slow, wicked smile touched her lips. She lifted

one long, soapy leg from the water. "I'm taking a bath."

Chris's gaze riveted on her shapely upraised leg. "I see that. Does this mean you're not angry with me anymore?"

"You could say that. I spoke to your brother today. He still had his key and he let me in." She ran a sudsy hand up her leg. "I hope you don't mind."

"Ah, no. I don't mind." Chris made a mental vow to give Mark everything he owned in thanks.

Chris watched, glued in place as she slowly stood up. White bubbles left silky trails in their wake as they meandered down her body. His blood pressure spiked and his heart practically stalled when she crooked her finger at him.

"Come here," she whispered.

He supposed his feet must have moved, because the next thing he knew, he was standing next to the tub.

"We're having a party," she said, reaching out her wet hands to unknot his loosened tie, "and you're waaaaay overdressed."

Chris stood perfectly still, his eyes fastened on hers, while she pulled his tie from around his collar and dropped it on the floor. Then she set to work unbuttoning his dress shirt.

Slipping the top button free, she said, "It occurred to me that we never went skinny-dipping." The second and third buttons opened. "While I realize this isn't a pool, it was the best I could do. We have all the skinny-dipping essentials—you, me, naked, water. And it does keep with our getting-wet tradition."

She raised her gaze, and Chris immediately drowned in her warm, chocolaty depths.

"If you have any objections," she said in a breathy

voice that oozed sensuality, "I suggest you speak now or forever hold your peace."

He recalled saying those exact words to her before he'd made love to her the first time. "The tub works for me."

"Good." She slipped the last button free. Placing her bath-warmed hands on his abdomen, she ran her palms up his chest.

With a groan, Chris tried to pull her to him, but she held him off, shaking her head.

"Not yet. There are a few things I need to say first." She eased his suit jacket from his shoulders. It landed on the floor next to his tie with a soft thud.

Chris swallowed and fisted his hands to keep them off her. "I'm listening."

Cupping his face between her hands, she kissed him gently. "I'm sorry," she whispered against his mouth.

"No. *I'm* sorry. I should have told you right away. I tried—"

"I know," she said, forestalling his words by placing her fingers against his lips. "And I want you to know I was sorry before I found out that you'd booked twenty-seven parties for the Pampered Palate. I had a long talk with Nana and she made me realize how wrong I was . . . and how foolish."

He brushed back a stray tendril of her hair. "I never meant to hurt you, Melanie."

"Of course you didn't. I was angry and hurt when I should have been proud of you for not compromising your principles and integrity, and grateful for your concern regarding my feelings." She brought his hand to her lips and kissed his palm. "I said some really hurtful things to you and I'm sorry."

The hell with not holding her. Wrapping his arms

around her, he dragged her up against him. Her breasts, warm and slippery from the bath, slid against his chest, forcing a groan from him.

He was about to kiss her when he noticed a tear glide down her cheek. "Hey, don't cry."

Another tear rolled down. "I'm not crying."

"Are, too."

"Am not."

He brushed away the tears. "Okay. Why are you *not* crying?

"I'm . . . overcome. What you did for me. All those parties. It's what changed the loan officer's mind."

"Glad to help." He ran his hands down her bare back and cupped her buttocks. "I'm not trying to rush you, sweetheart, but are you finished talking?"

"Just one more thing."

"What's that?"

"I love you."

Chris stilled. His heart seemed to stall, then jump back to life with an electric spark.

"I want you to know," she whispered, her big brown eyes swimming with more tears, "I'm not saying that because of what you did for me. I fell in love the instant I saw you. But I was so afraid."

"Of what?"

"Everything. That you'd turn out to be another Todd. Afraid I was falling too fast. But Nana straightened me out on that, too." She smiled. "She told me how long it takes to fall in love."

"Yeah? How long?"

"A moment. It only takes a moment."

"Well, I have to agree with her. That's about how long it took me to fall in love with you." He touched her cheek. "You're not afraid anymore?"

"Not unless you've changed your mind."

"About what?"

She dropped her chin. "Loving me," she said in a small voice.

He waited for her to look at him. When she raised her head, he cupped her face, her beautiful, tear-stained face in his hands.

"Not a chance," he said, his heart pounding with relief. "I love you. Completely. Totally."

"I love you, too. So much."

He huffed out a breath and smiled. "Thank God. Now, are you going to finish what you started here, or am I going to have to jump in the tub with my shoes and pants on?" He nuzzled her neck. "Something about you and water bodes poorly for my clothes."

She reached for his belt. "I'll finish."

He toed off his tassel loafers, peeled off his socks, and kicked them aside. Then he stood in an agony of anticipation while she slowly divested him of his trousers and boxers. The instant he was naked, he stepped into the steaming bath and lowered himself into the mountain of bubbles. Melanie joined him, settling her slippery body on top of his.

He held her tight against him, emotions swamping him from every direction. She loved him. He loved her. She was his. He was hers. And he wanted it to always be that way. Forever.

Tunneling his fingers through her hair, he gently pushed her head back until their eyes met. He saw all the love in the world shining at him from her big brown eyes.

"You're everything I never knew I always wanted," he said, unable to keep the husky note from his voice. He shook his head. "Does that make sense?"

A tender smile lit her face. "Perfect sense. You're everything I always wanted but was afraid to ask for."

"Seems like we're a good team."

"A perfect match," she agreed.

"So let's get married."

He watched her eyes widen to saucers. "Excuse me?"

"Marry me."

She stared at him, and he couldn't decide which word better described her expression—*amazed* or *horrified.*

He decided to hope for amazed.

When she continued to stare at him, bug-eyed and silent, he observed, "It seems I've left you speechless."

"You're serious," she finally said.

"Dead serious," he assured her. "Marriage isn't something I'd joke about."

"But you can't ask me to marry you in the bathtub!" she wailed.

Female logic. Go figure. "Why not?"

"Because someday our kids will ask us to tell them about how Daddy proposed to Mommy. How can we tell them we were skinny-dipping in the *bathtub?* Good grief. And how could we tell your mother and sisters? And Nana?"

"Oh, all right," he grumbled. He slid her off him, stood up, then scooped her up into his arms. Unmindful of the trail of water and soapsuds dripping behind them, he padded across the floor into his bedroom.

He was just about to lay her on the bed when she exclaimed, "Not here! You can't propose to me in bed."

"Why the hell not?"

"The same reason. What sort of example will we be setting for our children if we tell them we were in bed together when you popped the question?"

"Jeez. We don't even have these kids yet, and already they're giving me a pain in the ass." He looked around for somewhere she might deem appropriate and came up blank. "What do you suggest? I'm not about to lug you outside. We'll get arrested."

"We have to get dressed, Chris."

"Dressed?"

"Yes. We can't be naked."

He set her on her feet. "Who makes *up* these crazy rules? And the reason we can't be naked is . . ."

"Your mother, your sisters, Nana—they'll all ask me what I was wearing when you proposed. I cannot tell them I was buck naked."

Chris wasn't sure if he was annoyed or amused. "Can't you tell them you were so overcome with happiness, you forgot what you were wearing?"

"No can do. I'm not a good liar." She patted his cheek. "Besides, it's a girl thing."

Somehow he hadn't imagined his proposal going quite this way. Feeling very put-upon, he stomped to his closet and pulled out his robe.

Tossing it to her he said, "Here. You can say you were wearing Ralph Lauren."

She checked the designer tag and nodded. "Okay." She slipped the robe on and belted it.

He stalked to his dresser and grabbed a pair of Nike sweatpants. Grumbling under his breath, he jammed his legs into them. "Is this acceptable?"

"Perfect. Thank you. Now you may propose."

"Terrific. So what do you say?"

"About what?"

He took a deep breath and calmed himself. "About getting married. Yes or no?"

She raised her brows. "Wow. How *excruciatingly* romantic."

He dragged his palms down his face. "I'm sorry. But I've never proposed before. I wasn't aware all this damn protocol was involved." He took her hands and entwined their fingers. "I love you, Melanie. I want you to be my wife. Will you marry me?"

A brilliant smile lit her face. "Yes." She wrapped her arms around his neck and kissed him. "Now I'll ask you. Will you marry me?"

"Oh, no," he said, shaking his head. "If you're gonna ask *me,* we have to do it the guy way."

"The *guy* way?"

"Yeah." He untied the robe and slid it from her shoulders. Then he shucked his sweatpants, scooped her up, and carried her back to the bed.

Once they were lying in each other's arms, he said, "Okay. I'm ready. Go ahead and ask. Now when all my buddies ask me about popping the question, I can say we were in bed and naked." He kissed her nose. "It's a guy thing."

She laughed. "Will you marry me?"

He scrunched up his face and pretended to consider the question. "Well, let's see. On the plus side, you're really cute, sweet, and a great cook. Of course you're kinda bossy sometimes—ouch!" He rubbed his shoulder where she'd lightly punched him. "Okay! I'll marry you, Mel Gibson." He grinned. "Now there's a sentence I never thought I'd say."

She shot him a belligerent glare. "Wanna change your mind?"

He rolled them over until she sat astride him. "No way."

"When should we do it?"

He ran his hands up her body and cupped her breasts. "Hmmm. How about right now?"

"You want to get married right now?"

"No. I want to make love to you right now. We can get married tomorrow."

"Tomorrow?"

"Next week?"

"That doesn't give us much time to plan a wedding."

"How much time do we need?" he asked. "All you need for a wedding is a bride, a groom, and a minister. We have two out of three. How long can it take to find a minister?"

He rolled them again until she was under him, then settled himself between her splayed thighs.

"Besides," he added, running his lips down the length of her neck, "the wedding has to take place soon. Starting next month you'll be too busy with your new catering enterprise to take time off to get married. We need a couple of weeks for a honeymoon."

She moved beneath him, running her hands down his back. "Hmmm. Yes. The honeymoon."

"I vote for two weeks from now." He looked down at her dreamy expression. "How does that sound?"

"Perfect."

"Are we done talking now?"

"Yes."

He lowered his mouth to hers. "Thank God."

EPILOGUE

It poured on their wedding day.

The rain fell in a blinding sheet, but Melanie didn't care. Holding Chris's hand, they squeezed together under a huge umbrella and made a mad dash down the church steps and scurried into the white stretch limo waiting to whisk them off to the airport.

"Good grief," Melanie said, shaking raindrops from the full skirt of her simple ankle-length wedding dress. "Nothing like keeping with our tradition of getting wet. I've never seen such rain. Maybe we should build an ark."

"Relax," Chris said, settling himself next to her. "In a few hours our plane will land in sunny Florida. Then we'll board the cruise ship and spend the next week frolicking around the Caribbean." He kissed her nose. "I trust that meets with your approval, Mrs. Bishop."

Mrs. Bishop. Boy, did that sound nice. *Mrs. Bishop* smiled at her husband. "I can't wait. I've never been on a cruise before—except for our canoeing excursion. Hopefully this boat is a little bigger."

"Not to worry. I'll keep you safe."

"Hmmm. A week-long honeymoon, then as soon as we get home, there's another wedding to attend."

Chris smiled. "Nana and Bernie. Are they great together or what?"

"Perfect," Melanie agreed. "Although I think Nana scandalized the minister when she announced that she and Bernie *had* to get married. The poor man needed to sit down."

"He did look sort of pale," Chris said with a chuckle.

"At least I don't need to worry about the Pampered Palate while I'm away," Melanie said. "My dad is so excited about watching the place. I hope you won't mind if your new in-laws move to Atlanta."

"I won't mind at all. Having your folks around to pitch in at the Pampered Palate means more free time for you, and that sounds great to me." He slipped a handkerchief from his tuxedo jacket pocket and gently dabbed a few stray raindrops from her cheeks. Melanie watched him, and her heart skidded to a halt.

He was her *husband*.

Hers to have and to hold. From this day forward. How incredibly lovely was *that*?

She blew out a deep breath. Her gaze traveled over him from head to foot. Holy smokes. He looked so outrageously handsome in his black tux, she couldn't decide if she wanted him to keep it on forever, or if she wanted to tear it off him with her teeth.

"You okay?" he asked, halting his ministrations and giving her a searching look. "You look flushed."

Was she okay? She'd just married the most wonderful, gorgeous, incredible man on earth. *Okay* was a pretty lukewarm word to describe how she felt.

"I'm fine. I'm incredibly happy." She touched his

face with trembling fingers. "I can't believe we're married."

"You're legally stuck with me forever," he said, taking her hand and placing a warm kiss on her palm. "You don't mind that you're not Mel Gibson anymore, do you?"

Melanie heaved a blissful sigh and wrapped her arms around him. "Do I *look* like I mind?"

"No. You look beautiful. Stunning. The most perfect bride I've ever seen." He kissed her, tenderly at first, then with increasing ardor. Melanie's hormones sighed, *oooohhhhh baby!*

Several seconds later, however, she pulled back. "What was that noise?"

"What noise? I didn't hear anything."

Grrrrrrr.

Grrrrrr.

Chris frowned. "That's sounds strangely familiar."

Grrrrrr.

Silence.

"Uh-oh," Melanie whispered. "That didn't sound good. And have you noticed we're not moving?"

The limo driver lowered the smoke-glass partition separating them from the front seat and looked at them through the rearview mirror.

"Excuse me, Mr. and Mrs. Bishop, but there appears to be a, er, problem with the car."

"What sort of problem?" Chris asked.

"It won't start. Sounds to me like the battery's dead."

Melanie and Chris stared at each other.

Chris pinched the bridge of his nose. "I thought I recognized that growling noise."

A knock sounded on the rear window. Smothering

a laugh at Chris's expression, Melanie touched a button and lowered the window.

Nana and Bernie stood outside, huddled under the protection of a red-and-blue-striped umbrella.

"What's up?" asked Nana, sticking her head in.

"The battery's dead," Melanie answered.

Nana shook her head. "Jiminy Cricket. You two are always soaking wet or stranded." Pulling open the limo door, she said, "Come on. Me and Bernie will drive you to the airport." She marched off with Bernie, heading toward the lime-green Dodge.

Chris groaned. "Please tell me we're not going in the Dodge. Please."

Melanie laughed and kissed him. "Don't worry. With the way Nana drives, we'll definitely get to the airport on time. Besides, we started off in the Dodge, so it's only fitting that we finish there."

"That's just what I'm worried about—*finishing* there. Didn't you tell me Nana drove like a Mario Andretti/Mr. Magoo combination?"

Melanie framed his face between her hands. "Relax. This isn't the finish of anything. This is just the start. And lead-foot Nana's much better since she got her new glasses." She waggled her brows at him. "Besides, we can neck in the backseat. C'mon. Let's go before they leave without us."

Hand in hand, they dashed to the Dodge and settled themselves in the backseat. Melanie choked back a laugh at the look of utter relief on Chris's face when he saw that Bernie was driving.

Bernie turned around and grinned at them. "Where to, kids?" he asked in a chauffeurlike voice.

"To the airport, my good man," Melanie answered. "How long will it take?"

Bernie stepped on the gas and pulled out of the

parking lot at whiplash-warp speed. Grinning over his shoulder, he said, "Don't worry. We'll be there before you can say 'Kiss the cook'!"

The Only Sauce You'll Ever Need

The great thing about this recipe is that the ingredient amounts do not need to be exact. If you prefer more garlic, less onion, whatever—go for it! But *fresh* basil is a must—not dried. The amounts of ingredients listed below are simply guidelines. Don't panic if you use a little more or a little less of something.

12	ripe plum tomatoes
1	sweet onion
2-3	heaping tbs of minced garlic (for an easy shortcut, use the jarred kind from the supermarket)
1	bunch fresh basil leaves (approx. 3 dozen leaves)
1	cup good quality olive oil
	fresh ground pepper and salt to taste

1. Coarsely chop the tomatoes; drain excess juice. Place in nonmetal bowl.
2. Peel and chop onion; add to bowl along with the garlic.
3. Wash and chop basil leaves; add to bowl.
4. Pour olive oil over mixture; season with fresh ground pepper and salt. Stir gently with wooden spoon. Cover and set at room temperature for 2-3 hours before serving.

Unused portion should be refrigerated. Serve at room temperature with tostado chips for a deliciously different salsa. Spoon over toasted slices of Italian or French bread for an authentic *bruschetta* appetizer. Serve warm over your favorite pasta and sprinkle with Parmesan or Romano cheese for a light main course. Also delicious on salads and scrambled eggs or omelettes. Wonderful over your favorite fish. Use your imagination! And don't forget to tell your guests to kiss the cook! Enjoy and *bon appetit!*

ABOUT THE AUTHOR

Growing up on Long Island, New York, I fell in love with romance at an early age. I dreamed of being swept away by a dashing rogue riding a spirited stallion. When my hero finally showed up, he was dressed in jeans and drove a Volkswagen, but I recognized him anyway. We married after graduating from Hofstra University and are now living our happily ever afters in Atlanta, along with our very bright and active nine-year-old son, who is a dashing rogue in the making.